"So, you don't wish to become my wife?"

"No more than you wish to become my husband," Debra informed Rodare. "Love and marriage aren't fuel for farce."

"A farce?" As Rodare spoke, he thrust his fingers into her hair. "Be careful, Miss Hartway, you are in my house." He tilted her face as if it were a kind of offering and brought his lips dangerously close to hers. "Do you hear me? If you wish to be employed in my house, you will do as I demand."

"And if I don't?" she fought back.

"Then I shall prove to you that I am not a man to be provoked!" His breath stirred warmly against her mouth, and she was reminded too vividly of their earlier encounter. And deep inside her secret self she wanted just once more the hard possessiveness of his arms holding her to the power of his body as he took his fill of kissing.

Books by Violet Winspear

HARLEQUIN SIGNATURE EDITION
THE HONEYMOON

HARLEQUIN ROMANCE
1616—THE PAGAN ISLAND
1637—THE SILVER SLAVE
1658—DEAR PURITAN
1680—RAPTURE OF THE DESERT
2682—SECRET FIRE

HARLEQUIN PRESENTS
 492—NO MAN OF HER OWN
 566—THE MAN SHE MARRIED
 718—BY LOVE BEWITCHED
 734—BRIDE'S LACE
 854—SUN LORD'S WOMAN
1006—A SILKEN BARBARITY

VIOLET WINSPEAR

HOUSE OF STORMS

Harlequin Books

TORONTO • NEW YORK • LONDON
AMSTERDAM • PARIS • SYDNEY • HAMBURG
STOCKHOLM • ATHENS • TOKYO • MILAN

Harlequin Signature Edition published August 1988

ISBN 0-373-83207-9

Originally published in Great Britain in 1985

I have been taught that happiness is coy,
And will not come to all who bend the knee;
That faith is like foam upon the sea,
And hope a moth whose wings we may destroy.

Eric Mackay (1902)

CHAPTER ONE

THE first time Debra saw the house where she was to work she thought it was like a Charles Addams house and exactly the kind of place where a famous writer of historical novels should reside.

There it sprawled upon the granite cliffs, a powerful silhouette against the sunset sky, the caps of the corbelled-out turrets shaped like candle snuffers, the many windows reflecting the flaming rays of the sun as it sank into the sea.

Abbeywitch at the day's end, high on the cliffs of Lovelis Island, and making an indelible impression upon Debra. It seemed to her a house built to resist the sea winds, the howling storm and the unwanted intruder. A very private house that sheltered the passions of its inmates, the descendants of Don Rodare de Salvador who had a place in Cornish folklore as the Spanish captain who had abducted a young local girl while she netted shrimps from the rock pools of the island beach.

He had sailed off with her and they had returned two years later so their child could be born on Cornish soil. Repenting of his piratical ways, the Don had become owner of the island, and Abbeywitch had been built for his bride.

Out of the blue, Debra had been called into her employer's office and asked if she would like to go and work at Abbeywitch. She was employed by a publisher who was concerned that Jack Salvador's new book should be on the firm's autumn list. This might compensate the author for the recent loss of his young wife.

'I use the word compensation,' Harrison Holt said thoughtfully, 'but it doesn't really fit the case. Jack's wife was only twenty-three and with everything to live for, and the really hard part for the poor chap to accept is that Pauline drowned. Though a verdict of accidental death was recorded—who knows?'

His eyes dwelt for a long moment on Debra who sat facing him across his desk and she knew he was weighing up her character in relation to her look of youth, as if wondering if he dared plunge her into the deep waters of a family tragedy, made even more poignant by the fact that Jack had an infant son too young to ever remember Pauline.

Harrison Holt proceeded to inform Debra that Jack Salvador dictated all his work on to a tape-recorder, piling up the tapes which were then typed by a secretary into chapters. He would work in no other way and refused to allow the tapes off the premises so they could be typed into manuscript at the Columbine office.

'It seems that Jack's resident secretary had words with his mother and was dismissed—' the publisher paused, then leant towards Debra as if making a decision '—and we need someone there to put the book into manuscript form . . . someone who will slot into the household.'

'I would try to do so,' Debra murmured.

'At the present time, Jack is heaven knows where trying to get over the loss of Pauline.' Harrison Holt shook his head in commiseration. 'He seems to have lost interest in his book, but we certainly haven't, so will you go to Abbeywitch and do the necessary?'

'Yes, I'll go,' she quietly replied. Debra wasn't the kind of girl to gush in front of her employer, but she had been devouring the novels of Jack Salvador since her high-school days and she had often hoped that she might see the famous author if ever he came to call at Columbine.

But in her four years with the company she hadn't had the pleasure of seeing him and had scarcely dreamt that the chance to work under his very roof would come her way.

'When do you want me to start, Mr Holt?' She spoke in composed tones that didn't reveal her inward anticipation. She sat with her ringless hands folded together in her lap, looking what she had always proved to be, an efficient young person with a hint of reserve in her manner.

'As soon as possible, Miss Hartway. The Salvador house is a very fascinating one, and I'll telegraph Jack's mother and inform her of your imminent arrival.'

'I hope I shall get along with Mrs Salvador,' Debra ventured to say. 'Is she very much the matriarch?'

Harrison Holt spread his hands. 'The family is entrenched in its traditions, so my advice where Lenora Salvador is concerned is to tread warily. I know you're a diplomatic young woman. I've had good reports of you from various members of the company.'

'Thank you, Mr Holt.' Being given this opportunity to go and work on the book was like manna from heaven to a girl working in the city who often longed for fresh fields.

'Good luck,' her employer said, as if he suspected that she was going to need it.

Paddington Station teemed with people on the day Debra departed for Cornwall. She had a first-class ticket on the train appropriately called the Cornish Riviera and she intended to take lunch in the dining-car where she would bolster her confidence with a glass of champagne.

Though a girl with a self-contained manner,

she could at times be at the mercy of her
nerves and the job which awaited her at the
end of her journey was both an exciting challenge and a promising step up the career
ladder.

Debra yearned to be independent, her memory scarred by the way her mother had striven
so hard to make a living when she became
widowed at the age of thirty-two. There were
times when Debra had seen her mother rock-
ing on her feet from weariness, a woman of
quiet charm whose life had been sheltered by a
caring husband until one day he was there no
more to provide and protect.

Claudia Hartway's determination had been
handed on to Debra who was resolved that not
a single sacrifice made by her mother was
going to be wasted. She would make the
utmost of her career and make sure she never
had to depend on a man for her bread and
butter. And with this end in view, she had
become known at Columbine as an eager
beaver for work, loving the world of books
for its own sake as much as for the chance it
gave her to develop as an editor, until she was
looked upon as invaluable. Now, although her
editing skills were considerable, she had never
lost her ability to turn her hand to anything—
hence her new job!

As the train sped through the countryside,
she tried to imagine what Abbeywitch would

be like. She drew images in her mind but none of them, she suspected, was going to live up to the reality. Cornwall was a magical kind of place and it seemed to touch with its magic the things that were part of it. Wild and thrilling cliffs above the stern Atlantic that dashed high waves to the lonely beaches . . . not that in the summertime they would be lonely.

Today as she travelled west the train was filled with people on their way to enjoy the wonders of the Land of Merlin, as it was romantically called.

She sighed with expectation and leant her head against the white linen of her first-class seat. Columbine was paying her fare so she felt no qualms about the expense involved, and she felt so grateful to Harrison Holt for giving her this chance to prove her value to the company. It was a good publishing house to work for, go-ahead in its ideas and certainly ready to accept the fact that women these days wanted a career and were prepared to be as striving as the men.

She feasted her eyes on the passing scenery . . . how refreshing to see green fields and trees abundant with leaf, all the richness of corn and wheat growing high and untainted by the city grime that clung not only to walls and windows, but to the hair and skin of the workers in the shops and offices. It came from the exhausts of the cars and buses that fought

a losing battle with the giant trucks that
lumbered through the streets of London.

Upon learning that she was going to work in
the country for a few weeks, the other girls had
asked if she would be bored. As she was going
to an island, she would be unlikely to have a
television set in her room.

'Bored?' Debra had laughed at the idea.
'They repeat so many old programmes and
films during the summer they must think the
viewers dim-witted. I plan to make this the
working holiday of a lifetime.'

'Give me Malaga any day of the week.' The
editor who spoke had a sudden gleam in her
eyes. 'The sun is gorgeous and so are those
dishy-looking Spaniards.'

'There's a dash of Spaniard in Jack Salvador,'
Debra reminded her.

'But he isn't going to be there, is he?'

'True,' Debra admitted. 'But I shall see his
little boy.'

'My dear girl,' the other girl looked at her in a
rather mocking way, 'the kind of holiday fun
I'm planning on can only be had with big boys.'

As Debra reflected on the conversation, a
slight smile touched her lips. She got on well
with the other girls at the office, but she had
never accepted the offer to go on holiday with
any of them. If they had warned her that all
work and no play made Jill a dull girl, she
didn't really mind. She was saving her money

in a building society so that one day she would be able to take out a mortgage on her very own apartment. She would furnish it Victorian-style and love every square inch of it; it would be her haven against the world which was a playground for extrovert people rather than dreamy souls like herself.

It was a quiet thrill for her to be on the Cornish Riviera . . . it flew with her to the coast of Cornwall, and as her thoughts wandered along the banks of the Tamar, she remembered the holidays she used to spend in Devon with her mother's sister-in-law who, in her late thirties, had married a widower with teenage children. One of them had been a youth of nineteen and he had been quite willing to accept the shy admiration of a sixteen-year-old girl who had no brothers or sisters of her own.

Debra carried in her mind an image of herself at that age, hair in a long braid, long coltish legs and a tendency to blush when Mark paid any attention to her.

In her innocence, she had no idea the evening of the barn dance at Darlington Farm that he was using her to arouse the jealousy of the pert daughter of the local riding-master. Feeling grown-up in her green-check dress with the frilled collar, she had been thrilled to be seen dancing with the best-looking boy at the dance, with his shiny dark hair, his cowhand shirt and close-fitting denims.

He had promised they would dance again, but suddenly he had vanished from the big barn with the coloured lanterns hanging from the beams. So she went looking for him, and found him sprawled in the hay of an outhouse, his blue denims around his ankles, and oblivious to everything but the pert and panting girl who lay with him.

Debra had come down to earth with a thud and never again did she make the mistake of thinking other people were as romantic as herself, least of all young men who only looked god-like. As she grew into a young woman she saw Mark in all of them and was no longer impressed.

It took the house on Lovelis Island to impress Debra with its real and lasting splendour high on the towering cliffs. Home of the Salvador family, which was an Old Line one backed by substantial securities well able to afford the staff employed inside the great house and outside in the extensive grounds and the stables whose sleek horses were exercised daily.

Debra found it an unforgettable sight to see the horses cantering along the sands of the island beach, the surf churning about their long legs and splashing their silky hides. She longed to join the stable boys who rode them, but as yet she was a very new member of the staff and hopeful that she was going to fit in . . . and meet with the approval of Lenora Salvador.

The atmosphere at Abbeywitch wasn't ostentatious, but there was a solid air of comfort; a timelessness of a house removed from the feverish activity of city life so that at nightfall, there above the thrashing high tide, it had an air of isolation and mystery that soon captured Debra's romantic imagination.

There was nothing brash about the Salvadors. Their strain of Latin blood gave them depth and a suggestion of drama, so it wasn't surprising that one of them should wield a powerful pen while his sister should be an actress. Having seen Zandra Salvador in plays on television, it was exciting for Debra to see her in reality.

Debra's bedroom was on the same gallery as the nursery suite where Jack's baby son was in the care of Nanny Rose Jones. Debra felt grand sleeping in a four-poster with a sprigged canopy and the oaken ambience of her bedroom delighted her in every way.

The double doors of the windows opened upon a stone terrace that stretched to the verge of the cliffs themselves and it enchanted her to stand at the parapet and listen to the sea lashing at the rocks far down in the cove. Bride's Cove as it was called, where the boulders stood taller than a man, where long ago a skiff had slipped in among them and a real man had stepped ashore and found there a girl with the skirt of her dress high above her knees while she sought shrimps in the rock pools. He had swooped, captured her in ruthless arms and swept her off to his ship, and Debra wondered as she stood upon the terrace in the evening, if the girl had struggled very hard.

When alone on the terrace Debra released her long hair from its knot and let it blow in the sea-drenched air. She had ignored the persuasion of other girls and kept her hair uncut. 'It's your one claim to beauty,' her mother always said, brushing it to a nut-brown gloss. 'Your hair is something special . . . see how straight and thick it grows, and exactly the colour of chestnuts.'

Debra's mother had taught her how to plait it into an eight-shaped knot at the nape of her neck where it was held in place by the jewelled pin which Claudia Hartway treasured before she gave it to Debra. It was of real jade, a reminder to Claudia of exciting days when she and her husband had lived in Tokyo. Debra's father had been in the diplomatic service, but when Debra was still an infant a fatal heart attack had struck him down and she barely remembered him.

When Claudia brought her home to England they had been obliged to take in boarders for a living. But Claudia had managed to send

Debra to business college, and later on she had met a nice Canadian and had married him with Debra's blessing. From then on Debra started to live her own life, thankful that her mother had found contentment and security.

Debra herself was something of an idealist who suspected that the ideal lover was not a real person but a dream image who was unlikely to materialise in the flesh. She thoroughly enjoyed her work and reasoned that she had plenty of time to fall in love . . . there were so many other things in life apart from the fevers of physical passion, and she was savouring the delight of living on an island.

At night she was lulled off to sleep by the waves breaking on the shore and she grew to love the strange and mournful cries of the gulls, always in tune with the sea whether at high tide when it battered the stony walls of the cliffs, or when it had a more beguiling sound, distant and then near, strong and yet soothing, with the underlying threat of all powerful forces.

It was as if the gulls cried for the girl who had drowned in the water surrounding Abbeywitch. Those on the yacht the night of the party had searched frantically for Pauline and at last they had found her body caught among the rocks of Bride's Cove. The autopsy had proved that the battering of her face and body had occurred before she drowned, and the presence of alcohol in her system had seemed in accord with the verdict, that she had struck her head in falling from the side of the yacht.

It seemed to Debra that the sound of the waves would always remind Jack Salvador of his tragic loss. Only two years married and now he was a widower.

A week went by before Debra received word that Mrs Lenora Salvador requested her company for tea in the solar at three o'clock that afternoon. It sounded more like a summons than an invitation, but Debra had been expecting something of the sort. Upon her arrival at Abbeywitch she had been informed that Madam was in the throes of one of her migraines so they had been kept from meeting.

Now the summons arrived and Debra braced herself for the confrontation. She knew from Nanny Rose that since the departure of Jack Salvador's regular secretary there had been two replacements, but neither of them had met with his mother's approval. Debra was warned that Lenora Salvador was a difficult and demanding woman and it might be to her advantage to appear meek and mild if Debra hoped to find acceptance.

'I'm not going to be intimidated by her,' Debra rejoined. 'I'm here to work as an editor not to be a doormat.'

Nanny Rose laughed and looked Debra up

and down in her neat black skirt and pin-tucked shirt. 'I grant there's something a bit different about you from those others. A bit of class, I'd say. Madam's bound to notice, you mark my words.'

The solar was used as a sitting-room during the summertime, a boldly curving room with a range of wide windows and a barrelled ceiling. A table beside the hostess was attractively laid for tea.

'Do come and sit down, Miss Hartway.' Slanting dark-brown eyes appraised Debra as she crossed the room and sat down. 'You've met my daughter Zandra, have you not? Probably on the stairs as she's been coming and going? Zandra rarely walks if she can run, and rarely sits if she can pace about, preferably with a cigarette in her hand.'

Zandra was doing both those things as her mother spoke. She was tall, fashionably lean in culottes and a loose silk shirt, with dark shining hair that fell in a scroll to her shoulders, framing the sculptured planes of her face. Her eyes were like her mother's, with the slant to them that gave to their faces an individual look.

Those eyes flicked Debra up and down. 'So you're the latest in a line of adoring typists? Another female from a bedsitter who sits up half the night devouring my brother's chunky books—you'll be in for a real thrill when the video deal goes through, won't you? I guess you've heard that his best books are going to be filmed?'

'There was mention of it at Columbine,' Debra replied, her hands sedately folded in her lap as she met Zandra's rather insolent gaze. 'Your brother has a large following, Miss Salvador.'

'I'm not a Miss,' Zandra snapped. 'I'm divorced.'

'I'm sorry,' Debra politely murmured.

'Don't be, he was a silly ass with a beard and I should have heeded Mama's warning that he was no good for me. It's a family failing, both Jack and I turned a deaf ear to Mama when it came to choosing our soul mates. Tell me, have you met the precious infant?'

'Yes.' Debra smiled. 'He's very charming, and very forward for his age, so his nanny informs me.'

'He takes after his mother,' Zandra drawled.

'That will be enough,' Lenora reproved her daughter. 'Do you take cream or lemon in your tea, Miss Hartway?'

'Cream would be nice, thank you.'

'You don't need to watch your figure, eh?' Zandra was giving Debra a rather narrow look through the smoke of her cigarette which was clamped into a holder so the nicotine wouldn't stain her fingers. 'You look younger than the other typists who came here after Miss Tucker took to her heels following a scrap with Mama, which, incidentally, Jack is going to be furious about because he got on well with the old duck.'

'I couldn't possibly allow her to stay.' Lenora handed Debra her cup of tea, which wafted its fragrant aroma from a bone-china cup in an equally fine saucer. 'She called me an old witch! She accused me of making that silly Pauline's life a misery, and I did nothing of the sort! It merely irritated me, having to endure her chatter and the cheap music the girl was addicted to. And her clothes—she simply had no style, no finesse! When Jack was thinking of in marrying her, I just do not know!'

'Mama, you're not that old,' Zandra said in a teasing tone of voice. 'She was curvy and blonde and she got under Jack's skin.'

'He didn't have to marry her,' Lenora held a plate of tiny triangular sandwiches so Debra could take one or two. 'When I think of some of the delightful girls he's known, especially Sharon Chandler. My heart was set on Sharon for a daughter-in-law, and Jack knew it! Instead he had to go and marry that uneducated little dancer from a musical show, and I could have told him straight away that it was doomed; a man of Jack's powers in harness to that Sindy doll with her whispery voice!'

'Mama,' Zandra murmured, 'she is dead, and after all she was Jack's choice and even if you didn't care for her, I'm sure he did.'

Debra listened to the enlightening conversation and ate her sandwiches, which had a delicious salmon spread inside them. As Nanny Rose had hinted, the marriage which had produced young Dean had not been approved of by Jack Salvador's family, and even though Lenora doted on the boy she had despised his young mother.

Poor Pauline . . . Debra now had an image of her, a curvacious, child-like blonde who had danced for a living until meeting the famous writer of fine novels who, because of his lonely profession, would have found the young showgirl amusing and diverting and probably seductive.

Debra could well imagine the reaction when Jack Salvador had walked into the house with her . . . maybe he had carried her over the doorstep in the traditional way, only to be met by the snobbish disapproval of his mother! A widow very unlike Debra's mother, whose years of toil and unselfishness had paid off when she had met the charming, middle-aged man to whom she was now married.

Although Lenora Salvador was a beautiful, elegant and well-preserved woman, it seemed that a second chance at love had eluded her. She was like a diamond, Debra thought, a little too hard and cutting. As her daughter had reminded her, Pauline was dead, and in dying she had left her husband so grief-stricken that he had gone off, no one knew where, in order to try and recover from the loss of his pretty wife.

'Can't I tempt you to a cake, Zandra?' Lenora extended a plate with a selection of cream cakes on it. 'You used to love éclairs when you were a schoolgirl.'

'And look what all that cream and chocolate did to me.' Zandra waved the cakes away from her. 'I was such a podge that I got left out of all the most exciting activities at school and it hurt like hell. I swore I'd never be fat again— however I feel sure Miss Hartway won't say no to a sweet and creamy cake.'

'I'm afraid I shall,' Debra contradicted her. 'I haven't a sweet tooth, as it happens.'

'You do surprise me,' Zandra drawled. 'Miss Tucker lived on cakes and chocolate bars; she really believed in tucking into sweet things, a compensation, don't they say, for being an old maid?'

'I really wouldn't know, Miss—Salvador.' Debra's hesitation went unnoticed. It would have been impolite not to address her by name, and the actress's married title was not known to her.

'You've a boy-friend, then?'

Debra shook her head. 'I don't think it would worry me to be single.'

'You have to be kidding!' Zandra looked

scornful. 'It's true that men are hard to live with, but at the same time it's hard living without them. Maybe you don't attract them, eh?'

Debra's eyes dwelt on the sculptured face with the ironic and rather discontented mouth, an actress with a brittle kind of brilliance, as if her heart was never fully involved in anything she did. Never having been poor, she hadn't been tempered in the anxious fires of wondering where the next meal was coming from. Her success, Debra decided, was based on her appearance rather than her innate talent . . . it was her brother who had the more expressive and worthwhile gifts.

Zandra was reading Debra's thoughts in her large eyes, the kind with such a mixture of colours there was no telling their dominant colour until she was aroused to temper, when they turned green. A scowl darkened the classic face of Jack Salvador's sister.

'I suppose you think you're damned smart,' she snapped. 'And I suppose you keep your angel wings fastened down with sellotape?'

'Zandra,' exclaimed her mother, 'you do say the most astonishing things at times. Miss Hartway looks a sensible young woman to me; neat and clean, with sensibly arranged hair. Not every girl wants to be chased all the time.'

'Are you going to be chaste instead, Miss Hartway?' Zandra mocked. 'Quite frankly I wouldn't want your job on a gold plate; I'd go out of my mind having to type all those words, all those pages, with Jack suddenly deciding to make changes in the text. He isn't the easiest man in the world to work for, you know.'

'I expect he's a perfectionist where his work's concerned,' Debra murmured. 'His books reveal it.'

'Enthralled by his books, are you?'

'I certainly admire them,' Debra admitted.

'You'd better not get enthralled by Jack himself, isn't that so, Mama?'

'I've no intention—' Debra felt herself flushing at the very idea.

'All our intentions are good ones to start off with.' Zandra frowned moodily, as if recalling her marriage. 'Have you worked for our kind of family before?'

'I've only ever worked at the office,' Debra replied, not really intimidated by Zandra who, despite her mocking tongue, had a certain fascination which seemed to be a family trait. 'This is my first venture as a private secretary.'

'Then you're new to an Old Line family?'

'Yes, Miss Salvador.'

'We have our roots in the rollicking days of the corsairs who used to sail into Cornish waters and take whatever plunder they could lay hands on, including any likely-looking females. You may have heard how Bride's Cove came to get its name?'

Debra broke into a smile. 'Yes, your brother once wrote a book about your famous ancestor.'

'Infamous,' Zandra corrected. 'The daring Don Rodare became a sea rover because in Spain he climbed a certain royal balcony and visited a lady he shouldn't have visited. Following that escapade he had to make a bolt for it, so he took to the high seas and became as successful at pillaging as he had been at seducing ladies in high places.'

'Zandra,' her mother spoke in a flustered way, 'I wish you and Jack weren't so fond of bringing up the subject of that man.'

'I thoroughly admire the memory of the rogue,' Zandra laughed. 'I'd like to have known him, and I like to think that Rod and I have some of his genes in us.'

'Rodare certainly has,' Lenora agreed. 'I'm in no doubt that your half-brother has inherited a number of his traits. I'm relieved that Jack is more like my family.'

Upon mentioning her son, Lenora's eyes grew moist and she drew a lace-edged handkerchief from the white cuff of her well-tailored dress and touched it to her nose. 'Jack was always such a clever boy and I pray that Dean will take after him. Clever men, unfortunately, do have a tendency to make mistakes about women, it's a well known fact.'

Debra found herself silently agreeing with

this observation, for men of intellect did seem drawn to girls who were the opposite. But the name Rodare conjured an image of the Don. Though Nanny Rose had chatted about the family, she hadn't mentioned that Jack had a half-brother. As he didn't live at Abbeywitch, he was probably married and resident elsewhere.

It was certainly a fascinating family . . . rather like the cast of a play, its members a little more handsome and assured than their audience.

'Have you formed an opinion of Abbeywitch?' Zandra's voice suddenly broke in on her thoughts, edged by the condescension of someone who had grown up in grand surroundings and took them for granted.

'It's fascinating,' Debra replied. 'I've been told that sections of an ancient abbey have been built into it.'

'Perfectly true. The fireplace in the drawing-room is constructed from abbey stone, and some of the bedroom terraces are paved with it. And Jack's den, where you are working, is actually the cell where the priest of those days had his living quarters. We're rumoured to have a ghost, and a cousin of Mama's insists that she has seen it, but she's a rather dotty old dear who has never had a man in her life so she's inclined to get odd notions. She probably looks under the bed before getting into it in case there's a man hiding there.'

'That's no way to speak of Cousin Cora; she's a sweet woman and we all dearly love her.' Lenora glanced at Debra. 'Is your family living, Miss Hartway?'

'My mother is, madam. She lives with her husband in Canada on their farm and they're very happy. My father died when I was very young, that's why I feel for your little grandson. It's sad to lose a parent.'

Lenora Salvador seemed not to think so where Pauline was concerned, the tightening of her lips conveyed this.

'Poor Mama, you'd like to forget that Jack ever knew Pauline, wouldn't you?' Zandra brushed her fingers through her hair, her eyes glittering darkly. 'You'd like her memory to be swept away just as her ashes were that day Jack stood on the headland, at the very brink of the cliffs, and let the wind carry her ashes out to sea. It was pure theatre . . . he and I very definitely have drama in our veins, whereas Rod has the call of Spain . . . the deep southern heart of Spain.'

'His mother was Spanish so it comes naturally to him.' Lenora spoke rather waspishly. 'She was a Spanish gipsy and she danced in a *taberna*—it should have been Rodare rather than Jack who got entangled with Pauline.'

'Hmm, they would have suited each other,' Zandra said thoughtfully, 'except that Rod is more shrewd about women; they have one hell of a job catching him, he's too fly.'

'Anyway, it's a painful subject.' There was an edge to Lenora's voice. 'I bear the girl no grudge, but she wasn't one of us!'

Debra flinched from the cutting words . . . could none of these people at Abbeywitch have liked Pauline? Did they regard themselves as so Old Line that a girl from the chorus line was beyond acceptance? Or was it possible that Mrs Salvador was incapable of accepting any wife that her son brought home? She had spoken of a girl called Sharon whom she had deemed worthy of Jack, yet would she have turned against her had he made Sharon Chandler his wife?

Zandra clicked her lighter and lit a cigarette, puffing smoke into the air. Her mother tut-tutted and waved the smoke away from her. 'Do you have to smoke in here?' she demanded.

'I need to smoke, Mama. You may not have vices, but you must accept that your son and daughter aren't so saintly.'

'I don't pretend to be saintly,' a faint flush came to Lenora's face, 'but smoking is such a disagreeable habit and you're an actress and you should take more care of your throat, not to mention your lungs—you know what the habit does to people!'

'I know what not smoking does to me.'

Zandra wandered to a window where she stood in profile against the sunlit panes of glass. 'I wonder when Jack will decide to come home—has he written to you, Mama?'

Her mother shook her head. 'My son will come home when he's ready.'

Zandra gazed out of the window, smoking rather moodily and framed tall and striking against the glow of the sun. Debra couldn't help thinking that she should have been wearing a flowing robe instead of fashionable culottes.

'What if Jack was to bring home a new wife,' she suddenly said.

There was a palpable silence and then Lenora answered her daughter frostily. 'One must hope not!'

'All the same, Mama, it's a possibility we can't ignore. Jack does have an infant who needs a mother.'

'I'd never forgive him!' Lenora gasped. 'Not a second mistake!'

Debra sat there astounded by the statement. She had never heard such a selfish utterance and couldn't help but wonder if this woman had been on board the yacht the night her daughter-in-law had fallen into the sea.

'If you've finished your tea, Miss Hartway, you can go.' Lenora Salvador spoke abruptly to Debra. 'I assume you find your working and sleeping quarters satisfactory?'

'Yes, Mrs Salvador, I've everything I require.' Debra rose to her feet, murmured a polite good-afternoon and made her way out of the solar, leaving mother and daughter to speculate further on Jack Salvador's whereabouts and plans for the future.

Debra went downstairs in a thoughtful mood . . . she would have to ask Nanny Rose if Jack's mother had been a guest at that fateful party. She didn't bother to hide the fact that she had disapproved of Pauline, and Debra suspected that she was the kind of woman who might bear malice towards someone whom she thought of as being beneath her.

As Debra crossed the hall in the direction of the working den, as it was called, she found her gaze drawn to the towering portrait of the founder of the house. The dark eyes beneath the emphatic brows seemed to hold Debra to attention . . . there was proud dominance and a hint of devilry in that Spanish face.

Don Rodare de Salvador, whom Zandra had admitted to admiring, and whose ways her mother had said were inherited by the half-brother.

CHAPTER TWO

As the days passed and Debra established a working routine that no one interfered with, it dawned on her that she had been accepted by the *éminence grise* of the house and wasn't going to be discharged from Abbeywitch because she jarred on Lenora Salvador. A woman very much of her generation and class, who had also developed a prejudice against any young female who might affect her son Jack the way Pauline had.

Debra was faintly amused, for she was aware that in her neat shirts and skirts, with her hair in its chignon, and wearing the horn-rimmed spectacles that she needed for close work, she looked about as sexually threatening as a dove on a fence.

Thank heaven for it! She found Abbeywitch fascinating, and it made such a break to be working away from the sweltering city now that summer was coming. She didn't dare to hope that the job might become permanent, but she could look forward to a few weeks of bliss beside the sea, waking in the mornings to fresh air and only the sound of the seabirds, lifting and settling on the water, moving up and down like toy birds as the long waves curled towards the cove.

The den itself was a secluded room right at the far end of the hall, its high walls panelled with Spanish leather that was stamped with gothic crosses in saffron and black. Books and scripts and cassettes were stacked upon shelves in units that stood away from the walls, and the desk where Debra worked was in a big bay window that let in light that didn't quite penetrate to the far corners of the room, and sometimes she would glance up from the typewriter with the oddest notion that a pair of eyes were watching her while she worked.

Not forgetful of what Zandra had said, that long ago this room had been a cell where a priest had lived, Debra felt a sense of disquiet, but she kept it to herself. She didn't want to be labelled by Zandra as another dotty spinster who looked under her bed at night in case a man was hiding there.

It was odd hearing on tape the voice of a man she had never met. Jack Salvador had a deep and deliberate voice and if she closed her eyes he seemed to be in the room with her. She had no idea what he looked like for his books never carried a picture of him on the back of the jacket. In his view it added a sense of suspense that his readers had to imagine the way he looked. He never went in for self-advertisement and didn't appear on television in order to pro-

mote his books. Nor did he give interviews
to newspaper and magazine columnists.

He didn't need to do any of that, in Debra's
opinion, for he was an enthralling writer and
she had already written to Harrison Holt to
inform him that he wasn't going to be disappointed by the new book. It wasn't only
colourful and packed with detail, but it was
romantic as well, as if Jack's feelings for
Pauline had filtered into the story and added
impact to the interludes of passion.

His own love story was ended . . . he the
man of intellect who had fallen beneath the
spell of the showgirl whose attributes were
physical rather than mental.

A tragic romance, doomed to last but a short
while, its setting here on Lovelis Island as dramatic as anything Jack Salvador had portrayed
in one of his novels in which he interweaved
historical fact and fiction. It gave Debra a
sense of satisfaction to be working on his book.

She didn't see a great deal of Mrs Salvador
and her daughter, and this was something of a
relief. They were a rather disquieting pair, and
Debra preferred to take her meals with Nanny
Rose rather than sit constrainedly at the oak
table in the dining-room where the chairs were
very upright, matching the formality that the
matriarch insisted upon at the evening meal.

At the present time, Zandra had several of
her theatrical friends staying at Abbeywitch,

though they were absent most of the day, rehearsing a play at the Iseult Theatre on the mainland.

On Saturday afternoons Debra felt at liberty to go down to the cove, where she swam and lazed in the sun, disturbed by no one but the birds, securely aware that she couldn't be overlooked because of the guardian cliffs. They jutted in a brow above the beach, too high to shade the sands from the sun but making it impossible for the casual observer to gaze down on her, where she lay on her beach towel acquiring the tan that every town girl dreams of.

Debra had written to inform her mother that her stint as a private secretary on an island was turning out well, and that the house she was living in was built on high cliffs above the ocean. She had described little Dean to her mother, a grand little chap with his deep blue eyes and his infectious chuckle, too young to be aware that his young mother had lost her life in the glittering, churning sea which held such dark memories for Jack Salvador that he couldn't bring himself to come home until he could accept that he was never going to see Pauline again and hold her in his arms.

Pauline's death had been called an accident, but Debra wondered if a spiteful hand had pushed her into the sea while the dance music played. If she cried out the sound would be drowned by the music, and according to Nanny Rose the party on board the yacht had included Jack's mother. Family friends had gathered to celebrate Zandra's birthday, so Mrs Salvador had been persuaded to join the party, a lively one with not only dancing on deck but fireworks whizzing out over the ocean.

Down on the beach Debra would gaze at the water and wonder at the secret that the sea kept to itself. All that was left was a man's grief, and it would be a long time before the child of the marriage was old enough to ponder the mystery of his mother's death. By then the passage of time would have eroded the poignancy of it all, as the sea itself eroded the rocks along the shore and gradually turned them to sand.

After her swim Debra would stretch out and relax, lulled by the sound of the surf as it shuffled and foamed among the rocks. The sun-warmed air trapped the tang of the sea and the wafting scent of the ling and gorse that hung at the cliff edge, along with the white samphire and the figwort. The seagulls swooped, mewing like lost cats, their wings spread gracefully against the sky.

Debra had drifted off to sleep with the caress of the sun on her body, and it was her skin's awareness of shadow that awoke her. Her eyes fluttered open and she stretched her limbs with lazy indolence, which changed to sudden shock as her gaze focused on the figure which blocked out the sun by standing with long legs straddling her recumbent form.

There was a vibration in Debra's throat which felt like a scream that wouldn't emerge. This stranger had invaded the cove and every nerve and cell of her body was sending a signal of danger to her brain.

'This—this beach is private,' she managed to say.

'Then what are you doing on it?' he demanded.

'I have the right to be here.' The words jolted nervously from her throat. 'I work for the family who owns it.'

The eyes looking down at her swept her from neck to heel and in an attempt to conceal as much of herself as possible Debra made a cape of her hair, loosened from its knot after her swim so it could dry in the sun. As she did this the tall stranger narrowed his eyes until they were like slits of ebony.

'One of the maids, I presume?' His voice crackled with sarcasm. 'Does the lady of the house know that you lie down here without a stitch of clothing on?'

A wave of confusion and indignation swept over Debra. 'I'm Mr Jack Salvador's secretary—' And there she broke off with a gasp. It couldn't be, could it . . . the employer she had hoped to meet and impress with her efficiency in dealing with his book? If it was he, then how was she going to live down that he had found her shamelessly stretched out on his beach, with her clothes in a little mound beyond his firmly planted feet.

Damn, it looked as if her pleasant job was at an end!

'The secretary, eh?' Again he looked her over. 'The last time I was at Abbeywitch there was a fat little woman of fifty doing the typing, and I never caught her in your present predicament.'

'I thought for the moment—' Debra bit her lip. 'Who are you—are you a friend of Zandra Salvador's?'

'Do you think I look like an actor?'

The irony in his voice informed Debra that he had nothing to do with Zandra's theatrical friends, and she wondered if he might be the divorced husband whom Zandra had spoken of so contemptuously. But even as the thought occurred to her, she rejected it . . . he didn't strike her as the kind of man who would fail to live up to a woman's exciting expectations.

On the contrary . . . from the moment Debra opened her eyes and saw him towering above her, she had been picking up from him the most unsettling vibrations.

'Who are you?' she repeated.

'I assure you I have every right to be here. I

happen to be the owner of Abbeywitch,' he announced. 'You may have heard my step-mother speak of me—I'm Rodare Salvador.'

Debra caught her breath. She had assumed that Jack Salvador was the master of Abbeywitch and it came as quite a shock to hear this stranger announce that he was the master . . . and there was no denying the fact that he had a masterful air. He struck her speechless and all she could do for several seconds was stare up at him, a figure of confusion at his feet.

Her mouth worked, then the words came rather faintly. 'May I have my clothes, Mr Salvador, so I can get dressed?'

'By all means.' He picked up the bundle and dropped it down beside her and in a mocking way he turned his back and gazed out to sea while she hurriedly dressed. When he turned to face her, she was rewinding her hair into its coil.

He was copper-skinned and the Spanish ebony of his eyes were intent upon Debra, hitting the very centre of her nervous system and inducing two distinct feelings in her. She wanted to retreat hastily from him, and she also wanted to stay and defend herself against what he was probably thinking, that she was a shameless hussy and what the devil was she doing in the employment of his brother Jack. Secretaries who came to Abbeywitch should be comfortable bodies in their fifties who ate currant buns on the beach and knitted sweaters!

Debra agonised in silence, for she didn't want to lose her job and he had the power to dismiss her right now. Also he was partly Spanish and she had heard that Spaniards who saw foreign girls bathing in bikinis on their beaches had only one opinion of them . . . that they were there for the picking and weren't moral like Latin girls.

Oh lord, and he had come upon her without even a bikini to hide the more intimate parts of her figure!

He carried his cigarillo to his lips and drew on it, tall in a silky dark shirt worn with black doeskin trousers that hugged his long legs. There was strength and authority in every line of him; a kind of pantherish grace allied to the power and poise of a man accustomed to taking charge of a situation.

His face, Debra thought, was the kind which Yeats had written about: *Hollow of cheek as though it drank the wind. And took a mess of shadows for its meat.*

'I—I am off-duty,' she said, unable to bear his silence a moment longer.

'And do you always spend your off-duty time getting yourself an all-over tan?' he asked.

'The beach is sheltered.' Debra tilted her chin, as if attempting to pour her blush back where it couldn't be seen by him. 'I'm not an exhibitionist, but it's good to feel the sun and this is the first time I've worked in an oceanside house.'

'And do you enjoy your work?' Not by an inflection did his voice soften, it remained as coolly deep as those eyes in the coppery face. He looked as if he lived where the sun had bitten him to the bone.

'I like working at Abbeywitch very much,' she replied.

'You find it excellent board and lodging, no doubt, with seaside facilities thrown in?' Cigarillo smoke slid from his haughty Latin nose.

Debra drew herself up very straight and looked into the eyes whose ebony was so disconcerting. 'I can assure you, Mr Salvador, that I do my work thoroughly and earn my salary, and I naturally thought that I could use the beach—I didn't know it was your beach, of course, and that it was out of bounds to a mere employee. No doubt you would like me to leave Abbeywitch, so I'll go and pack my belongings—'

'You will stay exactly where you are, young woman!'

Debra obeyed him, though very much against her will. 'Haven't you finished telling me that all I appear to do is loll about on your beach, eat your food, and enjoy the comforts of your house?' Debra's eyes were green with temper . . . damned arrogant man! Standing in judgment on her ableness as a secretary just because he found her sunbathing, with her hair unbound from its tidy secretarial knot.

She touched a nervous hand to her knot; Rodare Salvador was looking at her hair as if recalling how she had caped herself with it when he had stood over her.

'My stepmother is usually the last woman in the world to be taken in by surface charm,' he said. 'How did you manage to persuade her that you were fit to be Jack's secretary? I'd have thought she'd have taken one look at you and sent you packing, as you're on the wrong side of fifty and have curves that haven't yet run together into a kind of doughnut. Tell me, what became of the other woman—wasn't her name Miss Tucker?'

'Miss Tucker said something that upset Mrs Salvador and she was fired.' Debra was all braced up to be fired herself, thinking how unfair it was that she and the former secretary should be given their notice, not because of inefficiency but because they had both managed to annoy a member of this high-and-mighty family. Secretaries weren't supposed to be seen or heard; the more they behaved like automatons the more they were appreciated.

'Do you happen to know what she said?' he asked curtly.

Debra hesitated. 'I—I think Miss Tucker made some reference to your brother's dead wife which Mrs Salvador took as an insult. She was dismissed in your brother's absence and several other secretaries were hired, and then fired, before I came to Abbeywitch.'

'And for some reason you clicked with Lenora, eh?'

'Mrs Salvador seems quite satisfied with my work, and I've enjoyed being here—'

'You can't be more than nineteen or twenty,' he rapped at her.

'I'm twenty-four.'

His eyes raked up and down Debra's figure in the sleeveless lemon-coloured dress, and he seemed both perplexed and annoyed by her. Feeling the same about him, she spun on her heel, picked up her beach towel and bag and walked away. 'Good afternoon, Mr Salvador!'

She had almost reached the handrailed steps that led up the cliffside to the headland when strong hands caught her by the shoulders and swung her around as effortlessly as if she had been a walkie-talkie doll.

'You have a temper, young woman.'

'Isn't that allowed either?' Her reaction to being touched by him was a mixture of wanting to pull away and being afraid in case a struggle resulted and she was brought into contact with his body. In the opening of his shirt his chest and shoulders looked formidable; his skin was the sheen of copper ore.

'The people who work for my stepmother are usually subservient.' His eyes moved over her face which was devoid of make-up because she had been in the water before stretching out to enjoy the sun. There was a glitter beneath the heaviness of his eyelids and Debra felt the warmth stealing from his skin.

This was more disturbing than anything else had been, and dusk was filtering down over the sea-grey cliffs and the sea. 'It's getting late,' Debra spoke rather breathlessly. 'Perhaps I should go and pack—'

'Packing to leave Abbeywitch is the last thing you want to do, eh?'

'I—I'd sooner go than stay on thorns, never knowing when I might do something else that I shouldn't—you see, Mr Salvador, I wasn't told that you were in charge of things.'

'I'm very much in charge whenever I'm here. What are you called?'

Her eyes widened, for he was more utterly arrogant than anyone she had ever met. 'Dogs and cats are called—'

'Enough of that.' He gave her a shake. 'Tell me your name.'

She wanted to tell him to go and jump in the ocean, but somehow he compelled obedience, not merely because he was so much bigger than she was, but because of that inherent force that was stamped into his features and alive in his eyes. Debra told him her name.

'Well, Miss Hartway, I'm not going to order you off my property because of your indiscreet exposure of yourself, but I am going to advise you not to do it again.' His gaze held hers. 'The times we live in are strangely menacing, and young women are vulnerable, even if they do choose to shout the odds about their emancipation and their rights. Anyone could have come down those steps, don't you realise it?'

'I—I never thought—'

'And that is the fundamental difference between the sexes, men act upon a thought, but you females react to a situation. You had been in swimming, eh, and when you emerged from the water the sun felt good on your skin so you decided to let every bit of you feel it.'

She flushed, for something in his voice informed her that he hadn't been unappreciative of seeing every bit of her; and Zandra had implied that he was the kind of man who enjoyed women without getting his wings scorched. It was the women, Debra thought, who felt the flame when Señor Salvador got near them.

'How is the young Dean?' he abruptly asked. 'The child is flourishing?'

She nodded. 'He's a charming little boy; it's such a shame that he should be left motherless.'

Rodare Salvador inclined his head, thickly capped by hair of a blackness such as Debra had never seen before . . . it was, she couldn't help thinking, almost wickedly black. 'Yes, as I indicated a few moments ago, young women can be at the mercy of many factors. You are fond of children, Miss Hartway?'

'I think they're quite nice, Mr Salvador, but I don't know a lot about them.'

'You have no brothers or sisters?'

She shook her head. 'No, I'm an only child; my father died when I was an infant.'

'I see.' His hands tightened a moment on her shoulders, and subjected to his touch Debra felt her heart quicken and she didn't want to feel this skin-tingling awareness of a man who had such a look of arrogance about him. He was too aware of his powers, as if he might brush people away like flies when they had served their purpose.

She wanted to draw away from him, and at the same time she didn't want to make it apparent that his closeness disturbed her, so she stood there as if unaware of his hands penetrating their warmth through the summery fabric of her dress.

'It's unusual to see a young English woman with a hairstyle like yours,' he said. 'It makes you look rather like a character from a Jane Austen novel.'

The remark startled her, but she quickly retaliated. 'There's more than a suggestion of Mr Darcy about you.'

'Indeed?' He arched a black eyebrow. 'You consider me a handsome snob, Miss Hartway?'

'I wouldn't call you handsome, Mr Salvador, but you're obviously a proud man who isn't very kind to people who bore you.'

'Do you also read the Tarot cards?' He spoke sardonically.

'You had my character weighed up in a few seconds, didn't you, Mr Salvador?'

'*Touché.*' His lip dented in what was no doubt his concession to a smile. 'So you are going to remain at Abbeywitch, eh? After leaping to the conclusion that I was going to send you packing?'

'Weren't you?' she fenced, flushing at the way he looked at her, as if he found her naïvely amusing.

'I don't interfere in my brother's business no more than he interferes in mine, so I wouldn't take it upon myself to dismiss his secretary. How do you like working for him?'

Debra stared at Rodare Salvador. 'Don't you know—?'

'Know what?'

'Your brother still hasn't come home.'

The ebony Latin eyes went narrow and the black brows drew together across the thrusting nose. 'But it's been weeks—you are telling me there's been no word from him, no indication that he's coming home? He has that child to consider! He has a duty to the living! What the devil has got into him?'

'Grief?' Debra murmured.

'Grief has to be overcome or it becomes a self-indulgence.' The strong, sun-darkened hands were abruptly withdrawn from Debra's shoulders. 'Come, the day is darkening and the tide is coming in, and I must speak with my stepmother.'

Debra mounted the steps ahead of him, glad of the falling darkness so those eyes of his couldn't dwell on her legs. When they reached the headland he came to a standstill, for there ahead of them, outlined against the last fiery rays of the sun, were the rooftops and turrets and great windows of Abbeywitch.

'Quite a sight, isn't it?' he said. 'Each time I return to the island I wonder why I leave it, but I'm a divided man, Miss Hartway. In the deep heart of Spain I have a *granja* where I live like my mother's people, but every so often I think about Abbeywitch and it calls to me, built as it is on these cliffs that rise from the sea itself. This wandering spirit has taken me back and forth since I was a youth, but it's unusual for my brother Jack to behave in such a way. Always he has put his work before anything else.'

'But along came Pauline,' Debra murmured. 'Your brother fell in love, Mr Salvador, and love can change people.'

The tall figure gazed down at Debra, a man far more Spanish in looks and outlook than his sister Zandra, and possibly his brother Jack.

The three of them had shared the same father, but Debra was inclined to believe that they shared little else. There might even be a certain undercurrent of enmity because Rodare had inherited Abbeywitch and yet chose to spend most of his time in Spain.

'What do you know of love?' He smiled slowly, sardonically. 'You look too young to have known the pangs and pleasures of a *relaciones amorosas*, apparent from the way you blushed down on the beach—ah, you catch your breath and want that encounter forgotten, eh? Do you think it's possible, *señorita?*'

Never in her life had Debra been addressed as *señorita*, which like many Spanish words was so provocative, and he attached it to a question which in itself was provoking.

'You won't say anything to your stepmother, will you, about seeing me nude on the beach—I don't think she'd understand?' This man not only managed to make Debra feel on the defensive, but he aroused other feelings to which she was a stranger. The men who worked for Columbine Publications had an attitude that was ambitious, their sights set on achievement in a modern world. Rodare Salvador seemed more attuned to the elemental fire of the sky as the sun dipped into the sea, where the waves surged to the shore with ponderous power, overwhelming the sands and the rocks.

'You may rest assured that I shan't say a word—it will be our secret, Miss Hartway.' Irony edged his voice as he glanced towards the sea, and when Debra looked at him, his profile was outlined against the dramatic beauty of the sky, broodingly strong and touched by a hint of melancholy. Was he remembering Pauline . . . or had he shared the family disapproval of his brother's wife.

'Such atmosphere,' he spoke almost to himself. 'If I were a writer or an artist I would find such surroundings of inestimable value to my work, and I'm sure this has been so for Jack. What do you think of his work, young woman?'

'I think he's one of the best popular writers alive today,' she said warmly. 'I—I just haven't the words to describe his latest book!'

'I imagine it thrills,' he said drily.

She smiled. 'Columbine are going to be enormously pleased with the book—I get so involved with the typing that sometimes I don't notice that the room is darkening as evening draws in, and then I—I imagine that someone has come into the den and is hiding among the shadows. I quickly switch on the overhead light and everything is back to normal again—'

Debra broke off, for she hadn't meant to confide the eeriness that crept into the leather-walled den with the fall of dusk, when she would quickly cover the typewriter and hurry to the nursery suite to be with Nanny Rose and little Dean.

'If you don't care for the atmosphere of Jack's den, why not work in one of the other rooms?' Abruptly he turned to face her, his shoulders spread wide against the afterglow. 'There's a small morning-room facing the library, so why not work there on Jack's book? I am aware that his descriptive powers can be effective.'

'No,' she shook her head, 'it would be childish of me to give in to fancies, and I'm all right most of the time.'

'You're over-imaginative, I expect.'

'I think I am,' she agreed. 'That's why I chose to work for a publishing house.'

'You have ambitions to become a writer yourself?'

'Oh no,' she said quickly. 'I love books, but I don't think I have it in me to be a writer of them. I was so grateful for the chance to work for your brother.'

'A touch of hero-worship, no doubt.' Abruptly her chin was enclosed by his hard fingers and he tilted her face so he could study it. The tide below them was crashing across the beach and hitting the cliffs as the sky turned to sable.

Debra felt her pulse beating with an intensity that was quite frightening and she had to subdue the urge to pull away from this man who had seen her with only her long smooth hair caping her body. She wished he was a stranger who would walk away from Abbeywitch, but instead he was the master who meant to stay awhile, and he had already implied that it wouldn't be possible for either of them to forget the way they had met down on the sands that were now possessed by the sea.

'Let us go and have dinner,' he said decisively, and they walked towards the house where lights were glowing behind the windows. 'Do you take your meals with the family, Miss Hartway?'

'No, I have them with Dean's nanny.'

'At your wish or my stepmother's?'

'Mrs Salvador suggested it, and it's what I prefer to do.' Debra spoke firmly. 'I like Nanny Rose and I—I feel more comfortable with her.'

'I'm sure you do, *señorita*.' But there was a rather hard note in his voice, and as they entered a sideway into the hall of the house the big chandeliers lit his face and reflected diamond-hard in his eyes. Instantly, in the big portrait of the Don Salvador who had founded the family, which hung against the dark richness of the panelled wall, Debra saw the man who walked at her side.

There was the proud arrogance in the shape of the head and the features; there the compelling look of authority, and the skin that a hot, fierce sun had tanned.

More than once Debra had stood and looked

at the portrait that commanded the attention of whoever came into the house, but she hadn't dreamt that she would ever meet such a man in the flesh.

'My infamous ancestor,' said Rodare Salvador, catching the look she flung at the portrait. 'He was said to have the blood of the Moors in his veins . . . very jealous men where their women are concerned, as Othello proved to the doomed Desdemona.'

And there in the eyes looking down at Debra, framed by brows and lashes of a wicked blackness, was the menace of strange places . . . the desires of a strong personality.

With a breathless urgency she said: 'Nanny Rose will wonder what's become of me—good night, Mr Salvador!'

'Good night, Miss Hartway.' He spoke with a slight note of mockery in his voice and watched as she backed a few paces to the stairs. 'Ours has been an intriguing introduction to each other. Please give the *hijito* a kiss and a hug from me.'

When she looked puzzled he briefly smiled. 'I use the Spanish word for little boy.'

'Oh—I see.' She stepped upon the stairs. 'Yes, all right.'

She turned and fled, obeying the impulse which had been clamouring in her from the instant she had looked into the Spanish eyes of Rodare Salvador.

CHAPTER THREE

BEYOND the parapet the sea had a breathless, sparkling beauty as the sun arose, with the seabirds flying on the crest of the waves to snatch their prey.

It had never been possible when Debra worked in the city to feel such a sense of expectancy in the day ahead, it merely came as a relief to reach the office after the usual subway scramble, the air in the streets still stale from the day before, the traffic fumes locked in by the tall buildings.

But here on the edge of the ocean the air was like a wine that went to her head so that she slept soundly and awoke hungry for her breakfast. She always had lunch and dinner with Nanny Rose, but chose to have her breakfast on the terrace. She never bothered the staff but went quietly to the kitchen to collect her tray and with a sense of luxury she would eat her eggs, bacon and toast while listening to the sea churning into the cove.

Although she had no need to work on Sundays, she chose to do a morning's stint at the typewriter. It helped pass the day and kept her from running into Zandra and her friends.

Several of them were staying at Abbeywitch and upon passing the drawing-room the other evening she had heard herself referred to as 'that mouse who pecks away at the typewriter in the den of mystery.'

Debra had to admit it was an appropriate description but it made her feel self-conscious, and it also made her aware of the actor who had tagged her as a mouse.

She knew him to be Stuart Coltan who had appeared in a television series about a famous dance-hall in New York which during wartime had been a rendezvous for servicemen and their girl-friends. Debra had enjoyed the series not only because it had been well-acted and lively, but because it had given her an insight into her father's life. He had seen action in Korea as a young man, sustaining the injury which had led to his broken health and his early death.

Stuart Coltan had played a young soldier in the series and much as Debra had enjoyed his acting and his skill as a dancer, she decided that in reality he was a rather brash American who liked to air his wit at other people's expense.

He seemed to be extra friendly with Zandra Salvador, and Debra was willing to bet that Zandra was the type of woman who demanded to be the centre of a man's attention. They certainly made a striking pair, and from the terrace Debra had watched them water-skiing, and going out in the launch to dine and dance on the deck of the big yacht belonging to the theatrical producer who was backing the show they were still in the throes of rehearsing.

Before starting her own work Debra went along to the nursery suite to wish Nanny Rose good-morning and to have a little game with Dean, who this morning had a new toy to show her, a clown with floppy legs and a bright red nose.

He held it out to Debra, his blue eyes beaming into hers. 'Dino,' he announced, his name for all his toys including his spinning-top and his teddy-bear with a bent ear.

'Isn't he a funny Dino?' she said. 'Did your uncle give him to you?'

Nanny Rose came over to the high-chair with Dean's bowl of cereal. 'So you know about Dean's uncle. No one had any idea he was arriving; he just turned up out of the blue looking as brown as a bullfighter and he popped into the nursery last night to take a look at his little nephew. He's that foreign-looking it's hard to believe he's half-brother to Mr Jack and Miss Zandra.'

Nanny Rose always referred to the members of the Salvador family in the old-fashioned way; she had worked her way up from a nursery-maid in the households of upper-class families and had been recommended to Jack Salvador by his publisher.

Debra smiled, but didn't mention her own disturbing encounter with Rodare Salvador.

'A pity it isn't the little lad's daddy who has come home.' Nanny Rose coaxed milky cereal into the child's mouth. 'The lord knows when he's going to return . . . I really start to wonder if he's gone and joined his poor love of a wife.'

'Oh—don't say that!' Debra exclaimed.

'You didn't see him, my dear, the day he scattered her ashes.' Nanny Rose gave Debra a significant look. 'Ashen-faced he was and he left Abbeywitch about an hour afterwards, speeding away in the motorboat like a man pursued by devils. There was such a to-do. Madam had hysterics and even Mr Rodare couldn't calm her down. And Miss Zandra got pie-eyed and went out on Firefly in that state and ended up breaking the mare's left foreleg. You should have heard the language Mr Rodare used! He had to go out with the gun and do the necessary, and when he came storming back into the house the chandeliers shook in the hall when he told those two women what he thought of them.'

Debra could well imagine the scene which had taken place. 'Nanny, I wonder why the family was so upset when none of them seemed to care very much for Pauline?'

'Perhaps they felt guilty.' Nanny Rose gave

Dean's chin a wipe. 'We all feel a touch of guilt when we lose someone we love, so just imagine what mother and daughter went through when Mr Jack went off as if he couldn't stand the sight of them.'

'But he left his little son behind.' Debra touched a finger to the child's milky cheek; he was sloshing about with his spoon and getting most of his breakfast over his face and bib. A man, Debra thought, would have to be in a very stricken state to do what Jack Salvador had done. This, after all, was Pauline's baby.

'There's no accounting for what folks will do when they're in a state.' Nanny Rose gazed at the little boy with a look of sadness in her eyes. 'I've been on this earth long enough to have learnt that people are the strangest of God's creatures, and that's a fact.'

And even as she spoke, the door of the nursery opened and in strode the boy's uncle. Debra felt a leap of her nerves, for here in the nursery he looked even more formidable than he had looked down on the beach. A cambric shirt was thrown open against his throat and he wore corded breeches and a pair of boots laced up the front to the knee. He brought a whiff of horse in with him and his shirt was generously splashed as if with sea water.

He gave Dean's nanny a courteous inclination of the head, then fixed Debra with a brief look that penetrated. When he turned to his nephew a smile quirked the edge of his mouth.

'How quickly a child loses the baby look,' he said. 'When last I was here Dean was so much smaller, just a bawling bundle of wants, now look at his chunky limbs and those mischievous eyes.'

Dean sat gazing up at his tall uncle, his mouth open like a cuckoo bird's so his nanny could feed him. 'Dino!' He turned in his high chair and waved a fist at his clown. 'Nice Dino.'

'Is that his name for me?' Rodare asked, amused.

Nanny Rose gave an indulgent laugh. 'That's the little lad's name for all his toys, isn't it, my duck?'

'You're a quaint *pequeño*, aren't you?' Rodare gently stroked a hand across the boy's dark hair, and in return Dean gave him a wide smile that revealed his tiny teeth.

'And already he has teeth,' Rodare exclaimed, as if he wasn't often in the company of very young children and didn't know a great deal about them. 'Such white little teeth, rather like grains of rice.'

A remark that touched Debra, though she was trying quite hard not to let the look and sound of this man get under her skin. He was a sudden and very alarming addition to the household, for she hadn't been prepared to meet in the flesh the living likeness to the Spaniard who had founded this family. Every muscular inch of him seemed to pulse with energetic life, as if he did take after his forebear in ways as well as looks.

Amused and intent he watched his nephew drinking orange juice from his Mickey Mouse mug, the boy's blue eyes fixed in turn upon his face. They seemed to Debra to be taking each other's measure, as if they were establishing their family bond.

'Joose,' Dean said, offering the mug to Rodare after he had taken his fill.

Rodare accepted the mug and solemnly raised it to his lips and swallowed some of the juice. 'Mmm, very tasty, *pequeño*.'

Dean glanced at his nanny with an eager smile, then he looked at Debra to see if she was impressed by his generosity. Utterly beguiled by him she took hold of his hand and kissed his plump fingers. 'You are a little gentleman, Dean.'

He nodded his head as if in agreement with her, and his uncle said musingly: 'Amazing in a child so young to have such innate good manners. He is quite a boy, I think.'

'He's Mr Jack's compensation,' Nanny Rose replied. 'Have you any idea of his whereabouts, Mr Rodare? He's making everyone so anxious the way he's behaving. After all, it's his duty to consider the living.'

'I quite agree, Nanny Rose.' Rodare gazed down sombrely at his brother's child. 'I had no idea Jack was still absent from Abbeywitch, and I shall have to look into the matter. I was very surprised when told that he was still away and had not communicated with his mother. As you rightly say, he has young Dean to consider.'

'I hope the poor man is all right,' Nanny Rose said worriedly. 'He wouldn't have gone and done something—foolish?'

'I think it very unlikely.' Rodare gestured in a very Latin way. 'No, he is in a morose mood that won't allow him to see reason. When we were boys he had a tendency to sneak off when he was upset about something, and the loss of Pauline was a great shock to him . . . perhaps he took some of the blame because they were quarrelling.'

Rodare glanced at Debra as he spoke, as if curious to see her reaction to his remark, and it did amaze her that Jack and Pauline had not been in sympathy, especially so soon after the birth of their son who should have been the living proof that they still cared for each other.

Debra's gaze dwelt on the handsome little boy, so unaware that he no longer had a mother and that his father was hiding away somewhere, either stricken by guilt or grief. Dean banged happily on his cereal bowl with his spoon, and Debra wanted to take him in her arms and hug him for Pauline . . . the girl from the chorus line who had never been accepted at Abbeywitch.

'Well, I have things to see to after my lengthy absence.' Rodare Salvador strode to the door. 'When I am less tied up, Nanny Rose, I shall take the *pequeño* to the zoo at Penarth. He looks as if he'd enjoy seeing the elephants and tigers, and someone has to stand in for Jack, eh?'

Directly the door closed behind him Debra sank down in the nursery rocker. It was as if a strong wind had swept through the nursery and left turbulence in its wake.

'So they were quarrelling,' she murmured. 'Jack Salvador and Pauline.'

Nanny Rose nodded. 'It was one of those marriages that never stood much of a chance. She had lovely long legs and could kick them high, but she didn't have a mind that could match his. It was based on physical attraction and to give his mother her due she knew this and would have preferred him to get Pauline out of his system without putting a wedding ring on her finger. That kind of attraction is far apart from love.'

'Then what is love?' Debra murmured, unable to believe that the cross-currents of sensuality that drew people together and then swept them apart were truly related to the mysterious emotion called love.

'I'm not smart enough to puzzle it out,' Nanny Rose retorted. 'I was a nursery-maid when I was fourteen and trained in the ways of being a nanny by the time I was twenty, and in those days a nanny was expected to stay single. The only young men in my life have been this sort.' She patted young Dean on the head. 'The only time they break my heart is when the time comes for them to go off to school. But over the years they go on writing to me and sending snapshots of themselves, and sometimes that's more than real sons bother to do.'

'Have you always looked after little boys?' Debra looked intrigued.

Nanny nodded as she took a flannel to Dean's face and hands. 'I'm good with lads so I select to nanny them. I had five sisters, you see, and by the time I left home to go and be a nursery-maid I'd seen enough of female tricks to last me a lifetime. I left the Welsh valleys with my suitcase in my hand and took a train to Somerset where I began my first job. A big grand house it was and I was so overwhelmed.'

'Didn't you ever want to fall in love and get married?' Debra asked.

'I suppose it crossed my mind when I was a romantic girl, but once I found out that I enjoyed being a nanny I stopped thinking about it. The best jobs in the best houses go to single nannies and I preferred that to chancing my arm with some young smart-alec who might make a drudge of me—I saw that happen to three of my sisters. Marriage can be a chancy business and no mistake.'

'It seems to be a mistake Rodare Salvador doesn't intend to make.'

'He's more like his mother's people than his father's, so he'll make sure he's got the right girl before putting a ring on her finger.' There was a dry note in Nanny Rose's voice, as if her years as a nanny to boys had given her quite a bit of insight into their ways. 'And I expect you can judge for yourself, Debra, that he won't be easily satisfied. He's got Spanish pride in him and he'll be a right challenge for the girl he settles on, and the Lord help her if she ever goes astray!'

'You sound like a Welsh soothsayer,' Debra laughed.

'I know how to read the tea leaves, my girl, so any time you want to know your fate I'll take a look at what lies at the bottom of your teacup.'

'I'm not so sure that I want to know my fate.' Debra rose to her feet and gave little Dean a cuddle. In response he laid his head against her breast and blinked his dark lashes at her, already showing signs of being quite a charmer.

'You're my boy-friend, aren't you?' she smiled at him, and Dean smiled in solemn response.

Some time later Debra was busily at work in the den when the door suddenly opened . . . she glanced up from the typewriter, taking off her horn-rims in order to see who had entered.

'Hi there.' Stuart Coltan closed the door behind him and strolled to her desk, wearing navy slacks and a sky-blue shirt that matched his eyes. Debra felt a flash of surprise at seeing him, and felt again that there was something disruptive in his personality.

'I'm very busy, Mr Coltan,' she said firmly.

'I really go for that crisp and efficient manner of British secretaries,' he drawled. 'It makes me wonder what it may be hiding.'

'All it's hiding, Mr Coltan, is the desire to get on with the job,' she retorted.

'On a Sunday?' He lounged against her desk and studied her hair in a ray of sunlight through the mullioned windows behind her shoulders. 'What a little glutton you are for work—is it all you live for?'

'When the work's enjoyable.' She had to admit to herself that close like this he was every bit as good-looking as on television, with thick dark hair that peaked above his eyes, a deep dimple in his chin, and a lean, agile body that gave every indication of his dancing ability.

'You really mean to say that you enjoy pounding that machine most of the day?' he quizzed her.

'I'm typing into manuscript Mr Salvador's latest historical novel and it's an enthralling piece of work,' she said warmly.

'D'you like being enthralled?' A suggestive note entered his voice and his blue eyes roamed her face. 'Y'know, you're not such a bad-looking chick when you take off those glasses, and I have to tell you that I go for the colour of your hair—what d'you call that shade of hair?'

'I'm sure I wouldn't know.' She perched her spectacles back on her nose and ruffled some pages of notes on the desk.

'It's called chestnut-brown, isn't it?' He smiled and showed a good set of teeth. 'After those big nuts that fall off the trees in autumn-time.'

'I've heard of a mouse being chestnut-brown.' She drily let him know that she had overheard his description of her.

'Aw, don't hold that against me.' He leant forward to take a folio out of the tray and received a smart slap on the wrist.

'Don't you dare touch any of those pages!' Debra gave him a severe look. 'I shall report you to Mrs Salvador if you tamper with her son's book. The book is confidential and not open to the public until the day of publication.'

'Is that a fact?' He looked quite unrepentant. 'I was just curious to see what sort of a typist you are—I might want a letter typed.'

'Then get one of your girl-friends to do it,' Debra rejoined.

'Does that mean you're exclusive to the brilliant writer?' He quirked an eyebrow. 'I must say you look an exclusive sort of chick.'

'Is that meant to be a compliment, Mr Coltan?'

'It sure is.' He looked quizzical, as if not often did he find himself in the company of a girl who wasn't prepared to react to him. 'I believe your name's Debbie?'

'It's Debra, and I don't let people use it unless I—like them.'

'Don't you get the feeling that you're going to like me?' He spoke with the brash confidence of a young man who had always found himself attractive to the female sex. 'I've been told that I'm appealing.'

'How good for your ego.' She gave the frame of her spectacles a push and hoped they would turn him off, well aware that men with a basic lack of sophistication were put off by girls in glasses. When at the office, she used them as a form of protection against the office wolves on the prowl. They definitely seemed to cool the libido in men who regarded girls as playthings, with not a thought in their heads beyond being the sport of the sex hunters.

'Haven't you ever tried contact lenses?' Stuart Coltan deliberately took the horn-rims off Debra's nose. 'It's a crying shame covering up those big eyes with old-maid glasses.'

'Give them back to me!' Debra felt a flash of anger. 'If you don't do so this minute I—I'll go and tell Señor Salvador that you're interrupting my work!'

'Am I supposed to quake at the knees?' he mocked, and looking undisturbed by her threat he perched her glasses on his own nose and peered at her. 'Take a letter, Miss Hartway—Dear Debra, how do you feel about letting me wine and dine you one of these evenings?'

'Are you going to believe that I'm not interested, Mr Coltan?'

'You've got to be.' He took off her horn-rims. 'I've an unbroken track record.'

'Congratulations.' She held out her hand for the return of her glasses. 'I don't wish to break my own record, which is that I never go out with wolves.'

'You can't imagine that I'm a wolf?' He looked mock astonished. 'Here, you had better have these back—you're not seeing straight.'

'I see through you even without them.' She accepted her glasses and replaced them. 'Now be a good boy and run away to your games, I have work to do.'

'Prim as a pussy in a collar, aren't you?' He laughed and glanced around the den, with its rather forbidding leather-stamped walls.

'Who used to reside here, the head of the Inquisition?'

'Back in the mists of time an abbey was built on this site and a Jesuit priest was attached to the Sisterhood. This was his cell.'

'Is that a fact?' Stuart looked genuinely interested. 'It sure feels like a great place for writing historical novels, but how do you feel about working alone here?'

It was a perceptive question and took Debra by surprise. She realised that there might be more to Stuart Coltan than agile good looks and a rather brash line in self-confident flirtation. 'I don't mind working here,' she replied.

He studied her a moment and then took in all aspects of the leather-walled room. 'There's a certain atmosphere about this place and I bet you've noticed it.'

'Noticed what?' she murmured.

His eyes met hers. 'As if it might be—haunted.'

'That's your actor's imagination at work, Mr Coltan.'

'Is it?' He quirked an eyebrow. 'I bet when you're alone here and the dusk is beginning to make shadows you start to get jumpy. I reckon it's a crying shame that you've been tucked away among all these books about the past. You shouldn't put up with it, kid. If you act like a mouse then all you'll get out of life is other people's stale cheese.'

'Thanks for the pearl of wisdom,' she rejoined. 'I was offered another room to work in, but I happen to prefer this one. It's quiet and tucked away and I don't disturb anyone with my typing—nor does anyone disturb me,' she added pointedly.

'Am I disturbing you, honey?' He made the query sound suggestive.

'You know full well that you're disturbing work, Mr Coltan.'

'What a let down, Miss Hartway, I did so hope that I was discomposing you.'

'It would take more than you to do that.' Debra rose to her feet and walked to the door, which she held open for his departure. 'Go and join your friends—especially Zandra. She'll have the bloodhounds out after you if you don't take care.'

'You don't have to worry about Zandra.' He strolled to the door and there he confronted Debra with his brazen smile. 'Your surname is a libel, do you know that? You don't know a thing about the ways of the heart.'

'Then that makes two of us, doesn't it?'

'Okay, Miss Heartless, but you haven't seen the last of me.' And as he passed by he quickly bent his head and planted a kiss on her mouth, then he sauntered off down the corridor, walking with the confidence of a young man who had decided that the world was his peach-tree and he was going to shake it for all he was worth.

Debra reluctantly smiled as she closed the door and returned to her typewriter. He was charming and insouciant, with a dash of East Side shrewdness which had already brought him a measure of success. Debra felt quite sure that he had already broken several hearts and gone casually on his way without looking back at the damage.

She slid carbons between sheets of manuscript paper and switched on the tape-recorder. Soon the sound of Jack Salvador's voice had dispelled the drawling tones of Stuart Coltan. She was into the third chapter of *Savage By Night* and the story grew stronger with each tape that she listened to. It saddened her that the author didn't come home to his little son and his new book, but if Rodare Salvador was right, then it was something to do with the failure of his marriage that made him reluctant to return to Abbeywitch.

Debra pondered the drama of it all as she worked away at Jack's fiction, and she couldn't help wondering if Pauline had deliberately drowned herself? Had Jack grown bored with her once the physical side of their marriage was satisfied and was that why he stayed away, because he was racked by doubt and the suspicion that his young wife had intentionally jumped from the side of the yacht?

Yet even as Debra reasoned it out, she couldn't quite believe that a lively showgirl would take her own life. It would be more feasible to imagine her taking a lover.

Debra's fingers paused on the keys and she gazed reflectively at the sun's rays picking out the sombre patterns on the jackets of her employer's many books of reference . . . the one piece of pattern that seemed to fit was that Lenora Salvador should be so sure that her clever son would in time find Pauline tedious, and it seemed to Debra that in self-defence Pauline would turn to another man to whom her blonde charms would appeal. A man, perhaps, who was less intellectual than her husband.

Debra couldn't pretend to be experienced in such matters, but she could see how the attraction of opposites could lead to unhappiness. Feelings of mutual attraction couldn't always be controlled, and the mere glimpse of someone could set the pulse racing.

That morning in the nursery it had happened to her when Rodare Salvador walked in. Her knees had gone curiously unstable and again he made her feel vulnerable even though he gave no sign that previously in his presence she had not been wearing a sedate blouse and skirt.

Without effort he made her aware of his forcefulness, to such an extent that she felt almost a sense of threat . . . as if her instincts were sending warning signals through her body.

There was no telling how long he meant to remain at Abbeywitch, and perhaps had they met in a less unconventional manner, then she might not be so sensitive to his presence in the house. At least, that was what she told herself.

Determinedly she pushed him from her thoughts and carried on typing, taken by surprise when a maid tapped on the door and carried in a glass of wine and biscuits on a silver tray.

'The master said to bring you these refreshments, miss.'

'Oh—thank you—!' Debra felt flustered by the unexpected attention and when the maid had gone she slowly raised the tawny wine to her lips and tasted it. It was utterly delicious and the first time she had been offered wine from the Salvador cellar which was deep beneath the house in the cool old cloisters which had been part of the ancient abbey.

Giving in to a sense of luxury, she sat in the windowseat drinking her wine and nibbling her biscuits, thinking to herself that along with more subtle and disturbing ways, Rodare Salvador had his share of Spanish courtesy. He knew to the hilt how to play the *hidalgo*.

Having savoured the wine, she held the empty glass up to the sunlight and watched the

myriad fine colours sparkling in the crystal.
How long, she wondered, did the *hidalgo* stay
when he came home to this fascinating old
mansion on Lovelis Island? This house whose
motto declared: *Let honour reside within.*

Could there possibly be a more romantic
setting for an island than this most evocative of
regions—the Land of Merlin, whose legends
and stories still haunted the very air? Cornwall
itself was almost an island, surrounded as it
was by the sea and the River Tamar. Though its
old Celtic language was seldom spoken now,
there was in the voices of its people a sound
like no other; a kind of depth and mystery.

Debra sat there with the taste of wine on her
lips, and her mouth wore a small, almost
poignant smile. In the city she had felt alone,
but here she felt akin to the sea as it tore itself
on the teeth of the rocks; she breathed honey
when the wind blew through the grasses of the
cliffs, great ledges of granite where the chough
had its nesting place.

She even loved the beach at low water,
when it was desolate and the sands were lit
strangely by the dying sun. Across the water
she would hear the bells of the Chapel of
Sacred Sorrows and combined with the duskfall
and the lapping sea they would create an indelible impression.

A little voice in the mind warned her not to
become too attached to Lovelis Island, but with

the optimism of youth she told herself that perhaps when Jack Salvador came home he would decide to employ her as his full-time secretary.

It would be so much more rewarding for her than working in the city where the rush and roar of the traffic had eliminated any sense of enjoyment for most people. It was part of Debra's nature to like natural things and she found the ambience of this island more exhilarating than anything she had ever known before.

With each passing day there seemed to be something expectant in the very air she breathed and with all her heart she longed to stay. She returned to the typewriter, feeling today less of a stranger in the house which long ago the piratical Don Rodare had built for the bride snatched from the sands and carried on board his ship with his other booty.

It was no wonder, she told herself, the Salvador men were unconventional in their ways. Debra glanced across at the silver tray on which stood the crystal wine glass and she felt the strangest of feelings go tingling through her veins.

Was it possible . . . oh no, her reason for wanting to stay at Abbeywitch couldn't be related to that proud personage who chose to spend most of his time in the deep warm heart of Spain! The very idea alarmed her and her fingers were as if petrified upon the typewriter keys.

It wasn't only that she had never met his like before, it was that she distrusted the emotions which gave rise to physical attraction. That distrust had taken root in her when she was at a very impressionable age, and though she could be detached about it all in a book, she didn't know that she could face the reality of it . . . least of all in relation to Rodare Salvador.

She typed rapidly and her heart almost kept pace with her flying fingers. She wanted the thought of him to go away, but it was as if his every feature had become a fixture in her mind. Dark, aloof, fascinating . . . it was as if the wine he sent to her had contained a potion that cast a spell over her.

She firmly told herself that when she was through with her work she would take a brisk walk along the headland and let the wind blow these schoolgirl notions out of her head.

Getting ideas just because he behaved with Spanish courtesy and sent her a glass of wine to refresh her! She smartly tapped the key with the exclamation mark upon it.

CHAPTER FOUR

EVENING had fallen and as Debra crossed the court to the side entrance a light rain was coming down. The combination of moisture and lights sheened her hair as she stepped into the great hall. She shook the moisture from her wind-blown hair and her eyes were still alight from the fantastic sunset which she had watched from the brim of the high cliffs.

'Buenas tardes, señorita.'

She swung round with a catch of her breath, expecting to see the tall figure who had been in her thoughts as she walked in the wind and rain. But it was Stuart Coltan who stood running his gaze over her slim figure which was warmly encased in a fluffy jersey and hip-hugging pants. 'That set your nerves jumping, didn't it?' he jeered. 'You thought I was El Rodare.'

'Oh, it's you,' she said in a cool tone of voice, and she proceeded across the hall to the staircase.

'Whoa there!' Stuart leapt forward and caught her by the arm. 'You don't have to be in such a hurry.'

'Do you mind letting go of me?' She

attempted to shake off his hand.

'I rather like the feel of you,' he rejoined. 'What do you call that fluffy stuff?'

'Angora wool.'

'Feels real nice.' He stroked her and she very quickly slapped his hand.

'Look, Mr Coltan, I thought I'd made it plain that I don't play your kind of games.'

'Maybe you did, honey, but that was in working hours and now it's time to relax. I thought I made it plain that I like you—you're a girl with class, aren't you?'

'I'm a girl who happens to be particular,' she said frostily. 'I don't wish to lose my job by being caught with you. We both know that Zandra Salvador wouldn't like it.'

'Why should it concern Doña Zandra if I want to talk to you?' There was a wicked glint in his blue eyes as he spoke. 'She's at least ten years older than me.'

'I feel that wouldn't stop you, Mr Coltan, not if you found a woman attractive.'

'I certainly find you attractive, with that chestnut hair undone by the wind.' His hand tightened on her waist and he pulled her against him before she could resist. 'There's to be a party to welcome home the master of the manor and I'd like to share the evening with you. Come on, live a little or you'll turn into an old maid.'

'What a terrible fate,' Debra mocked,

pushing a hand against his chest in an effort to lever herself away from him, but he had the strength and resilience of a dancer and she found herself his very unwilling captive.

'Release me, Mr Coltan,' she said firmly.

'You scared of men and emotion?' he asked, an inquisitive gleam in his eyes as they stroked over her face.

'It takes more than someone like you to make me scared!'

'Someone like El Rodare, for instance?'

Every separate nerve in Debra seemed to give an alarming little jump. 'You'd better mind he doesn't hear you calling him that.'

'You sound in awe of him.' The laughter left the vivid blue eyes and they probed her features. 'Relax, kid, he doesn't know you're alive. The girl he'll be squiring tomorrow evening is the daughter of Morton Chandler, one of the Cornish bigwigs. D'you imagine you can compete with her sort?'

'Is her first name Sharon?' Debra asked thoughtfully.

'That's the lady.'

'I had the idea she was Jack Salvador's girlfriend before he met and married Pauline.'

'Maybe she was, but now she has her eye on his half-brother and it's no secret that the Salvadors would like her in the family. She has what they consider the three essentials: face, fortune and finesse. Be warned, Debra, you and I might amuse these people but we don't really fit in. No more than Pauline did.'

'Did you know her?' Debra eyed him curiously.

'Casually,' he replied. 'She danced in the chorus line of a few of the television shows I starred in. Pauline was a climber, but she lacked the streak of ruthlessness that creates people like the Salvadors. Don't pretend you haven't taken a long look at El Rodare.'

'I—I know what you mean.' From the first moment Debra had looked at Rodare Salvador he had seemed to have an almost barbaric detachment from gentle feelings; a high-and-mighty man, proud of his bloodline even if he had forebears who had strayed from the path of virtue. He probably knew that he was the living image of the family founder.

'You and I are amusing outsiders, honey, but that doesn't mean that we have to be subservient.' Stuart Coltan gave a scornful laugh. 'So how about putting on your party dress tomorrow evening and keeping me company?'

'I—I don't know what to say—' Debra was hesitant, and yet something inside her responded to the idea of dressing up and being a person in her own right instead of being the quiet mouse in the den who got on with her work and bothered no one. 'I haven't been invited to the party by Zandra and I'm not the sort to stroll in with the casual assumption that I'm wanted.'

'You'll be strolling in with me,' Stuart said airily, 'and I've handled tougher propositions than Zandra in my time. She isn't as tough a chick as she likes to pretend, you can take it from me.'

Debra felt sure that she could take it that the good-looking and insouciant Stuart could handle most females. 'Won't she want you to keep her company?' Debra asked.

'Sure, she'd like my company, but the producer of our show is invited to the soirée and he'll expect the VIP treatment, which means that she'll have to be attentive to him.'

'I see.' Debra looked directly at Stuart and once again she found herself thinking how attractive he was, and yet he didn't stir her pulses in the least. 'Are you involved with Zandra?—I hope that doesn't sound as if I'm prying but I don't want her thinking that I'm trying to take you away from her.'

'Honey babe,' he drawled, 'you have my permission to take me away from all other women.'

'I bet!' Debra scoffed. 'Seriously, is Zandra attracted to you?'

His smile answered for him. 'I play up to her because I'm ambitious and she has connections in the right places, but the real truth is that I don't feel drawn to thin brunettes who live on cigarettes and salads.' He looked Debra over in his impudent way. 'You're just the right height for me; you come to my shoulder and I bet we'd dance a dream together. Do you dance?'

'As a matter of fact I do.' Her smile was just a little grave. 'My mother always liked to dance and though, after my father died, we never had much money in the kitty she paid for me to have lessons. I started when I was twelve and went on with them until I was seventeen. My interest grew less when I became interested in my secretarial training. I had made up my mind that I wanted to work for a publishing house and I wanted to be good at my work. Yes, Mr Coltan, I dance, but I don't know many of the modern steps. My teacher was more intent on the Astaire and Rogers type of footwork.'

'But that's great!' Stuart's blue eyes burnt with enthusiasm. 'I go for that myself and consider that it beats all the honky-tonk stuff danced at the disco places. That's for kids!'

Suddenly in his enthusiasm he took Debra by the waist and whirled her around the hall. Involuntarily she fell into step with him and there they were, waltzing around the hall of Abbeywitch when the master of the place suddenly appeared on the scene and stood regarding them, his eyebrows raised.

'Stuart—' All at once Debra caught sight of the tall figure who sardonically watched them. 'Please let's stop!'

'Why should we ever stop?' he grinned. 'You dance like a breeze, do you know it? You're good, honey!'

But even as Stuart paid her the compliment, Debra felt herself stumbling over his feet, and although this brought him to a halt he didn't let go of her.

'We're practising for the party tomorrow evening,' he informed Rodare. 'This hard-working kid wasn't given an official invitation to the party so I decided to remedy the oversight.'

But the Spanish gaze was upon Debra's flushed face. 'I had no idea you were over-looked, Miss Hartway. I understood from Zandra that all the young people would be attending the party.'

'It really doesn't matter,' Debra made an effort to pull away from Stuart. 'I didn't expect to be invited, *señor*, and Mr Coltan is only fooling around.'

'So I noticed.' The dark eyes flashed in Stuart's direction. 'The pair of you dance well together.'

'Kind of you to say so,' Stuart drawled. 'Even though women weigh less than men they aren't always light on their feet, but Debra is like a swan. She's wasted at the typewriter in that mysterious room where she works, but I guess you Salvadors don't regard the feelings of the hired help with much consideration.'

'It's presumptuous of you to say so.' Rodare swept Stuart up and down and his dark eyes held the tempered glitter which Debra had noticed down on the beach. 'It also seems to me that you are putting pressure upon Miss Hartway with regard to the party my sister has arranged.'

His gaze returned to Debra, who had begun to feel like a bone of contention between a pair of bristling hounds. 'Is this young man trying to persuade you against your will?'

'No—that is I'm not sure—'

A black eyebrow was elevated above those glittering eyes. 'You must know one way or the other whether you want his company or not?'

'I suppose so,' she agreed, 'but it's my business, isn't it? I think I'm entitled to decide for myself.'

'Are you now?'

'I most certainly am, Mr Salvador.'

'Look here,' Stuart broke in, 'this kid works all hours, even on a Sunday, so I think she's entitled to a bit of fun.'

'Provided by you?' Rodare spoke curtly. 'I'm wondering at her wisdom in allowing you to provide it.'

'Holy James, you talk as if I'm not to be trusted with a girl,' Stuart expostulated.

'Maybe you aren't, with a good girl.' Rodare spoke quite deliberately. 'If Miss Hartway is stirred by your looks then I have no argument, but I venture to say that you exceed her in worldly knowledge, so be careful, Mr Coltan. I have my eagle eye on you!'

'Who the devil do you think you are?' Stuart demanded. 'Debra's off duty right now and free to be with me if she wants to be.'

'Miss Hartway is a responsibility of mine while she's employed in my house. She isn't here to provide my sister's friend with amusement, and we both know what I mean by that word, don't we?'

'What damned arrogance.' Stuart was almost snorting with temper. 'This isn't Spain, where the girls are kept behind iron grilles and expected to tease but never touch. Debra isn't a Spanish *señorita!*'

'Quite so.' The Spanish eyes flicked Debra's hair and face. 'But I venture to say that neither is she very experienced where men are concerned. There is a saying, the hand always reaches for the peaches that cling to the tree.'

'Not just my hand, I bet!'

'Meaning?' Rodare thrust lean hands into the pockets of his doeskin trousers and the action opened his shirt a little wider across his chest, the bronzed skin firm against the muscles, holding Debra's gaze until she realised that she was gazing and quickly looked away. Stuart was right, she told herself. The man was arrogant and she didn't really

appreciate being spoken about as if she hadn't long left the schoolroom and didn't know why the bee flew to the flower and why the birds built nests in the trees. Peaches, indeed!

'Meaning,' she interjected, 'that I can take care of myself and don't need either of you snarling at each other over whether or not I go to Miss Salvador's party. She hasn't invited me, so I shan't be going.'

'Debra,' Stuart looked annoyed, and also rather crestfallen, 'you promised—'

'I did nothing of the sort and you know it. I'd feel out of place, anyway—'

'And why is that?' Rodare curtly demanded.

'Because as you said, *señor*, I'm employed here; I'm not a guest like Mr Coltan. It's really of no consequence; I'm quite happy to read a book, and you have an extensive library, Mr Salvador.'

'Books!' Stuart threw up his hands. 'Honey, no wonder you have to wear those owl-rims when you're working. Soon you'll be wearing them all the time.'

'Which should make me safe from the likes of men,' she said rather heartlessly.

'Of course you'll go to the party.' Rodare spoke in his firmly decisive way. 'It was never in question, and I'm merely reminding Mr Coltan that while you reside beneath my roof I act in a guardian capacity and that means that if any harm came to you at the hands of a

Salvador guest I would deal with him in no uncertain manner. It's a matter of honour.'

'Holy James,' Stuart exclaimed, 'don't you ever stop being the high-and-mighty Spaniard? Zandra's right when she says you're the image of that ancestor of yours, the one in the big portrait in the hall. You make the rules and crack the whip, but I bet like him you're not above breaking a few.'

'I make the rules that apply to this house,' Rodare declared, 'and if you feel you can't abide by them, Mr Coltan, then I suggest that you pack your belongings and leave, *pronto*.'

'Of course Stuart isn't leaving!' High heels clicked on the parquet of the hall floor and Zandra joined the trio, her hand reaching out to clasp Stuart by the arm, her fingernails a deep and fiery red. 'He happens to my guest, Rod, so come down off your damned high horse and inform me what he's supposed to have done to make you breathe fire and sulphur.'

'Your half-brother seems to think I'm out to seduce the typist,' Stuart informed her, his eyes cutting like a blue facet across Debra's face. 'All I was doing was asking her to be my date tomorrow evening—'

'Your what?' Zandra asked, with a deadly kind of quietness.

'Now don't you start,' Stuart laughed. 'I've got to have someone to keep me company while you're sweet-talking the producer-man.'

'Is that a fact, Stuart?' Zandra gave him a blazing look which she suddenly turned on Debra. 'And what do you say to all this, Miss Hartway? Are you longing to keep him company while I'm unavailable?'

Debra was longing to dash up the stairs in search of the common-sense company of Nanny Rose.

'I think Mr Coltan is enjoying a joke at my expense,' she said quietly. 'I rarely go to parties and only when I'm invited.'

'I have invited you.' The voice of Rodare Salvador overrode her softer tones. 'I'm perfectly aware of how hard you have been working on my brother's book and I agree with Mr Coltan that you deserve a little fun—so long as he behaves himself!'

'Well, of all the nerve!'

'Rod, you damned well suit your name!'

The two voices blended together in their annoyance with the tall and inflexible master of the house.

'It's all right,' Debra started towards the stairs, 'I wouldn't dream of intruding.' And she ran up the staircase with the fleetness of a young hare, afraid that Rodare might come leaping after her, snapping those white teeth and commanding her to do as she was told. She hurried along the gallery, telling herself that Zandra was a snob and a jealous one, that

Stuart was an inveterate girl-chaser, and Rodare a man who liked to impress his authority upon everyone.

When she walked into the nursery her eyes were intensely green and her pulses were leaping with temper. Stuart Coltan was nothing but a nuisance, and she couldn't imagine what had made her think she was falling in love with Rodare Salvador. Lord help the woman who allowed herself to become his possession!

'Hello, my dear.' Nanny Rose was giving Dean his evening bath, her stout figure enveloped in a towelling apron so the boy's splashing wouldn't penetrate to her uniform. He seemed to have a great love of water and bathtime gave him the opportunity to flood the floor and half-drown anyone who came near him.

'Dibby,' he shouted when he caught sight of Debra. He flung a plastic boat at her in his enthusiasm and when water splashed all over her shoes she had to laugh, feeling a sense of release at being here in the bright and soapy atmosphere of the nursery.

'You look all flushed up.' Nanny Rose handed her a towel so she could wipe her legs. 'Whatever's the matter—your hands are shaking?'

Debra could feel the disturbing tremor not only in her hands but in her knees. 'I'm annoyed,' she admitted. 'I don't think I've ever

met such a high-and-mighty devil as Rodare
Salvador!'

'I see, so that young man has put the green
devils in your eyes, has he?' As Nanny Rose
spoke she cocked a warning glance at Dean.
'Not again, my lovey, you play with your
boaties in the bath.'

Debra sat down in the rocking-chair and
broke into a reluctant smile. 'He'd arouse the
devil in a nunnery,' she said.

'I daresay he would—going to have a cup of
tea with me?' Nanny Rose switched on the
kettle.

'I'd love a cup of tea.' Debra spoke from the
heart.

'Nothing like it for settling the nerves.' Tea
spoons clinked in saucers and from the direction of the bath came the joyous sound of
splashing as Dean dive-bombed his boats in
and out of the water. A contented child with a
caring nanny who had no idea that his young
mother was dead and his father perhaps at the
other side of the world, licking his wounds.

'I'm afraid, duckie,' Nanny Rose measured
tea into the pot, 'that Mr Rodare is the sort who
brings lightning in with him. Sometimes in the
valleys you come across that sort of man—I
was acquainted with one when I was just a slip
of a girl. He sang like an angel in the local choir,
but was always at the centre of any trouble at
the pit. A big, dark-haired chap, with fire in his

eyes. Every girl had her eye on him and yet at the same time he scared them silly. Then killed he was, when a gas explosion took place down in one of the tunnels. He could have saved himself, but according to one of the lads who did manage to get out, David *bach* stayed to try and help the trapped pit ponies and died with the poor scared creatures.'

Nanny Rose opened a tin of biscuits and poured out the tea. 'I see something of his look in Mr Rodare. They are men who play on the imagination. They are men whose words and deeds always seem that bit more significant—so what's he been doing to upset you, my lass?'

'He's been throwing his weight about.' Debra sipped her tea, which was always extra nice here in the nursery because Nanny Rose used good tasty Indian tea rather than the China tea which the Salvadors preferred.

Debra described the scene which had taken place down in the hall. 'Stuart and the *señor* were snarling at each other like a pair of angry hounds,' she sighed, 'and there I was in the middle of them. Then Zandra appeared and things got bitchy. I took to my heels and scampered upstairs, for the last thing I want is arguments over whether or not I go to this party Zandra has arranged. If she had wanted me there I would have been asked. It was Stuart's fault I got dragged into the argument, and Rodare Salvador obviously felt obliged to issue an invitation . . . along with a strong hint that Stuart behave himself because he thinks I'm too naïve to be able to take care of myself.'

Debra broke off in exasperation. 'You'd think I was about sixteen years old and had no experience of life to hear that man issue commands! He made such an issue of it, and it was as if he deliberately enjoyed baiting Stuart.'

'Not going soft over that young American, are you?' Nanny Rose regarded Debra with a frown. 'He's a bit too good-looking and he knows it, flashing those blue eyes of his at every creature in a skirt. He even comes in here with his charm turned on, and I'm old enough to be his mother!'

'Does he often come to the nursery?' Debra looked intrigued. 'I can't picture him being fond of children, least of all a year-old infant such as Dean.'

'You can't always tell about people, as I've learnt over the years.' Nanny Rose went and lifted Dean out of his bath and, wrapping him in a towel, brought him wriggling to her chair, where she sat rubbing him dry.

Debra sat and watched, thinking to herself that Dean's blue eyes were as bright and daring as Stuart Coltan's, and because he had the dark Salvador hair and eye-lashes he was a most appealing child to look at.

'Are Jack and Rodare alike in looks and ways?' she casually asked.

Nanny Rose considered her question, then in a thoughtful way she shook her head. 'I wouldn't say so, Debra. Mr Rodare is of his mother's people, not only in the way he looks but in the way he thinks. Mr Jack takes after his mother, but that isn't to say he isn't a very nice man—perhaps a mite too nice, if you get my meaning? The sort of chap to be snapped up by a showgirl on the lookout for a meal-ticket that would put caviar on her bread.'

'Was Pauline that kind of a girl?' For some reason Debra felt disappointed; she had hoped that Lenora Salvador was in the wrong when she implied that the young dancer had married Jack in order to gain money and status. Debra had romantically hoped that it had been one of those breathless love affairs which had ended tragically because it had been fated to do so.

She gave a crooked little smile. 'I suppose I read too many books, Nanny Rose, and real life isn't like fiction, is it? Real people are very complex, almost frighteningly so.'

'That may be the case, my ducky, but don't you turn into one of those women who won't dare to love because the very dangers of the involvement are too much for them to face. That's what some people lose sight of when they tend to deride "old maids", as they sourly call them. If I know anything about single women it's that they're a mite too romantic in their ideas, and a mite too ready to be self-sacrificing when it comes to family or career.'

'So in your heart, Nanny Rose, you do regret a little that you never married and had a family of your own to raise?'

'Now and again it crosses my mind.' Nanny Rose had put the sleepy Dean into his pyjamas, and she carried him to bed where he snuggled down with his floppy-eared teddy-bear. Debra gazed down at him and wondered how Jack Salvador could stay away from this affectionate little boy who needed him. Even if he blamed himself for the failure of his marriage he shouldn't allow that blame to include his son.

She bent down and kissed the rosy cheek. 'Sleep tight, little boy, and may the angels guard you.' It was a little prayer her mother always murmured to her when she was an infant.

She stayed a while longer with Nanny Rose, then bade her good night and went along to her own room. As she switched on the light and gazed around her, her usual pleasure in the room was diluted tonight by her troubled thoughts. Restlessly she wandered out on the terrace, a jacket flung round her shoulders in case it was still raining a little. But the rain had gone away and the sky had a refreshed look, the stars in silver clusters above the sea. She breathed deeply of the night air and felt a restoration of her spirits.

Despite the undertow of drama which

seemed to haunt the atmosphere of Abbeywitch, she wouldn't have changed places with anyone. She felt strangely elated to be here, and all at once her mind was filled again with the dark and dominant figure of Rodare Salvador.

Debra knew that someone less sensitive than herself would accept his invitation to the party, even if he did make it out of courtesy alone.

Suddenly she shivered and drew her jacket closer about her figure. With a touch of panic she ordered herself to stop thinking about the master of this great house, a man to whom she could never mean anything other than the secretary of his brother; a man who at some unexpected moment would return to Spain and forget her very existence.

But Rodare Salvador was the type of man who didn't merely saunter into a girl's thoughts, he invaded them. Her fingers closed upon the stonework of the terrace and she stood there a long time, willing the wind to blow from her mind his tall, persistent image.

It was sheer madness to allow herself these thrills of fascination. It was begging for heartache to fall beneath the spell of someone who barely knew she was alive. She was the little mouse in the den, and she had better remember it!

With a last look at the stars Debra returned to her room and closed the terrace doors. She drew the curtains and prepared for bed. A slim romantic paperback awaited her on the night-table and she hoped it would relax the relentless hold which the *hidalgo* had upon her imagination tonight.

She was seated at the dressing-table in her wrap, passing a comb in long strokes through her hair, when someone rapped upon her bed-room door. Sometimes Nanny Rose came in for a chat, or it might be the young maid who liked to talk about her boy-friend who spent all his wages on his motorcycle and wouldn't save up to get engaged. Debra didn't hesitate to go and open the door.

She retreated with a gasp, for Rodare Salvador was standing tall in the corridor and he had a look of sombre elegance in a burgundy velvet jacket, his lean fingers holding a cigar from which the smoke drifted aromatically.

'Ah, I see you are upon the verge of going to your bed.' His Latin eyes took in comprehensively the honey-coloured wrap that she wore, her hair caping the silky fabric.

'Yes, I am about to go to bed,' she said nervously. 'What do you want, *señor*?'

He carried his cigar to his lips and drew on it, and Debra was desperately aware that he had previous knowledge of the shape and texture of her beneath the wrap, and she had to fight with herself not to draw the lapels together across her bare neck, a gesture that would indicate her extreme awareness of him.

His eyes flicked the slim bareness of her neck. 'You seemed disinclined, Miss Hartway, to accept an invitation to my party, so I came to impress upon you that you are expected to attend. I shall be most annoyed if you are absent, and people have been known to get very nervous when I'm annoyed.'

Because Debra was fighting his alarming attraction; because she had to conceal every indication that his air of Latin distinction made her legs feel weak, she answered him as if she disliked everything about him.

'You call it an invitation but it's really an order, isn't it, *señor*? You feel compelled to make it plain to me that I wasn't deliberately left off the guest list, but we both know that I was, and I really don't mind in the least—'

'I do mind,' he interrupted her, 'and I am making it very plain that you are to join us.'

'But I'm not a guest, *señor*.' Debra was determined not to be overruled by him; she didn't really want to see him being charmed by the young woman named Sharon who was coming as a very much wanted guest. 'I am here at Abbeywitch to work on your brother's book and I no more expect to socialise with you and your family than does Nanny Rose. I would feel very much out of things.'

'That is nonsense!' He gestured with his cigar and looked so haughty and Spanish that he made Debra feel gauche and very conscious that her hair was hanging about her face and shoulders in a way that intensified her youth.

'It isn't nonsense, a-and I won't be bullied—'

'Bullied?' he took her up, his eyes glittering. 'I don't like the sound of that word.'

'I don't suppose you do,' she said bravely, 'but it seems to me that you're using your position as head of this house in order to make me do something I don't want to do.'

'You would be so unable to enjoy yourself at my party?' He looked astounded, as if never before had a slip of a girl dared to oppose one of his whims. 'Not even with the handsome Stuart Coltan there to dance with? Surely he has every female in the house eating out of his hand?'

'I stopped eating out of anyone's hand a long time ago, *señor*.' Debra strove to look haughty. 'I realise that you imagine me to be not long out of the schoolroom, but I've been earning my own living for several years now and I'm quite capable of taking care of myself and making my own decisions.'

'And so you have decided to throw my invitation back in my face, eh?' He drew on his cigar and watched her through the smoke, with eyes so unreadable it was impossible to tell whether he was annoyed or casually amused by her.

'That's putting it rather strongly, *señor*,' she

murmured. 'I'm merely saying that I understand why your sister omitted my name when
she made out her list. I'm employed here.'

'So you keep informing me.' His glance
drifted over the room beyond her shoulder. 'I
see you have been given a comfortable room to
sleep in, but I am not too sure that you have a
restful room in which to be employed, least of
all on one of Jack's books. It is rather isolated
from the rest of the house.'

'And that makes it ideal,' she said firmly.
'I'm able to concentrate on what I'm doing and
I don't get interrupted.'

'Not even by Stuart Coltan?'

'No—that is, he did look in this morning out
of curiosity.'

'Yes, I would say that young man has a great
deal of curiosity about young women who fail
to swoon at his feet.' Cigar smoke made the
Spanish eyes look devilish for a moment. 'You
would inform me if he became a nuisance, eh?'

'No,' she replied.

'No?' A black eyebrow elevated with astonishment. 'But it would be my right to know.'

'Your—right, *señor*?' Almost without awareness Debra closed the lapels of her wrap across
her throat.

'I happen to be the master of this house,' he
rejoined, 'and I take it upon myself to safeguard those who sleep beneath my roof. That
you address me as *señor* is proof, Miss

Hartway, of what you see in me. You see my partiality for the ways of my mother's people; for their code of honour and their rules of hospitality. I was born in Spain and I grew up there when my parents separated and my father took a second wife. Jack and Zandra were born here and I expect you wonder why Abbeywitch is mine?'

She nodded, and even as her mind warned her against him, she was held by her own curiosity and his curious charm. He was as impossibly beyond her reach as a planet in the sky, but never had she felt so fascinated by anyone. He looked like no other man she had ever seen, and he had a way of speaking that made his slightest remark seem significant.

Debra was quite certain now that he had the air of a Goya *grande*, and if he commanded people to do things it was because nature had made him that way.

'It is a known fact,' he said, smoke curling from his lips, 'that men turn away from the children of a broken marriage, almost as if they blame the first wife for the failure. This is probably related to the fact that first love has something magical about it and when the magic fails it's often the fruit of the marriage that takes the bruising.'

He shrugged the firm, burgundy-clad shoulders. 'I was never easy to bruise, but my mother was—however this house and the island can only be inherited by the eldest child and so Abbeywitch became mine, much to my stepmother's ire. Had I been vindictive on account of my own mother and her unhappiness I would have emptied the place of Lenora and her brood, but too much of me is Spanish and there are a lot of rooms.'

He smiled briefly and his eyes flicked Debra's hair which glistened in the wall-lighting. 'There is a moth,' he murmured, 'which has wings the colour of your hair. It comes to the bougainvillea which shades my Spanish house and trembles there among the creamy blossoms, so vulnerable that its wings can be crushed by a fingertip. Tell me something, Miss Hartway, do you wonder what I do for my living?'

'No—' She supposed him a man with a comfortable income, and somehow he didn't strike her as a business tycoon.

'Perhaps you think me rich and idle, eh?'

'No, I can't imagine you being idle, *señor*.'

'True enough.' He shrugged off the very thought. 'I am a *padrino*, *señorita*, which in Spain is almost a profession. I act for people who need advice and fortunately I came into enough money to enable me to do what I like best to do. I expect my occupation strikes you as unglamorous beside that of my brother?'

'It's different.' She found herself smiling into the dark eyes, a moment so confusing that she held the edge of the door for support. Dear lord, she was falling headlong into infatuation with this man and it would be mortifying if he sensed his effect upon her. Swiftly she replaced her mask of polite reserve and drew back a step into her room.

'I really must go to bed,' she said nervously. 'I've worked a good few hours on the book and my eyes feel heavy.'

'No, you must never overstrain the eyes, nor must you make of your life all work and no diversion. I shall expect to see you in your party dress tomorrow evening at eight . . . is that understood?'

Overwhelmed by feelings she was trying not to feel, Debra gave in to his dictate. 'Very well, *señor*, if you must have your way.'

'There are certainly times when I must have my way.' He inclined his dark head. *'Buenas noches, señorita.'*

She closed the door as he strolled away, and when she went to bed her knees still felt rather wobbly. She lay there with the curtains drawn open and watched the distant sparkling of the stars. The sea could be heard washing the rocks that littered the shore, and though there had been nights when the sound had rocked her off to sleep, tonight she was made restless by it.

Pressing her face into her pillow, she desperately told herself that she couldn't allow what she was feeling to have the name of love. She was infatuated with the dark authority of the man, and even though she was unworldly in some ways, she had instincts that told her to beware of his subtle charm . . . an edge of steel showed through the velvet in which it was encased.

He was of the *hidalgo* class of Spaniard and no doubt used to casting his spell over girls like herself. Girls he could entrap in those dark eyes, beckoning them on until they found themselves in his arms. Debra burrowed into her bed and tried not to see his face, tried not to remember his voice, but it was as useless as trying to stop the sea from beating the rocks of Lovelis Island.

She lay there and there was no way she could stop herself from remembering the cadence of his voice when he had spoken of her hair and related its colour to that of a moth that clung to the bougainvillea of his Spanish dwelling.

She knew of her own unfledged wings, but she couldn't allow herself to be a tremulous moth drawn into his dark flame . . . she would burn like mad and all he would feel would be a haughty amusement.

What should she do about the party? She lay and pondered the problem, and when she finally fell asleep she dreamt that she was dancing, but she couldn't be sure if she danced with Stuart Coltan or the *señor*.

CHAPTER FIVE

THE long casement windows were ablaze with light, but out there on the headland of the island the winds of the wild huntsmen seemed to howl.

Before bracing herself to go downstairs, Debra stood at her windows and heard the wind whipping the sea across the rocky strand way below the house; it was as if the elements were trying to get at the occupants of Abbeywitch . . . as if some sad, demented creature was angered by the sound of music wafting from the windows.

Debra couldn't help thinking of Pauline who had loved to dance, and who had been far too young and vital to perish in the sea. Did the souls of the young linger to haunt the environs of the place where they had died? It was down there among the cruel rocks that Pauline had been found, her long pale hair floating in the water, her slim and lifeless body turned marble-white in the light of dawn. In a hushed voice Nanny Rose had related the details to Debra who, as she stood there in her long-skirted party dress, felt indescribably sad on an evening when she should be feeling light-hearted.

It seemed that the party tonight was the first to be held at Abbeywitch since Jack's wife had died.

With a catch of her breath, Debra took a final look at herself in the mirror, seeing a wide-eyed figure in the charming simplicity of a white dress which set off the colour of her hair. Tonight she had arranged it at the crown of her head with the jewelled Japanese pin, and the styling revealed the slim grace of her neck and shoulders. Her only adornment apart from the pin was a pearl pendant, glowing and silky against her skin and shaped like a small pear. It had been bought by her father from a Japanese pearl-diver during the time he and her mother had been resident in Japan, and because she had been only a tot the pendant had been put away until Debra was grown up enough to wear it. Actually, there hadn't been too many occasions but Debra had decided that tonight was an occasion she both feared and yet had to face.

She had the certain feeling that Rodare Salvador would come to fetch her if she didn't put in an appearance. His deep sense of Latin courtesy wouldn't allow him to shrug her off, and the last thing she wanted was to be marched to the party in the grip of one of his firm brown hands.

Oh no, she didn't want to be the cynosure of

all eyes but wanted to slip in among the guests and hope not to be noticed by *el señor*. But even as she was thinking this there was a rap upon her door and her pulse leapt like a frog on a lily-pad. She went reluctantly to the door and opened it, and her relief was tinged by a little stab of disappointment when she saw Stuart Coltan standing there, looking very striking in a white tuxedo over dark trousers, his pale pink shirt set off by a dark string tie. On any other man the outfit might have looked theatrical, but Stuart had the kind of dashing good looks that could carry off whatever he chose to wear.

'My,' she murmured, 'you look ready to take part in a tropical extravaganza.'

'So you like the jacket.' He smiled and smoothed a lapel, and those blue eyes of his didn't miss a detail of her dress. 'You look *très charmante*, if I may say so? I was half inclined to wonder if you'd put on the owl-rims and have your hair bunned.'

'I was half inclined to do so, Mr Coltan.' She had been very tempted to make herself look dowdy, but something deep inside her had swayed her away from the idea. She would show Zandra and her friends that she could look attractive even if she did a job that shut her away in an office all day. Even if she couldn't afford expensive dresses as often as Sharon Chandler, she knew that her white dress was impeccably styled, the fabric soft and fluent, and the pearl on its slim chain a real one.

Debra tilted her chin and felt sure she was a credit to her parents; she had healthy hair and good teeth and her hands were nice. A beauty she had never pretended to be!

'When are you going to start calling me Stuart?' he demanded, taking her by the shoulders and giving her a slight squeeze. 'We aren't living in the days of Jane Austen when even the matrons addressed their husbands as Mister.'

'Isn't it a pity that we aren't?' Debra drew determinedly away from his touch. 'They were such gracious times compared with what goes on these days.'

'Sure, fine for the upper middle classes.' Stuart's eyes narrowed into slits of steely blue. 'The poor were dirt beneath their feet, and the marvellously erudite Miss Austen wrote mainly about her own class; the fine ladies and gentlemen who had nothing better to do than flirt behind their fans and their glasses of Madeira.'

Debra lowered her gaze, for it was true what Stuart said.

'Surprised that I've even opened a book?' he mocked.

'Of course not.' Debra knew very well that self-educated people often read far more books than those who were fortunate enough to have parents who could send them to college.

'You had better believe it.' He firmly tucked her arm through his. 'We're two of a kind, you and I, honey. We have instincts in place of a university degree and we can go as high as we want to.'

'You might be ambitious,' she protested. 'What makes you think I'm equally so?'

He shot a side-smile at her as they walked down the grand staircase, arm in arm, her long white skirt brushing the dark material of his narrow-fitting trousers. 'You're here at Abbeywitch, aren't you? The Salvadors are landed gentry, and here you are among them, looking like a princess.'

'Your talent for flattery is inexhaustible,' she rejoined. 'There has to be a dash of Irish in you, Mr Coltan.'

'For sure there is,' he laughed. 'My great-grandfather was a real wicked lad from the old country; I believe they threw him out in order to save the chastity of the girls of County Mayo. He landed up in New York harbour, never made a penny that he didn't spend, and married himself a little lacemaker. There, now you have my family history you can start to call me Stuart.'

'Is Stuart your real name, or adopted for the stage?'

'Does it matter, honey?'

'Not in the least.'

He laughed softly to himself, as if he thought it did matter to her that he kept his real name a secret.

'You're very conceited,' she informed him.

'Am I?' He didn't seem to mind in the least that she thought so.

'You really believe that every girl you meet falls in love with you.'

'Love?' He gave her a wryly amused look. 'Now there's a word to conjure with . . . what do you think it means?'

'What it says, I suppose.'

'Two lonely souls drawn to each other by a fine thread of fate into an everlasting devotion?'

'You're being sarcastic,' she accused.

'Why not, when it's a lot of romantic tosh. You've been reading too many books, honey. Don't confuse fiction with reality or you'll land yourself in trouble.'

They reached the foot of the stairs as he spoke the words, and the way he looked her up and down informed Debra that he thought her naïvely amusing and about ready to be taught the real facts of love.

'Have you ever had a boy-friend?' he asked, in his impudently assured way.

'I think you know the answer to that question, Mr Coltan, so why ask me?'

'It isn't every girl who would admit such a thing.' His eyes glinted with a hunting light.

'You're a bit of an innocent, aren't you?'

'Oh, I'm not so innocent that I'll allow you to singe my wings,' she retorted.

'You might enjoy the experience.'

'I doubt it,' she said, with spirit. 'A short while ago you said I was ambitious and in a way you're right. I like the business of books and I want to develop my skills as an editor, but I'd stand little chance of doing that if I allowed myself to be carried away by your blarney . . . in more ways than one. I'm not a flighty little fool, Stuart. My head is firmly set on my shoulders.'

'So you're going to settle for all work and no play,' he scoffed, 'and end up a lonely spinster?'

'I expect that will happen,' she agreed. 'Quite frankly, I can't see much wrong with it, especially when I think of Pauline Salvador and the way she ended up. No one gave that marriage much chance, did they? No one in this house accepted that poor girl and they wonder why her husband has gone off by himself.'

'Perhaps she's on his conscience,' Stuart said, his eyes narrowing. 'There's hot blood in the Salvadors and he may have caught her playing around.'

'Would Pauline do that!' Debra gave him a troubled look. 'She had the little boy to consider, and despite what everyone thinks, I don't believe she married Jack Salvador for money and position.'

'How would you know?' Stuart gave a short laugh. 'You never met Pauline and you have the tendency, honey, to judge people as if they're characters in a book. Real people, my dear girl, can be very unpredictable. They don't behave to a prescribed pattern, and do you honestly believe that anyone ever really knows anyone else? I doubt if we know ourselves from one day to the next.'

'That might well be true,' Debra agreed, 'but Pauline had Jack's baby and surely that proves something?'

'What exactly?' He looked directly into her grey eyes with their vagrant tints of green, and the edge of his mouth was cynically quirked.

'That they loved each other.'

'Sainted James, you are innocent, aren't you?'

'I—I know what you're thinking.' Debra wanted to walk away from his jeering, but at the same time she didn't want to walk in among the party guests all on her own.

'What am I thinking?' Stuart demanded.

'That babies don't come from the heart.'

'Isn't it a fact?' he drawled.

'If you're such a cynic, Stuart, why do you bother to go and play with little Dean in his nursery?' This frankly puzzled Debra, for not a thing about Stuart Coltan indicated that he had the slightest interest in young children. He seemed to her a young man who was busy enjoying himself and quite detached from the more serious aspects of life, including a little boy whose mother had drowned and whose father left him in the hands of other people.

'I knew Pauline, so why shouldn't I be interested in her nipper?' Stuart pushed his hands into the pockets of his jacket and his gaze drifted from Debra and settled on the dominant portrait of Don Rodare de Salvador in its huge baroque frame; he wore black and silver and his eyes were dark and alert in his lean Spanish face. 'I'm not immune from feelings, Debra. You've got the wrong idea about me. I bet I've a softer centre than any member of the Salvador clan, especially the present-day *hidalgo*.'

Her own eyes had focused on the portrait and she gave a start when Stuart mentioned the man who so much resembled the Don Rodare who had founded the family into which a showgirl had married, her young life doomed, it seemed, from the moment Jack Salvador had carried her over the threshold of Abbeywitch.

Her start became a shudder when Stuart suddenly gripped her by the shoulder. 'Is that it?' Stuart's breath was hot against the skin of her neck. 'You've got your eye on the *hidalgo*?'

'Don't talk nonsense—!' Debra wrenched

away from him, but he pursued her and before she realised he had trapped her in one of
the alcoves of the hall, out of range of the
chandeliers and therefore shadowed. Stuart
caught her roughly against him and before
she could protest he had his mouth on hers,
insistent and expert and entirely unwanted.

Maddened in case Rodare Salvador saw
them, Debra drew back her foot and kicked
him on the shin, right on the bone with the toe
of her silver shoe. It made him let go of her and
instantly she whirled out of his reach and fled
towards the sound of music and people . . . a
breathless young creature in georgette, unaware that she had the look of a deer fleeing
from a fire as she entered the high-ceilinged,
wide and panelled room where the party was
in progress.

She stepped forward quickly as Stuart
loomed up behind her, and in that instant her
gaze fused with that of an even taller figure in
matt-black evening suit and striking white
shirt. His skin had something naturally gold
about it and more than ever he looked as if he
had stepped out of a Goya painting. He stood
framed by tall embrasured windows draped in
flame-coloured curtains . . . black, gold and
flame of the Inquisition, striking in Debra a
chord of awareness more intense than anything she had ever felt before.

A burning sensation ran over her skin and

she had a wild desire to turn and run and not stop running until she was as many miles as she could get from that darkly brilliant gaze . . . compelling as the flame that traps the moth.

'That music is driving my feet crazy!' Debra didn't resist as Stuart propelled her to the centre of the room where the parquet floor had been waxed so the guests could dance. A group of professional musicians had been hired and they were excellent, with a lilt to their playing that Debra recognised.

'That's Georgie Dane,' she breathed, her eyes fixed upon the young man playing the piano.

'Sure is.' Stuart smiled as they moved to the easy rhythm, to the lilting touch of those fingers on the keys. 'I knew he and his group were entertaining at the St Regis in Newquay and I suggested to Zandra that she get them for the party. I'm full of great ideas, eh?'

'If you say so.' Debra felt herself smiling, her annoyance with him dying away. He was good to dance with, and being here with him among the throng of dancers was safer than being within reach of Rodare Salvador. She didn't dare to look in the direction of the windows where he seemed to stand apart from the fun and chatter . . . rather like a monarch amused by his subjects!

'Don't look now,' Stuart murmured in her

ear, 'but our haughty host has just been joined by a package I'm sure he'd like to unwrap.'

Debra strove not to look but her curiosity overcame her caution. Her heart gave a thud when she saw that Rodare had been joined by a dazzling young blonde, and that his dark head was bent to her in a listening attitude and he seemed to have lost awareness of the other people in the room.

'Is that Sharon Chandler?' Debra asked, feeling quite certain that the girl in the satin gold dress with the low neckline was the girl whom the Salvadors would welcome into their family with open arms.

'You bet your sweet life it is.' Stuart openly quizzed the girl in gold. 'She looks expensive, which was something poor Pauline couldn't achieve even on Jack's money. That was one of the reasons why the haughty Lenora didn't like her. The landed gentry judge girls not by their nice natures but by their pedigree. Breeding is paramount, then daddy's bank account is taken into consideration, and finally if her riding-seat comes up to standard she has the rosette pinned on her.'

As the Georgie Dane group moved into their version of *I Don't Want To Set The World On Fire*, Debra was swung breathlessly close to where Rodare was still in deep conversation with Sharon. She caught the deep sound of his voice and saw the girl watching him intently, and it was natural discipline that kept her in step with Stuart.

'You can take it from me,' he went on, 'Lenora didn't like it one little bit when her darling Jack got himself involved with a high-kicking filly from the chorus line. Anyway, it looks as if the *hidalgo* plans to remedy his half-brother's mistake. Just look at the way that girl is looking up at him!'

'He's so tall that she can hardly help it.' Debra spoke as casually as she was able to, for those two figures superimposed upon the flame-coloured curtains were in every way a foil for each other. The girl was like a golden bloom which the man had plucked for himself, and those beckoning dark eyes of his seemed to be holding her in thrall. If Debra hadn't been so fair-minded she would have taken an instant dislike to Sharon Chandler, but there was no denying the girl's good looks and the lissom charm of her figure in the dress that glistened like golden moonlight on water.

'They are well matched,' she murmured.

'Made for each other,' Stuart said drily. 'I see Lenora bearing down on them . . . Holy James, she's actually smiling!'

Debra took a quick look and saw Lenora kissing the girl on the cheek. Rodare stood looking on and Debra had her gaze upon him just a second too long . . . suddenly his eyes had hold of hers, then they raked over her in

Stuart's arms and she could have sworn that mockery flicked the edge of his lip.

Debra felt herself tingle with resentment. Did he expect her to sit in one of the alcoves like Jane Eyre, eyes cast down and looking a picture of demure servility? Was that why he had wanted her at the party, so she could see him with Sharon Chandler?

She wanted to walk out of the room, but if she did depart he might assume that she was envious. Obviously she was meant to feel like the little typist whom his sister Zandra hadn't felt worthy of an invitation. Already she had caught the sharp attention of Zandra, who looked rather like a tigress in a dress of honey and brown stripes. The raven-dark hair was bunched at her nape in a diamond circlet and there were diamonds in her earlobes.

'I—I didn't want to come to this party.' Debra couldn't quite keep the tremor out of her voice. '*He* insisted.'

'El Rodare?' Stuart raised an eyebrow so high it almost reached into his hairline. 'You mean he got you on your own and insisted?'

'He came to my bedroom—' Debra broke off, realising at once that the words sounded invidious. 'What I mean—'

'I think I know what you mean.' Stuart stared down at her, seeing her as if through the eyes of the other man, the one who was master of the house. She didn't dazzle the male eye with blonde hair and the kind of blue eyes that clung to a man as if he were the god of light. Debra had a more subtle attraction . . . that of unalloyed innocence.

'Did he try to push his way in?' Stuart was scowling, and at the same time leading her off the floor in the direction of the buffet.

'No—nothing like that,' she protested. 'As if he would!'

'I bet it was on his mind!' Stuart reached for two flutes of champagne from a passing waiter and handed one to Debra. 'Come on, you don't imagine he's any different from other men just because he gives you all that high-and-mighty talk about the honour of the Spaniard being bound up with hospitality. That's just his line and bound to get to an innocent like you, who has probably read all about the noble Knights of the Round Table and other romantic tales. They talked a lot about honour, but that didn't stop Lancelot and Tristan from seducing the fair ladies.'

'I don't intend to be seduced by anyone,' Debra said indignantly. 'Just because it's always on your mind!'

'That's slander,' he said, but without rancour. 'Mmmm, this is splendid champagne—nothing but the best for the Salvadors. What they've splashed out on Krug and caviar tonight would keep me in lunches for quite a few weeks. Let's go to the buffet and help ourselves to some of that delicious food.'

What was laid out on the long white-clothed table made Debra feel hungry, and following Stuart's example she took a plate and a fork and helped herself to whatever took her fancy. From the moment Rodare Salvador had looked at her in that mocking way, Debra had decided to look as if she was having the time of her life. She would gobble down this plate of food even if it made her feel bilious; she would laugh at Stuart's nonsense, and dance whenever he asked her to.

They were standing side by side, sampling the caviar, when Zandra made her way towards them with a tigerish glitter in her eyes. 'I expected you to come and say good-evening,' she snapped at Stuart, and the glare she gave Debra was enough to curl the smoked salmon. 'Perhaps you had something better to do, is that it?'

'You know I like to dance,' he drawled, 'and you seemed busy with Van Allen. This is great caviar, you should try some.'

'Are you enjoying it?' Zandra snapped at Debra.

'Yes, thank you,' Debra said politely.

'One assumes that you've never had it before?' Zandra was in such a temper that she didn't even pretend to be polite. She looked Debra up and down and it seemed to fuel her anger that Debra looked cool and charming in her white dress set off by her chestnut hair, jade-pinned.

'No, I've never had caviar before,' Debra agreed. 'It reminds me a little of the cod's roe I always took home for my supper on Friday evenings.'

Debra heard a spluttering sound as Stuart nearly choked on a swallow of champagne.

'Is that meant to be funny?' Zandra demanded.

Debra looked wide-eyed and shook her head. 'Fried cod's roe is delicious, especially with chips and a cup of tea.'

'You impertinent little typist!' Zandra was fuming. 'You weren't meant to be at this party, for we don't usually invite the staff!'

'Zandra!' Stuart was abruptly unamused. 'I don't know what's got into you, but if you want to pick on someone then choose me. I'm used to dealing with the tantrums of actresses—they're inclined to be touchy if the spotlight isn't on them the whole time.'

There was a flash of diamonds and Stuart caught and gripped Zandra's wrist a moment before she struck him. She glared at him, he stared at her, and Debra quickly walked away, heading into what she thought was an alcove and found to be an archway into a conservatory that led off from the immense ballroom.

The dance music followed her into the green sanctuary, with its domed glass ceiling, masses of indoor plants, and pale lilies spinning on the pond where gold fish swam lazily beneath the heart-shaped leaves.

Debra drew a shaken breath. Oh lord, what a scene! Zandra was hopelessly in love with Stuart and he quite obviously didn't feel the same way about her. He had a certain charm, but he used people and he had casually hinted that he had ingratiated himself with Zandra because he was ambitious and she had social and theatrical connections. They were the main attraction where he was concerned, and despite the way the actress had spoken to her, Debra couldn't help feeling a kind of sympathy.

Hadn't she herself felt a stab of unwanted jealousy when she had glanced across the dance floor and seen the girl in gold holding the attention of Rodare Salvador.

It was a hateful feeling and Debra sank down into a fan-backed cane chair and drank from the champagne flute which she still held in her hand. She wanted her nerves to get back to normal. She wanted to be again the cool, composed girl she had been while working in London. She wanted to dislike that haughty Spaniard for the way he had looked at her while she danced with Stuart. Anyone would think he had caught her in Stuart's arms for a more intimate purpose!

She sank back in the cane chair and it creaked

a little, and, as if in answer, she caught a movement at the other side of the foliage; there came a click, then a drift of aromatic smoke, followed by a definite footfall.

He stood there suddenly, the man who caused her a similar kind of desperation to that which his half-sister suffered at the hands of Stuart Coltan.

'I didn't think it would be long,' he remarked, 'before you took to cover. Are you in hiding from that young predator?'

'It was your sister, *señor*, who made me take to my heels.'

'She also saw you dancing with Coltan, eh?'

'I'm afraid so.'

'Why be afraid, Miss Hartway?'

'You know why, *señor*.' The Spanish way of addressing him came so naturally to her lips, and in view of the many exotic plants surrounding them, they might have been alone together in far away Andalucia. It was such a fantastic notion that she blamed it on the champagne.

'You think my sister was impolite to you because she has taken a fancy to Coltan, eh?'

'Yes.' Her wide-apart eyes were upon his Latin face, wreathed in the smoke of his cigar, and she wondered why he was in here instead of enjoying the captivating company of Sharon Chandler. She wondered why he wasn't dancing when he looked as if he would dance with all the expertise of his Spanish blood.

'Have you also taken a fancy to that young man?' he asked.

'Do you think I have, *señor*?'

'We say in Spain that people who dance well together have an affinity with each other.'

'How interesting.' Debra ran a fingertip around the rim of her champagne flute, but more as a distraction from his eyes than from an attempt at provocation.

'Most things Spanish are interesting, *señorita.*' He said it without arrogance but with a decided touch of pride, a man who had long since decided that he was more attuned to his mother's people than his father's. He had the proud stance of the race, a male dominance accentuated by his dark evening wear . . . an imposing man of honour who could, perhaps, be merciless as the matador.

'Intriguing,' he murmured, 'that scattered through our blood are instincts we are helpless to control; feelings and urgings derived from the roots of our existence. No one is an island though we go through this life in total detachment . . . what does that realisation do to a mere girl such as yourself?'

'Oh, why ask me, *señor*?' She gave him a cool look. 'I am merely the little typist who wasn't meant to be at this party.'

'Zandra said that to you?'

'Yes.'

'Then come,' he reached for her hand and drew her to her feet, 'come with me and we'll show Zandra that you have my seal of approval.'

'No—' Debra pulled back, her fingers tensed and straining in his grip. 'I am only in this house to do a job of work and I would much sooner go to my room.'

'The night is young,' he mocked, 'and at my welcome-home party I'm entitled to have my own way. Come, I want to dance!'

The very words seemed to bring Debra's heart into her throat. 'I—I don't think we should—your stepmother won't like it if she sees you dancing with me—'

'If I wanted to dance on my head in my own house I would do it.' Inexorably he was forcing Debra to go with him, into that room where the music played and where everyone would see them together. Holding her inescapably by the hand he extinguished his cigar, and she said desperately:

'I shouldn't think you'd want to dance with someone you despise!'

'Say again?' He rapped out the command, a dark and alarming figure above her slenderness in the pale, softly clinging fabric. Her nostrils tensed to the woody spiciness of *L'Homme Est Rare*, and her heart palpitated as his free hand closed upon her waist.

'I—I saw the way you looked at me—when I

was dancing with Stuart.' He had seared her skin with that look, and now when he touched her Debra felt it to the bone.

'And how, exactly, did I look at you?' he demanded.

'As if you thought me—cheap.' It hurt to say the word.

'That, my young woman, is a confounded lie!'

'It isn't!' she said hotly. 'You told me to come to your party, but I wasn't expected to behave like a guest—was I?'

'You are talking rot.' With a strength that shocked her, he pulled her so hard against him that she felt the pressure of hardened saddle muscles, and the very next instant she was bent over his arm and his eyes were piercing hers, dark as midnight and holding all the mystery of his maleness, a man unknown to her until their meeting on his beach where he had seen her stretched upon the sands with not a stitch on her body.

She felt again, as she had felt then, helpless to move, magnetised by his eyes and weakened by his look of power.

'Strange creature that you are, with eyes that change their hue and sometimes hold silver or shadow.' His breath was warm on her skin, smoky from his cigar, and his lips were almost touching hers. 'Why would I think you cheap, *señorita*?'

'Y-you are proving it—right now.' Her lips shook and her body was more his possession than her own . . . she was the moth in the flame and tormented by this game he played with her.

'Would my kiss be less welcome than a kiss from Coltan?' he murmured.

Her heart gave a jump . . . he knew . . . he had seen her with Stuart in the alcove and believed she had wanted to be there. 'Do you spy on everyone who comes into your precious house?' she asked breathlessly.

'Spy?' he breathed. 'Now that is an accusation I won't tolerate, and you will pay for it!'

His gaze and his arms held her locked to him, and then he lowered his head and his black hair fell upon his brow and she felt his mouth crush itself against hers. There in the dim green jungle of the conservatory a kind of savagery was let loose in him, as if he wanted to prove to himself that her innocence was a mask and that he could make her respond as her true self—a girl who used demureness to lure men to her.

She felt the heat of his hands through her dress, felt the wild beating of her heart as the pressure of his mouth drew from her a response she tried so desperately not to feel. Even as her outward self tried to strain away from him, her inner self was all warm and clamouring as his lips travelled down her slim, soft neck into the contour of her collarbone where they slid a kind of fire along her skin.

She could feel herself trembling against his closeness, nostrils and nerves quivering at the masculine scent and feel of him. She died and came alive again at his almost deliberate roughness when he raked his hand from her neck to her hip . . . as if he contemplated ripping off her dress.

Instead he pushed her from him, scanning her disorder with expressionless eyes, hooded and in shadow with his thoughts. There was no sign of triumph to make her feel more ashamed than she did feel, because he knew as well as she did that he had drawn her into his kiss and halfway into total surrender to him.

Hating him . . . hating herself . . . she dragged the back of her hand across her mouth. 'Y-you decided down on the beach that I was cheap—now you've proved it to yourself, haven't you?'

He raked his hair back into place. 'The trouble with women,' he said, 'is that they attack with words and don't stop to think that men retaliate with action. You called me a spy. Did you think I would accept that without retaliating?'

A shiver ran over Debra, caused by the sense of chill that follows extreme excitement. 'Y-you chose to judge me. You saw me with Stuart and drew your own conclusions.'

'Did I really?' His expression was sardonic. 'It would seem that you and I are set on misreading each other, Miss Hartway. I wonder why that is?'

'You know why.' She spoke hardly above a whisper . . . it was damnable that of all the men in the world she should be misjudged by this man. She knew he would never stop believing her to be slyly brazen behind a demure posture. She felt certain that every Spanish bone in his body was firmly resolved in her disfavour. She felt equally certain that he wouldn't have kissed Sharon Chandler in such a rapacious way . . . he would handle her as if she were made of petals. A golden flower of a girl, bred in a hothouse and accustomed to every care and attention.

A burning resentment took the chill out of Debra's bones and she turned to leave the conservatory.

'Just one moment!'

She paused but didn't look at him; her body hummed with expectancy as she stood in the dim lighting that made her dress seem more green than white.

'You and I are going to dance, are we not?'

'I—I don't want to—' She was poised for flight, the jade jewels glinting in her hair, aware of her tormented inner self but unaware of her elusiveness. She protested as he caught her by the wrist.

'Why are you being—cruel to me?' She couldn't stop herself from asking, but she could no more look at him. To look into his eyes was to see herself in his arms again.

'Don't exaggerate.' He drew her to the archway that led back into the ballroom. 'You have danced with Coltan and now you are going to dance with me, it's as simple as that.'

'But why?' She raised her gaze only to the level of his chin and saw that it was set with determination. 'Do you want your mother to dismiss me from my job?'

'She is my stepmother, and when I am in residence at Abbeywitch the orders come from me.'

'You are ordering me to dance with you?'

'I am now.' He swung her among the dancers and once again there was no escape from his arms; she had to submit to his dictate and her only defence was to look as polite and indifferent as if she were dancing with a stranger.

But no more did he feel like a stranger. Her body reacted to his touch and her senses were attuned to him so she became quickly aware that they were moving in perfect harmony through the movements of the dance. She knew also that they were being watched; that they couldn't be anonymous out there on the floor. In a state between torment and enjoyment she followed where he led, past a group of people with Lenora at the centre, and then past Zandra and the silver-haired Van Allen.

It struck Debra all of a sudden that other couples were leaving the floor so that soon she and Rodare were dancing alone. She could feel him controlling her every step, making her body obey him even if her mind was in rebellion.

All at once the dance band slid into a rumba, and Debra felt herself carried along by the sheer verve of the Latin American music. She sensed right away that the rhythm was deep in Rodare's Latin bones and so she abandoned herself to him . . . to the sheer delight of a partner so strong and pliant.

For panting seconds at the finale of the rumba it was as if they were welded together, and then people began to applaud and this brought her down to earth. She broke free of his hold on her and ran headlong from the ballroom, pursued by the sound of clapping and laughter.

Maybe some of the party guests thought it had been arranged, but as Debra fled to her room all she could think of was that Rodare had ruined her job at Abbeywitch.

She wouldn't be allowed to stay now he had managed to make her look like a little upstart . . . a replica of Pauline in the eyes of his stepmother and sister. The look on their faces had been ominous, and as excitement drained out of Debra she felt the sting of tears and wished she had kept to her resolve not to attend the party. With biting candour Zandra had said she wasn't wanted, and now she had really landed herself in hot water.

As she withdrew the Japanese pin from her hair and felt it uncoil to her shoulders, she had a mental image of herself dancing with Rodare in front of all those people. The very thought of it took her breath away, but now she was left with the regretful feeling that he should have danced the rumba with Sharon Chandler. That would have seemed natural to his family and friends, but in dancing with a member of the hired help he had caused eyebrow raising and speculation.

Was that his nature? Debra decided that it was . . . that he pleased himself and right now wouldn't be sharing her troubled feelings. He was his own master and didn't have to consider himself in relation to an employer.

Debra put a hand to her throat and it was then she discovered that her pearl pendant was no longer on its chain about her neck . . . the silky little pear was gone and though she quickly undressed and searched her clothes was nowhere to be found.

One half of her wanted to rush downstairs in order to search for the pendant, but the other half was reluctant. She would have to wait until the morning. It could have come undone while she was in the conservatory . . . Rodare had not been gentle with her during the course of that kiss.

She gave a shiver and put on her wrap. Why couldn't he play his games with Miss Chandler and leave her alone!

CHAPTER SIX

IT was after midnight when Debra heard the launches departing with the guests who were returning either to the mainland or to the Van Allen yacht. Various close friends of the family were staying over the weekend and it was at least another hour before the house fell quiet and the vagrant laughter and chatter ceased.

Debra turned restlessly in bed and lay staring at the moonlight on her terrace. She longed for the morning to come so she could go and search for her pendant; if a member of the staff found it, then it would be taken to Lenora, and Debra could see herself standing before Mrs Salvador and being made to feel that her behaviour at the party had been reprehensible.

She pummelled her pillows in an effort to get comfortable and wondered why some people were such snobs. What did they imagine made them superior to other people? It could only be too much conceit and ego that made them that way, pumping them up with too many pretensions about themselves. Lenora and her daughter were bound to dislike anyone who was without airs and phoney graces, and that was probably why they hadn't liked Pauline.

In a way Debra wasn't sorry that tonight was probably her last night at Abbeywitch. She thought the house and the island were lovely, but it was better that she didn't see Rodare Salvador every day. Inevitably she would find herself having to fight his attraction, and the power he could exert.

He stirred her physically and she didn't want to be another Pauline; a plaything for another of the Salvador men to enjoy as a novelty.

Debra was drifting off to sleep when the house telephone tinkled beside her bed. It was there because she occupied the room in which Miss Tucker had slept, and sometimes at night Jack Salvador had required his secretary to take notes.

Wondering if Nanny Rose was calling her, Debra lifted the mouthpiece and spoke her name.

'Did I wake you from your dreams?'

A frown puckered Debra's brow. 'What do you want, Stuart?'

'I have something of yours, honey, and I wondered if you'd like me to bring it to you?'

'My pendant?' she exclaimed.

'The very same,' he drawled. 'I'm holding it in my fingers at this very moment, a perfect pear-shaped pearl on a golden chain.'

'Where did you find it?' She felt a glow of relief that the pendant was safe; it was a link with the father she couldn't remember and the last thing she wanted to lose.

'Down beside the goldfish pond in the conservatory,' Stuart informed her, and a note of curiosity had entered his voice. 'What were you doing in there, I wonder, and how did this little trinket came loose from your neck?'

Debra flushed as she remembered. 'I went in there for a breather—I'm so glad it's found.'

'Did someone special give it to you, Debra? Was the donor of this pretty object a very special friend?'

She could easily have told him that her father had been the donor, but she needed to put an obstacle in his way. 'Yes—I was worried when I found it was missing.'

'Then you need worry no more, honey, I'm on my way to your boudoir with your *gage d'amour*.'

'No—' She felt a lurch of panic. 'It can wait till the morning—' She broke off, for the telephone had clicked and was purring in her ear. Hastily she cradled it and slid out of bed, fastening her wrap around her with a very secure knot. She hastened to the dressing-table and tidied her hair . . . it would have to be Stuart Coltan who found her pendant and though she wanted it back in her keeping, she didn't want that young man getting the idea that he deserved a reward for finding it!

When he knocked upon her door she

opened it a mere couple of inches and peered out at him. He was clad in a Paisley robe with a cravat arranged at the throat and his dark hair was smoothly combed. One of his hands was deep in his pocket, as if he held there the pearl and chain.

'I—it's kind of you to bring my pendant.' She tried to sound composed but felt a nervous urge to laugh at his imitation of a roué who expected to be invited into her boudoir. 'May I have it, Stuart?'

'You may have anything you wish.' As he spoke he was eyeing what he could see of her through the few inches of open door, her chestnut hair mingling with the pale mauve fabric of her wrap. Then slowly he withdrew his hand from his pocket and the pearl on its chain hung teasingly from his fingers. 'A very pretty object indeed.'

Somehow he managed to make the words insinuating and Debra no longer felt like laughing. She slid her hand through the gap between them. 'I'm glad you found my pendant, Stuart, now may I have it?'

'Exactly the shape of a tiny pear, isn't it?' He swung the pearl in a tantalising way. 'I can't help feeling curious about the guy who gave it to you . . . someone special, eh? Someone who knows you well?'

'Intimately.' The word sprang to her lips like a weapon of defence, anything sharp enough to keep Stuart Coltan at a distance. As she expected to leave Abbeywitch in the morning, she didn't want to return to Columbine with her character in total ruin.

'So that's the way of it.' He released the pendant as he spoke, just short of her outstretched hand so the pearl and chain dropped to the floor. With a catch of her breath Debra let go of the door and she was bending down to retrieve the pendant when Stuart quite deliberately placed his slippered heel on the pearl and bore down on it with all his weight.

'Don't do that,' she cried out. 'How dare you—oh, take your foot off! Take it off!' She pummelled at him but he only laughed, and Debra couldn't bear it that her precious gift from her father should be treated in such a way.

She stood up and with her eyes blazing slapped Stuart across the face with all her might. 'You nasty little boy,' she said furiously. 'I suppose you're getting back at me?'

'Back at you for what?' He rubbed a hand against his cheek and still he kept grinding her pendant with his heel.

'You know!' Debra could feel herself trembling with temper that verged on tears. 'You know all right!'

'I'm sure I don't know what you're getting at, but I'll tell you this—you aren't quite the demure little mouse you make out to be.'

'No,' she agreed, 'but you're every bit as caddish as I thought you.'

'Caddish?' he jeered. 'Is that the kind of outdated word Jack Salvador uses in his precious books? Is he as outdated in his tastes as his big brother?'

'And what do you mean by that remark?' Debra had to clench her hands in order to keep herself in control; she could hardly bear it that her precious pendant was trapped beneath his careless foot.

'The rumba!' he mocked. 'If he'd thought you could manage it he'd have led you into a *paso doble*. My, my, what an exhibition.'

'At least I didn't trip over his feet,' Debra retorted.

'Implying that El Rodare is a better dancer than me?' Stuart's eyes narrowed and there wasn't a vestige of his charm to be seen; at that moment he looked almost feral. 'Anyway, what would you know? I suppose you felt flattered by his attention, but take it from me neither Zandra nor her mother were impressed. That exhibition reminded them of the way he used to dance with Pauline—that surprises you, doesn't it, Miss Coolheart? Jack's the academic one, but El Rodare with his Latin blood likes to trip the light fantastic . . . makes you wonder, eh, what else he and Pauline liked to do together?'

Debra's nerves felt as if they were jerked on

strings . . . in a way she wasn't surprised that Rodare had found Pauline stimulating to dance with, but her innermost self felt shocked by the suggestion that he may also have been her lover.

'What a nasty thing to say!' She gave Stuart a disgusted look. 'You must have a very low mind to even think it.'

'Because Pauline was his sister-in-law and he likes to act the honourable *hidalgo*?' Stuart gave a jeering laugh. 'It's about time you took your nose out of books and took a real look at people. You might discover that some of them aren't quite the heroes you take them for.'

'I'm not such a greenhorn as you seem to suppose,' she rejoined. 'Not for a moment was I fooled by you. I could see that you're only out to please yourself and you don't care who gets hurt so long as you get what you want out of life. You're self-centred!'

'Isn't everyone?' he scoffed. 'When you realise that every single person is bound up in himself then you stop having illusions. You start seeing straight and you head for your own goal and don't get side-tracked by some false emotion that singles someone out from the crowd. Take it from me, we aren't put on this earth to be boxed up with one partner and one set of emotions. We're here to live as much life as we can manage, not to go stale in a cage, looking at the same old face, hearing the same old opinions year in, year out. I'd go nuts and I'm honest enough to say so.'

'You're entitled to your opinion,' Debra agreed. 'I don't think I want to discuss the philosophy of life with you. Right now I think you're behaving like a petty little boy who breaks someone else's toy just for the pleasure of it. I don't call that being grown up. I think you've quite a long way to go before you become an adult.'

He stood scowling at her, then with a shrug he turned on his heel and walked off. It gave her a heartfelt sense of relief to see him go, and when she picked up her pendant she cradled it in the palm of her hand as if it had been desecrated. Anxiously she examined the pearl and found to her distress that the silky surface of it had been damaged along with the gold attachment. She felt choked up and as the emotions of the entire evening welled up in her, tears brimmed in her eyes.

When a hand suddenly touched her on the shoulder she thought Stuart had returned and she whirled round, words and tears spilling over. 'You swine, leave me alone—' She broke off, for the male figure confronting her was Rodare Salvador.

His eyes raked over her tear-streaked face. 'Why are you crying, and who did you think I was?' he demanded.

'I—' But she couldn't speak, his sudden

appearance on top of her scene with Stuart
seemed to let loose an avalanche of tears and
once again she ran from him, into her room.
But this time he followed, closing the door
behind him. He came and stood behind her
and clasped her heaving shoulders with both
hands.

'Who has done this to you, eh? Has Zandra
been to see you? Has she said something to
upset you?'

Debra shook her head and tried desperately
to control herself. She wasn't a weepy person
as a rule, but she couldn't seem to stop the sobs
from tearing at her throat.

'Come!' Rodare propelled her to the bed and
sat her down on the side of it, then he strode
into her tiny bathroom and in a few moments
returned with her face flannel and wiped away
her tears as if she were a child. He poured her
some water from the carafe on the bedside
table and made her take a few sips. In a while
he brought her to a state of semi-calmness and
she was able to tell him what had occurred. He
opened her clenched fingers and took the pearl
and chain out of her grasp. He examined the
damage and she heard him mutter a word
which she didn't understand.

'So this came undone while you were with
me in the conservatory?'

She nodded and didn't meet his eyes. 'T-the
catch is a little stiff a-and I couldn't have

fastened it properly. I don't wear the pendant all that often, you see.'

'I shall have to confront Coltan about this.'

Debra pushed the hair away from her brow as if it weighed on her. 'I'd rather you didn't, *señor*. I'm leaving, aren't I, so he isn't likely to bother me any more?'

'You are leaving over this?'

This time she was compelled to look at him. She shook her head and felt certain she must look wretched with her swollen eyelids and disordered hair. 'You know I can't stay. Your stepmother and sister will want me to leave.'

'Why so?' His eyes dwelt intently on Debra's face and he seemed to her more foreign than ever before in the neat environs of her bedroom; his Latin swarthiness was intensified and even his voice seemed extra deep. She noticed that he was wearing a robe and she wondered why he had been in the vicinity of her bedroom. Had he looked in on his young nephew, who might have been disturbed by the extra noise in the house?'

'I—I think Zandra and her mother are annoyed by me,' she replied.

'Is their annoyance of such importance that you intend to leave Jack's book in less attentive and considerate hands?' he asked, and as if he felt that he was threatening her with his height he sat down beside her on the bed, so that instantly she became aware that the upper part of his body was bare beneath the heavy dark silk of his robe. She could see the swarthy skin of his chest and the black hair across his pectoral muscles, producing deep within her a clenching awareness of him as a man.

A man she was very much alone with in the depths of the night.

She lowered her gaze and bit her lip rather painfully. 'I don't want to leave my work unfinished,' she said, a quake in her voice. 'I have enormous respect for your brother's book, but when you found me crying you asked if Zandra had upset me. You know how displeased she and your stepmother are. I—I shouldn't have been at the party, you know that!'

'Do you imagine that I worry about those two women and their ideas of social acceptance?' Abruptly he reached out and taking Debra by the chin made her look at him. Her lashes fluttered wildly and his touch increased her awareness of him. 'You came as my guest in my house and too bad if I offended their sense of propriety by dancing with you. Everyone else seemed to enjoy our performance.'

'I don't imagine Sharon Chandler did.' The words emerged before Debra could suppress them; they had been waiting to leap from her lips and were all part of her emotional state tonight. She had never felt such a mixture of feelings churning about inside her before.

'Let us get something straight.' His hand moved itself to the nape of Debra's neck, enclosing it warmly beneath the cape of her hair, and his big frame seemed to loom closer. 'I don't live my life in subservience to other people and what they expect of me. I am my own person and I don't choose to bow my neck to any woman. I wished to dance with you and so we danced. Why on earth you should feel guilty about it, I do not know.'

'Simply because I work here, *señor*, and the members of your family are conscious of their social position.' All the time she spoke Debra could feel his thumb in movement against the skin of her neck, and she knew that if he were to lean forward and take her lips she would be helpless to resist him. She felt his power like an intoxicating Spanish wine, dark and rich with ingredients that went to her head. It added to her confusion that he probably knew how his close presence on her bed was affecting her.

'You simply mean they are snobs,' he mocked. 'That they haven't the wisdom to know that in Spain a beggar may have the pride of a prince if he also has a sense of honour and abides by it. That is why I love Spain, *señorita*. That is why I choose to be there more often than I am at Abbeywitch. In my absences Jack is master, but where is Jack, I wonder?'

'Probably alone and brooding,' she murmured, and all at once she recalled Stuart's insinuation that Jack's wife may have been involved with Rodare. She couldn't bear to believe it, and yet Pauline had found herself in need of a refuge against the in-laws who despised her because she worked as a chorus girl and wasn't a social butterfly like Sharon Chandler.

Debra gave a sigh. 'Poor Pauline,' she murmured. 'One moment her life was filled with bright lights, and the next she lay dead among the cruel rocks. Isn't it a good thing we don't know what fate has in store for us?'

'It certainly keeps us from going mad,' he said drily. 'Have I convinced you that you have no need to leave Abbeywitch?'

'I—I don't know.' She looked at him and saw how very Spanish he was; that soon he would leave Abbeywitch and if she stayed she would be like Pauline, at the mercy of Zandra who couldn't endure Stuart Coltan to look at another girl. At the mercy of Lenora Salvador who until her dying day would assume herself to be superior because her elegant and useless hands had never been put to use.

'Wherever Jack may be, I know he's relying on someone to do their utmost for his book.' Rodare gave her a compelling look and his strong hand cupped her head so her hair was flowing over his fingers. 'You won't let him down, will you? I can't believe that you are the sort of girl to be easily intimidated—you defended yourself well enough when we met for the first time on the beach, remember?'

Oh yes, she remembered every detail and the memory made her realise that right now she was clad for bed beneath her wrap. Her skin warmed and she felt a blush running over, showing itself through her fair skin so he couldn't help but notice her heightening of colour. Something seemed to spark in his eyes, and then like a portcullis his lashes came down and his eyes were guarded again.

'We danced well together, eh?' A smile quirked the edge of his mouth. 'I wonder how you would perform the *paso doble*? Have you ever tried it?'

She shook her head and thought of what Stuart had said. 'I know it's an exciting dance, but I quit dancing school before I could start the Latin American course. The rumba is fairly simple.'

'But most enjoyable. Why did you run away—were you suddenly overcome by shyness?'

She smiled diffidently. 'I felt I had showed off enough, and I could see that Mrs Salvador and Zandra were displeased. I—I know what they were thinking.'

'Do enlighten me, Miss Hartway, what were they thinking?'

'That I was—flirting with you.'

'*Dios*, how that must have scandalised them.'

'I know you're amused,' she said defensively, 'but I've now been at Abbeywitch long enough to have learnt that your stepmother never approved of Pauline, so she's bound to be annoyed if she thinks I'm stepping out of line. You must have seen for yourself the way she was looking at us!'

'I had no need to look,' he drawled.

'Do you always suit yourself regardless of other people's feelings?' Debra asked him quite seriously.

'Whose feelings do you refer to, *señorita*, your own or my stepmother's?'

'Both, *señor*. You made me dance with you, and you knew she would disapprove, so you can't blame me if I think you please yourself most of the time.'

'Do you think I am bothered by your opinion of me?'

'No—'

'I wonder?' He leant a little closer and searched her eyes and she felt his breath fan warm across her face. 'It rarely comes as any surprise to me that young Spanish girls have a certain innocence, but whenever I return to England I find innocence a commodity which soon will have antique value. Can you wonder at my first reaction when I came upon you on the beach? Always when I return I take a stroll along the sands and there you were on my beach, bare as a peeled shrimp—ah, you don't care to be reminded of it, do you?'

Debra had gone rigid in his grip . . . once again, as in the conservatory, she had the feeling that he was trying to delve into her personality and make her fit into the pattern of the experienced English girl who couldn't be over twenty and still a virgin.

'You seem to like reminding me,' she said tensely. 'Why should you be shocked if you believe that all English girls are shameless? You should have taken me in your stride, like those topless holidaymakers on the Costa Brava.'

'You were a little more than topless,' he mocked. 'Of course, had we met in my brother's office then I might have been fooled into thinking you a sedate young spinster. What a pity!'

Debra stared at him and felt her heart thudding away in her innocent frame and there seemed no way she could hit back at his big, powerful, threatening form. He seemed to be able to take the initiative in any situation and she wished she could make him feel less sure of himself.

'The sooner you go home to your pure Spanish girls the better,' she said. 'I was getting along fine with my job before you came and spoilt everything—now your family will think that I throw myself at men, and I don't! I didn't want to dance with you—you forced me into it—oh, I wish you'd leave me alone!'

'Do you imagine I came to your room on purpose? I looked in on my nephew, and there you happened to be and you were crying. I showed for you the same concern I would show for any other guest in my house—' Abruptly he broke off as the door was thrust open and Lenora Salvador swept in, outrage written all over her face.

Her eyes took Debra in, still captive in Rodare's grip, there on the bed. The look of anguish which Debra flung at him could only be misread like everything else. How was there any way to explain his presence in her bedroom, and even if he attempted an explanation his stepmother wasn't in the mood to believe him . . . the look she was giving them made Debra tingle to the roots of her hair. She felt sure Lenora wanted to grab her by the hair and throw her out of the house.

'Zandra warned me!' Lenora's lips were thin with rage. 'She said you had been seen coming in here—you, Rodare, with your proud talk about the ways of Spain and how the men respect the honour of the women. I don't see you living up to your proud boast!'

'I came in here—' He paused. 'I came to propose to Debra.'

The incredulous look on his stepmother's

face was no match for the look which Debra turned on him. And then with haughty indignation Lenora spoke again.

'You can't be serious, Rodare? You know the terms of your father's will—the terms which have always existed. It's because of them that you have stayed a bachelor.'

'Exactly. When I marry I must settle here at Abbeywitch or renounce my right to the property. Only a saint or someone insane would give up his birthright, so I shall abide by the terms of *padre*'s will and make my home here with my bride.'

Debra listened and decided that Rodare had to be insane and she was about to make some kind of a protest when he tightened his arm so powerfully around her and gave her such a warning look that she bit back her protest and bewilderedly wondered why he should make such a statement to Lenora.

What on earth was he doing . . . was he protecting his Spanish standards of honour because his stepmother found him in the bedroom of his brother's typist?

But I'm not a typist, Debra thought indignantly. I'm an editor, and a good one, and I'm not putting up with this nonsense!

She was about to speak out when Rodare silenced her in the most effective way . . . he planted a kiss on her mouth. Then imperturbably he returned his attention to Lenora, rising to his feet so he towered over her.

'It's high time that I took a wife and settled down,' he said. 'As the saying goes, a man without a wife becomes selfish while a woman without a husband becomes fastidious. What is the matter, Lenora? How disapproving you look.'

'Can you wonder?' She cast an icy look at Debra, sweeping her eyes over the disorder which Rodare had caused. 'I refuse to believe that you seriously mean to marry someone who is employed in the house! I know you have an odd sense of humour, but you are going a little too far, Rodare. The girl might take you seriously!'

'I hope she does,' he rejoined. 'You are taking me seriously, are you not, Debra?'

Debra met his eyes and she wondered what he would do if she did take his crazy proposal seriously. She decided to give him a dose of his own medicine and said softly: 'Of course I am, Rodare. I can't wait to marry you.'

Something flickered in his eyes, but his face remained imperturbable. 'There you are, Lenora, you have your answer. Debra is all eagerness to become my wife.'

'I daresay she would be,' Lenora snapped back at him. 'You happen to have money and land and she probably set out to be seduced by you from the moment she laid eyes on you. You've allowed yourself to be taken in just as

Jack was, and you'll live to regret it. For heaven's sake, Rodare, pay her off and let her go!'

Debra flinched and realised that the joke had gone far enough. 'Mrs Salvador,' she started to say, and was brusquely interrupted by Rodare.

'Perhaps, Lenora, I should suggest that you leave Abbeywitch if you can't bring yourself to live under the same roof with my wife. I know *padre* was generous to you in his will so you can well afford your own apartment. I daresay you could share it with Zandra.'

Lenora stared at him as if she couldn't believe her ears, then she carried her silk handkerchief to her nostrils in her habitual gesture of the grieving widow. 'I never thought I'd live to hear you speak to me in such a way, Rodare. That girl is changing you just as Pauline changed Jack. Why are the pair of you drawn to girls beneath your station?'

'Perhaps it runs in the blood,' Rodare retorted.

'You—you're insulting,' Lenora gasped.

'And so are you.' His face was dark and hard. 'Do you think it's kind for Debra to sit and listen to the things you've been saying? Do you think it's ladylike?'

'Do you think it gentlemanly to creep into her bedroom while we have guests in the house?' Lenora retaliated. 'That's why I came to warn you—we don't want a scandal, do we?'

'How could there be a scandal when I intend to marry Debra?'

'For God's sake, Rodare!' Debra had had enough of sitting there listening to the pair of them. 'As if you have to marry me—the whole thing is ridiculous!'

'There you are.' Lenora looked triumphant. 'These working girls don't expect proposals of marriage when they're caught with a man. Your trouble, Rodare, is that you've lived in Spain too long. You don't have to feel obliged and Miss Hartway knows it. Give her a cheque.'

'I wouldn't touch his money with a barge-pole,' Debra flared up. 'I'm going to pack my suitcase and I'm getting away from Lovelis Island before I finish up like Pauline.' She scrambled off the bed and hurried across to the cupboard where she kept her suitcase, but halfway there Rodare caught up with her and swung her to face him.

'Do you really want to leave?' he demanded.

'I can't wait to get away,' she retorted. 'I came here to work on a book and didn't expect to find myself being spoken to as if I'm a—a slut. I've never played around with men in my life a-and I won't be accused of it! You know very well that we weren't playing around!'

'Really, Miss Hartway,' Lenora's eyes flicked her up and down, 'if being in the arms of a man on a bed isn't playing around, then please tell me your definition—it must be quite hair-raising.'

'I—I was crying.' Debra sought for the words that would take the look of contempt off Lenora's face. 'I was upset about something and Mr Salvador was trying to make me feel better—'

'I'm sure he was,' Lenora drawled. 'I am certain that Rodare is very good at making young women feel better—that was certainly the way it looked when I walked in.'

Debra blushed vividly and couldn't stop herself, seeing the scene as it must have looked to Lenora who had already decided earlier in the evening that Debra, as an employee at Abbeywitch, had overstepped the mark by performing a rumba with the master of the house. If the situation hadn't been so threatening then it might have been amusing, but never had Debra felt less like laughing.

The threat simmered in Rodare's eyes and in the way he was gripping hold of her. He hated the way they had been caught together, she realised, especially as he had been so quick to warn Stuart Coltan that if he did anything he shouldn't beneath the roof of Abbeywitch, he would find himself in trouble.

Debra suspected that Stuart was at the bottom of this predicament she found herself in. She had the feeling he had been lurking about when Rodare had visited the nursery; he had waited and watched and seen Rodare follow her into her room, and he had then gone to Zandra and hatched mischief.

'Oh, does it really matter?' Debra sighed. 'It's really only a storm in a teacup. I'll leave and the whole thing can be forgotten.'

'Not by me.' Rodare spoke in a voice of iron. 'You may recall what I said, Debra, and I meant it. While you reside beneath my roof I guard your name . . . there is no way I can let you leave with mud on your name. It's a matter of pride.'

'This isn't Spain, señor—' Debra had grown frightened by his manner, and all too well she remembered the scene down in the hall, when he had told Stuart that he made the rules that applied to this house and he expected himself as well as other men to abide by them.

'Spain is where a Spaniard happens to be,' he rejoined. 'I repeat, I can't allow you to leave. I must put things right and that means you must marry me—whether you want to or not!'

'What utter nonsense, Rodare. As if *her* good name matters?'

He swung round to face his stepmother and he looked as if he were barely holding himself in check. 'You have said all I wish to listen to, *señora*. It's time to say good night, so please leave!'

She stared at him a fraction longer, then with

a shrug she turned to leave, saying as she went:
'Play the gallant fool if you feel you must, but
you'll regret it—regret it with all your heart,
just as Jack did. Fools the pair of you! Making
wives of girls who don't fit into our way of life.
Girls of a lower class!'

She significantly left the door open behind
her and Debra stared at the opening as if she
wanted to dash out . . . out of this house which
she had entered so innocently, unaware that
she would find herself in a situation such as
Rodare Salvador proposed.

'It is nonsense,' she said to him. 'People
these days don't get married to avoid a scandal, and no matter what your stepmother sur-
mised or said, you and I know that we've done
nothing wrong.'

'Of course we know.' His look was sombre
and very Spanish. 'But everybody else will
think otherwise, and in all conscience I can't
allow other people to put a wrong interpret-
ation upon our behaviour. You see, the curse
of a Spanish heritage is that honour and duty
are deep in the bone, there in the marrow, and
I am quite unable to watch you leave this
island labelled as my partner in a grubby
little episode.'

'There was no episode—least of all a grubby
one,' Debra protested. 'Why should I expect
you to—to marry me? Only people in love get
married.'

'In Spain,' he said deliberately, 'love is not always the reason, as in this case. We have been caught so we pay the price!'

'You can't make me marry you—' Debra backed away from him. 'You're behaving just like the other Don Rodare, and you know it!'

'Not quite like him.' Rodare took a step forward in time with her every backward one until she had nowhere to go but out on the terrace in the chilly night air. He came after her and without any hesitation swept her up into his arms and returned her to the bedroom, where he held her and scanned her face.

He gave a brief laugh. 'Come, don't look so petrified by the idea. Don't you find anything about me worth being married to? I have sufficient funds for the two of us and, after all, what is love? We say in Spain that love doesn't happen, it has to be made.'

He dropped her to her feet. 'Your eyes are almost out of your head, so go to your bed and sleep will repair your shattered emotions.' He strode to the door and flung a few last words over his shoulder. 'Tomorrow I shall start to arrange matters and you had better write to your mother to inform her that you are going to become a wife. *Buenas noches*, Debra *mia*!'

'I'm not yours,' she protested.

He turned in the doorway to regard her as she knelt on the bed in an attitude of appeal. 'I think I know you better than most,' he said, 'so in that context you are mine. Does the thought frighten you?'

'It frightens me that you're always so sure about everything,' she rejoined. 'You—you take things for granted.'

'I am taking you for granted, eh?'

'Yes—you think I shall tamely do as you say a-and marry you.'

'You will marry me because you have no choice.'

'I do have a choice.' Her eyes were pure green as she looked at him across the room, seeing in him everything she could intensely love if she allowed herself such madness, but seeing also a man whose pride enforced his proposal of marriage. It was the proud boast of his house *Let honour reside within* and Rodare felt duty-bound to stand by that statement.

'And what choice is that pray?' He was drawn up to his full height, looking every inch the *hidalgo* to whom his name as well as hers was of the utmost importance . . . exceeding that of two people being madly in love with each other, swept by all the passions and not just a passionate sense of honour.

'I respect your wish to respect me,' Debra's voice softened, 'but you must be realistic, *señor*. When you marry you must marry a girl who will fit into your way of life. I have a career—'

'You have a responsibility,' he broke in.

'Oh, in what way?' She looked perplexed.

'You were responsible in the first place for my presence in your bedroom.'

'But I—I didn't ask you in. I didn't ask for your sympathy, *señor*.'

'You didn't repudiate it when I gave it.' He withdrew her pearl pendant from his pocket and swung it in his fingers. 'I shall have this repaired for you, but tell me who gave it to you in the first place?'

'My father,' she said simply.

'And would your father be happy if he knew that his daughter left her place of employment with a black mark against her name?'

'No—but you exaggerate, *señor*. The rules in England aren't quite so definite as those in Spain and you must be aware that your stepmother had already decided that I should be dismissed.'

'Dismissed because you danced with me,' he said ironically. 'The more we talk, *señorita*, the deeper we find ourselves embroiled—fate has decided for us, wouldn't you agree?' And he gave the smile that was never more than half realised, his gaze brilliant and unavoidable, his dominance accentuated by his haughty Latin nose.

'Fate,' she murmured, and her head was slightly bowed so the lamplight played upon the subtle highlights in her hair, a glossy cape around the shoulders of her pale mauve wrap.

She gave an emotional shiver, for it was as if fate had taken a hand and placed her within dangerous reach of a man she would never meet again if she left him as she secretly planned to do.

'Run away from me,' he menaced, 'and I shall follow you.'

'But why?' she asked.

'Because I stand by my word!' He inclined his head like an eighteenth-century courtier, then the door closed behind him and Debra was left alone to remember every detail of his face as he had spoken those words.

'Rodare,' she whispered. 'Oh, Rodare, you devil—you beloved devil!'

CHAPTER SEVEN

'WHAT do you think I should do, Nanny Rose?'

Debra hugged young Dean in her arms and gazed across at the older woman with a hint of hope in her eyes that Nanny Rose would be able to solve the problem she had brought to the nursery quite early. Beyond the open windows the birds could be heard, but the sunlight was fitful as the occasional large cloud rolled above the sea.

'Perhaps you should listen to your heart,' came the reply to Debra's anxious question. 'You may not get the answer you hope is the right one, but you'll get an answer if I'm any judge.'

'But I daren't—' Debra broke off. 'You think I've fallen for him, don't you?'

'Aye, you've fallen a good deal of the way,' Nanny Rose agreed, but the look in her eyes was gentler than her tone of voice. 'I could see it happening—you so untried, and Mr Rodare so big and dominating, with those Spanish ways of his. And now he wants to marry you!'

'I—I told you why, Nanny Rose.'

'So you did, ducky.'

'But don't you think it's impossible?'

Nanny Rose thoughtfully poured two cups of tea from the brown glazed teapot she had treasured through many households where she had worked as a nanny. 'It's time he settled down and to my way of thinking a kind-hearted girl like yourself would be better for him than the Chandler girl, for all her beauty and worldly ways.'

'They belong to the same social circle and she is stunning.' Debra ruminated. 'I was watching them together at the party and they looked well-matched.'

'So you don't think you're a match for him?' Nanny Rose placed Debra's cup of tea in front of her and removed the reluctant little boy to his high-chair. She gave him a rusk to nibble and sat down at the table, her eyes upon Debra as she stirred her tea.

Debra shook her head. 'I'd no more fit into his life than Pauline fitted into his brother's—look what became of her! Perhaps her death wasn't an accident. Perhaps she took her own life. The facts were never firmly established, were they?'

'The thing is,' Nanny Rose sipped her tea, 'Mr Rodare would take better care of a wife than his brother.'

'You mean he'd be more possessive.' Debra had to smile. 'He'll never stop being three-parts Spanish—his spine went like a ramrod when Mrs Salvador made her suggestive remarks. I knew instantly that he couldn't bear them. He not only looks as if he's stepped out of the eighteenth century but he has the duelling instinct and I can see him with a rapier in his hand, defending his honour among the misty trees at dawn.'

Debra's smile gave way to a sigh. 'But it's no joke and I think I must leave Abbeywitch.'

'I don't see why,' Nanny Rose said unexpectedly. 'You're more akin to this house than Madam herself, and ten times more akin to it than Zandra. You've taken to the place, haven't you?'

'Yes,' Debra confessed. 'I think I could stay here for ever, but Rodare has only proposed to me out of a sense of obligation and I can't let him marry someone he doesn't love.'

'All the same it's tempting, isn't it?' Nanny Rose said shrewdly. 'It isn't every girl who gets the chance to get her hands on a man like him—granted he's a proud devil, but he's every inch a man and I bet the very thought of him stirs up your blood. Marry him and make him love you, girl!'

'Marry him and make him hate me!' Debra jumped to her feet. 'I'm going to pack my things and I'll get Mickey Lee to take me across to the mainland in the launch. I shall miss you, Nanny Rose—you and little Dean.'

Debra went to the boy's high-chair and, when he smiled up at her, she caught her breath, seeing in him a fleeting resemblance to the man she had to run away from.

'Your daddy will come home soon, sweetheart.' She bent and kissed his cheek and right away he put his chubby arms around her neck and got rusk crumbs in her hair. She started to laugh, but tears rushed into her eyes and sent her running from the nursery. If this was love, she thought wildly, then it was a weepy business and no mistake. Once in her room she grabbed a paper handkerchief and scrubbed her eyes dry, and this time there was no one to stop her from packing her suitcase. Quite soon it was loaded with her belongings, and now she had to hope that she could get down to the boathouse without attracting Rodare's attention.

She mustn't see him again. His effect upon her was too unsettling and though she had sought Nanny Rose's advice she couldn't take it. To be loved by Rodare would be wonderful, but to be married to him *sans* love would be impossible. The very fact that he had stayed a single man so long was an indication that he valued his freedom and the fact that he could spend lots of time in Spain. It had come as quite a surprise to Debra that when he took a wife he either lived permanently at Abbeywitch or gave up his inheritance. It was an entailment that probably went back to the first Don Rodare and had been enforced ever since so the eldest son had to abide by the terms if the house and the island meant anything to him.

Debra buttoned her jacket and for the last time she went out on the terrace and walked to the parapet that overlooked the sea. A wind had arisen and the clouds were ripped like chiffon and the sea itself had a metallic sheen. It was as if the day matched her mood of melancholy and even as she stood there a spot of rain splashed her cheek, warning her that she had better be on her way.

She closed the terrace doors, picked up her suitcase and walked from the room where only a matter of hours ago Rodare had said emphatically that he couldn't allow her to leave Lovelis Island with mud on her name. Well, she was leaving and she didn't feel in the least besmirched . . . she thought him gallant but where was the love . . . the subtle thread that led from one heart to another and joined two people together?

Debra knew herself, she was a romantic with longings to be loved just for herself. She wasn't afraid of passion but she wanted it linked to tenderness and empathy.

She reached the hall without being seen; it was still quite early and the family and guests were either taking breakfast in their rooms or were in the morning-room with a newspaper. Mickey Lee who worked as boatman for the family always took the motorboat to the mainland in order to collect mail and newspapers, so Debra felt confident that he would be down at the boathouse pottering about. He was the housekeeper's son and slightly retarded, still having the mind of a boy in his tough frame.

Fingers tense upon the handle of her suitcase Debra hurried beneath an archway shaded by a mass of greenery and her nerves gave a jump as a black raven alighted on a branch, sharp of eye and beak, reminding her a little of the way Lenora Salvador had regarded her when she entered her room and saw what she took to be a clandestine affair between her stepson and Jack's secretary.

It would take a more open mind to believe otherwise and Debra knew that Lenora had narrow and rigid views about people and their station in life and to her way of thinking a man of means didn't consort with a secretary, and it was that factor rather than anything else which had so offended her.

Debra felt quite sure that had Lenora come upon Rodare in a compromising situation with Sharon Chandler she would coolly have looked the other way.

Debra made her way down the cliffside steps, breathing the scent of stonecrop and rock-spurrey, seeing grey seals poking their heads above water, not far beyond where the surf foamed and bubbled. The wind blew cold against her face and she caught the sound of a curlew, the storm cryer. She hurried along the sand towards the aged boathouse which looked as if it had been constructed from wreckwood; small windows peered from the bleached walls and from inside she heard the sound of hammering.

Hitching her shoulder-bag she made for the open doorway, hearing behind her the waves as they unfurled themselves on the beach with a hiss and a roar, spraying the air with moisture. A dracaena tree rattled its leaves, looking not unlike a cabbage palm, and again the curlew called.

'Mickey!' She stood in the doorway of the boathouse and saw someone large bent over the hull of a rowboat. 'I'd like you to take me across to the mainland; I'll pay you!'

The figure straightened and slowly turned to face her. He regarded her in silence for a few seconds and then came towards her, holding a claw-hammer in his hand.

'You're the Miss who works for Mister Jack,' he said, and his smile was strangely flickering for it revealed a silver tooth near the front of his mouth. He was hulking and Debra knew that he took part in wrestling bouts, a still very competitive sport in Cornwall. Debra tried not to shrink away from the bulk of him and that strange smile.

'That's right,' she said. 'I was working for him up until today, but now I'm leaving and I have to get to the mainland so I can catch the train for London. I would be grateful if you'd take me in the launch, and I'll certainly pay you for your trouble.'

'But, miss,' his brow wrinkled, 'you can't leave work without your pay certificate. You won't be able to get another job.'

'I—I'll send for it,' she assured him.

'So you know where Mr Jack is staying as well?' His brow cleared and he took a step nearer to her, a confidential air about him. 'The others don't know. His Ma and his sister, they don't know, and I didn't even tell when Mr Rodare came and asked me. Me and Mr Jack, we played together as boys. We were friends!'

Debra gazed up into the big craggy face in which the eyes were curiously guileless and she felt a rising excitement. So Jack Salvador hadn't gone away without telling someone of his whereabouts and that person was big Mickey Lee who could probably keep a secret because he retained a childlike trust in his friends.

Suddenly her own need to get away from Cornwall as soon as possible took second place to seeing Jack Salvador so she could impress upon him the fact that he was needed by his little boy. Though Dean was still only an infant, he was a bright and inquisitive child and he would turn his affection to other people if

Jack continued to stay away from him. A rift would grow between them and to Debra's way of thinking that would be a great pity, especially as the child's mother was dead.

'Mickey,' she stepped forward and took him by the arm, 'you're right about my pay certificate, I should collect it from Mr Salvador, so I think it best if you take me to him. I wouldn't want it to get lost in the post, and if that happened it would cause a lot of bother.'

He nodded in agreement, and glanced at her slender hand upon his arm; for several moments it seemed to fascinate him, then his eyes slid to her face again. 'You leaving because of *her*?'

'You mean Mrs Salvador?'

'No.' He shook his head and his gaze travelled to the waves splashing the shore where the rocks stood dark against the sullen sky. 'She wasn't golden any more when they found her, she was all white like the marble tombstones in the churchyard of the Sacred Sorrows. You can hear the bells across the water when the wind is right—shall I show you where they found her, miss?'

And before Debra could quickly say no, he began to take long strides along the beach where the wind had torn seaweed from the rocks so it was scattered across the sand like drowned hair. Debra followed in the wake of Mickey Lee, for she had to conciliate him if she was to persuade him to take her to Jack Salvador.

He approached a jagged line of rocks where large pools of water would be deep enough to drown someone when the tide swept in, and there he paused and pointed with the claw-hammer towards one of the pools. 'The tide left her there.' Mickey Lee stared downwards as if he still saw Pauline floating there, battered and lifeless, her hair like the seaweed on the sands. 'She was stony-drowned and there was no more laughing in her eyes.'

Abruptly he swung round and Debra noticed how hulking and dark he looked, as if chiselled from rock himself. She realised how alone with him she was, here on the beach which during her first weeks on the island she had freely used without realising any danger until Rodare had ordered her to take care.

She gave a sudden shiver and couldn't help but wonder what would have happened had it been Mickey Lee who had been standing over her instead of Rodare, seeing her not with Rodare's worldly eyes but with eyes which had noticed Pauline's golden looks.

'We must be on our way, Mickey.' Debra infused a note of authority into her voice. 'It's going to rain and I want to see Mr Salvador as soon as possible so I can collect my pay certificate. Come along!'

She turned and hurried back towards the boathouse, aware of him lumbering along behind her, that horrible-looking hammer in his hand. She was glad when he discarded it in order to stow her suitcase on the motorboat and then hand her in. The motor chugged into life and they were off, bouncing over the waves as they headed in the direction of the nearest mainland harbour which was at Penarth. She couldn't ask Mickey too many questions or he would guess that she hadn't any idea where Jack Salvador was staying.

Jack's family presumed that he had gone abroad, but as he was obviously in touch with Mickey he was more than likely in Penarth itself, needing to be near his son and yet unable to face a return to the island where everything reminded him of Pauline. In love with her or not her death was haunting him, and Debra knew from working on his book that he had a strain of sensitivity that other members of his family seemed to lack.

Debra had to include Rodare; she knew of his power and his pride but she doubted if he was a sensitive person.

'It's a shame you're leaving,' Mickey said at last, as if being on the water had lightened his mood. 'Mr Jack will be ever so sorry because he told me he was glad he had you working on his book.'

'That was nice of him.' Debra tried to look at

ease, as if she were on her way to see a man she
knew rather than someone who in person was
a stranger to her. She knew Jack's voice, for she
had listened to it often enough. She admired
his work, but beyond that she wouldn't have
known him had she passed him in the street
. . . unless, of course, he resembled Rodare
physically.

There wasn't a thing about Rodare that she
would forget easily. The way he looked and
spoke and carried himself, just a hint of a
swagger in his walk.

'Why are you leaving?' Mickey wanted to
know.

'Because I've had an argument with Mrs
Salvador—the same as Miss Tucker. She isn't
an easy person to please, I'm afraid.'

'I keep well out of her way.' Mickey scowled,
and spray stung Debra's face as the motorboat
sliced its way through the heaving sea. Overhead the sky was like armour-plating, heavy
and dark with the threat of a downpour.

'The likes of her can't fire me because Mr
Rodare is master of the house and what he says
goes!' Mickey nodded to himself, his brows
heavy and dark over his eyes. 'She don't like
me and I don't like her, but there ain't a thing
she can do about it. Never wept a tear she
didn't, but it's known hereabouts that witches
don't cry!'

'You mean at the cremation?' Debra

murmured. 'Were you there, Mickey? Did you see Mr Salvador scatter the ashes?'

'I was hanging about,' he growled.

'You liked Pauline, didn't you? She was kind to you, Mickey?'

'She didn't treat me like I was a dog, like the other two do!' All at once a sly smile passed over Mickey's face. 'Miss Pauline liked the men and I could tell you something if I had a mind to, but you'll only go and tell Mr Jack. Women can't keep secrets, not like I can.'

'Is it a very deep secret?' Debra could feel her own excitement and tried to control it. She had to look and sound casual or she would send Mickey Lee back inside his shell. She believed he was being talkative because he had sometimes seen her chatting with his mother.

'Deep as the sea,' he grinned. 'There's no one can come up against the sea and beat it, miss. She got punished, that's what!'

'Why should Pauline be punished, especially in that terrible way?'

'People get punished when they do a wrong thing,' he said ominously. 'She didn't ought to have gone with someone else behind Mr Jack's back—they didn't know I saw them rolling and laughing on the sand, her gold hair all untidy and him all over her! She was wed to Mr Jack and it weren't right, and I'll tell you something else, miss, I'm not the only one who knows what she got up to.'

'You mean Mrs Salvador, don't you, Mickey? She knew that Pauline was playing around with another man?'

'She'd be bound to find out,' he muttered. 'She's got nothing better to do than to stir up the pot, the old witch!'

Debra felt tempted to ask Mickey who he had seen with Pauline on the beach, but they were rapidly approaching the harbour of Penarth and he had to guide the motorboat in and out of the chopping seacraft until the motor chugged to silence and the boat was secured to the quay.

Light as a cat for all his bulk he leapt to the wet steps and held out a helping hand to Debra, which she accepted, feeling the welt of rough skin across his palm. She followed him up the steps to the cobbled pavement, feeling the rain in the air and the way it intensified the smell of fish. A huddle of stalls stood beneath awnings where women were doing their shopping and enjoying a gossip.

'Let's go straight away to Mr Salvador.' Debra drew up the collar of her jacket and wished she had worn a warmer coat. 'He's staying here in Penarth, isn't he?'

'At *The Cap And Bells*.' He gave a laugh that was more like a growl. 'No one knows but me, for it ain't the kind of place the two ladyships are likely to call in at—' Abruptly he paused and stared down at Debra with his brow furrowed. 'D'you reckon I ought to take you there, miss?'

'Of course,' she said briskly. 'I'm not a ladyship, am I?'

'You won't split on him, will you?'

'The thought never entered my head, Mickey.' She wasn't lying to him, but she did harbour the hope that she could persuade Jack Salvador to return home for the sake of his son. Why on earth did he stay away from Dean . . . did he suspect that the child might not be his?

'Come on, then.' Mickey strode across the road and Debra had to hasten her steps in order to keep pace with him. The rain was also coming down harder, and by the time the Tudor-like edifice of *The Cap And Bells* came into view, Debra could feel her hair plastered to her scalp and she was almost out of breath.

They went in through the hotel entrance and mounted a flight of stairs with faded carpet on them; the old oaken stairs creaked with age and the atmosphere of the place was musty and somehow forlorn up here on the landing where Jack Salvador had taken a room and was hiding away from his family.

Mickey Lee tramped to the end of the landing, his heavy frame inducing such creaks from the floorboards that Debra feared an imminent cave-in. They came to a door with a yellowed plaque on it which announced that this was the Green Mantle room, and it made Debra feel sad that the writer of books which had a vast and eager readership should spend hour upon hour brooding alone in this place with his memories.

She glanced at Mickey, who was staring at the door in a hesitant manner. 'I don't know if I've done right,' he said, shaking his head.

'You've done right, Mickey,' she assured him, and taking the initiative Debra knocked upon the door. It didn't open right away and she was raising her hand to try again when it was flung open. 'About time, I thought you'd gone to pick the hops—' The words broke off and a moody pair of eyes looked Debra up and down. 'Who the devil are you?'

'Hello, Mr Jack.' Mickey shuffled Debra's suitcase from one hand to the other. 'Miss had to come and see you on account of her pay—'

'What pay?' Dark brows meshed themselves above the moody eyes. 'I thought I told you to stay away, Mickey—and who is this girl?'

'I'm Debra Hartway and I have to talk to you, Mr Salvador.'

'Hartway?' He thrust a hand through dark hair grown overlong at his nape. 'It rings a bell—ah yes, you're with Columbine and you're working on my book. Harrison wrote me; I have a box number, you understand.'

'You've got to give Miss her pay certificate,' Mickey insisted. 'I wouldn't have brought her otherwise, Mr Jack. You know I can keep my mouth shut and I never let out a murmur, not even to Mr Rodare, and you know what he can be like if he gets a bee in his helmet.'

'Yes, Mickey, I know my brother and his ways.' A kind of weariness had replaced Jack's irritability. 'Miss Hartway, what is all this about? What are you doing here when you're supposed to be working on my book at Abbeywitch?'

'I—I'm not working on it any more, Mr Salvador. It didn't work out—'

'My mother's been interfering again?' he groaned. 'Oh, lord, why didn't you make women *sans* speech and suspicion? So, Miss Hartway, you've quit the job, but what are you doing here? Why have you persuaded Mickey to bring you to me? What do you think I can do?'

'You could give me a little of your time,' she replied.

'For what purpose?' Fleetingly his eyes were as vivid as Rodare's, making Debra's heart jump.

'For the sake of your son,' she dared to say. That momentary glimpse of Rodare made her aware that she was trespassing and that he would be justified in telling her to mind her own business. She was braced for this, but pain twisted his mouth and for a moment his eyes were bleak.

'You have your nerve,' he murmured, then

as if taking a decision, he turned to Mickey. 'Be a good lad and make yourself scarce, Mick. I want to have a few words in private with Miss Hartway.'

'Right you are, Mr Jack.' Mickey Lee seemed relieved rather than excluded. 'Shall I leave the suitcase?'

'Yes, leave it, Mick. Go down to the bar and have a drink.' Jack took out his wallet and gave Mickey some money. 'Mind you lay off the whisky, eh?'

Mickey gave a nod and a wink. 'I'll keep to cider, Mr Jack, and have a pastie with it.'

'You do that, Mick—and don't take the boat back to the island for an hour or so.'

After Mickey had lumbered off down the stairs, Jack invited Debra into his room and was about to close the door when the barmaid appeared with his drink on a tray. 'Will you have a drink, Miss Hartway?' he asked.

Debra declined and he closed the door. He gestured to a wing-back chair which, like the other furniture in the room, had seen a lot of wear. But it was comfortable enough and Debra was glad to sit down, because all at once she felt a reaction from having nerved herself to come and confront Jack Salvador on an issue that was very private to him.

He lounged with his drink against one of the stout twisted posts of the bed and she saw that his glass contained a colourless liquid that was probably vodka for a silver-skinned onion was floating in it.

'Cheers!' He raised his glass, then took a deep swallow. 'So my mother has taken exception to you, Miss Hartway? May I ask why?'

Debra was at a loss, for she couldn't blurt out that his mother had caught her alone with his brother in the middle of the night and jumped to the obvious conclusion.

'I think the truth is, Mr Salvador, that she is so unsettled by your long absence that she isn't quite herself. She tends to—to misjudge people.'

'So she has misjudged you, eh.'

'I—I'm afraid so.'

'And you put her edginess down to the fact that she misses me?'

'Of course she misses you—isn't that natural?' Debra studied him and decided that when he was shaven and groomed and clad in a suit he would look distinguished. He was tall but lacked the look of power which made Rodare so much more formidable, and because his hair was flecked with a little silver he didn't seem quite so swarthy. It was also very apparent that the hot sun of Spain wasn't burnt into his skin; he had the drawn look of a man who had been lurking in the shadows a little too long and Debra felt a stab of compassion for him.

'You stare at me, Miss Hartway.' He sampled some more of his drink. 'Are you looking for a resemblance to the child?'

'There is a family resemblance,' she murmured. 'Only today I caught a glimpse of your brother in Dean.'

'How interesting, and do you see glimpses of Rodare in me?'

'Of course—'

'You imagine it,' he said curtly. 'Rodare has inherited strong Spanish traits, both physical and mental, and the only thing we have in common is our pride. Do you see pride in me, Miss Hartway?'

'Yes, Mr Salvador.'

'So now you know why I've stayed away from the island and caused my mother such— anguish.' A most unamused smile twisted his lip. 'I suppose you are going to tell me that I have no right to absent myself from my son, am I correct?'

'Yes.' Despite the various emotions which she sensed were smouldering in him, Debra found she could meet his eyes with more ease than she could ever meet his brother's. 'He's a charming little boy and if you stay away too long you'll miss the fun of seeing him start to toddle and talk. Why punish yourself?'

'You imagine that's what I'm doing?'

'I think you are.'

'You don't know me, Miss Hartway, so how

can you presume to know why I hide myself away in this dreary little pub instead of enjoying the comfort of Abbeywitch? I surmise that you read a lot of books and maybe take me for a sacrificing hero.'

'I—I think you're sacrificing your rights as a father in order to brood.'

'Brood?' he took her up, little angry lights agleam in his eyes. 'Let me put a case to you, Miss Hartway. How would you feel about infidelity?'

Debra winced . . . so all the rumours and innuendoes had been correct, Pauline had taken a lover and Jack Salvador was unsure about the part he had played in the production of Dean. Yet she had seen that glimpse of Rodare in the boy . . . a realisation that suddenly took on ominous shadings. Oh God, was it suspicion of his brother that made Jack hide away with his hurt and angry pride? Was Stuart Coltan's insinuation a valid one, that Rodare and Pauline had liked to do more than dance together?

She gazed dumbly at Jack Salvador, and then rose to her feet. 'I had no right to come here,' she said. 'I tricked Mickey Lee into bringing me and you've every right to be annoyed. I'll go now. I'm on my way back to London.'

He tossed back the remainder of his drink. 'Stay and have some lunch with me—quite frankly I hadn't realised how much I have missed the company of someone kind and rational. This old pub lays on a good luncheon and you need something to eat before the train—you are set on taking it?'

She nodded.

'Anyway,' his eyes were intent upon her face, 'you will take lunch with me?'

'That's kind of you, Mr Salvador.' Debra was hesitant, but there still remained the faint hope that she could make him see reason where little Dean was concerned. It wasn't as if he had stated definitely that Dean wasn't his son, and even so it wasn't just for an adult to lay any kind of blame upon a mere baby.

'I'd appreciate the company.' He rasped a hand across his unshaven jaw and gave her a wry sort of smile. 'If you'll give me about fifteen minutes to turn myself back into a civilized human being?'

'Of course.' She watched him take a change of clothing from the bureau and then he vanished into the adjoining bathroom from whence came the rushing sound of the shower. Debra walked to the window and gazed down into the cobbled yard of *The Cap And Bells* where the rain was making puddles. She had a feeling of unreality; so much had occurred in her life in the past twenty-four hours that most of it was hard to take in.

Now she was off the island it almost seemed possible to believe that she had dreamt of

Rodare's proposal of marriage rather than experienced it.

What, she wondered, had been his reaction when he found out that she had left Abbeywitch? He had threatened to follow her if she left, but Debra didn't think he would go that far. The impulse which had driven him to propose to her would have lost its impetus overnight and she felt sure he would be relieved to find her gone.

Whatever her feelings for him, she had never really got to know him and she suspected that Jack Salvador was right when he spoke of her as being the kind of person who wanted men to be like the heroes in the books she had read.

Even as she smiled a little a sigh took its place. Rodare was a man like any other and in her mind's eye she saw him dancing with Pauline as he had danced with her last night. Pauline the golden girl, as Mickey Lee had called her, fitting her lissom dancer's body to Rodare's and looking so blonde in contrast to his darkness. Leading him into desire even as he led her through the rhythms of the dance?

Pain twisted Debra's mouth as she had seen it twist Jack's. She didn't doubt for an instant that there was Salvador blood in little Dean, and she couldn't help but wonder if Pauline had flung in Jack's face a secret so unbearable that in his fury he had struck her and caused her to pitch into the sea.

'What a day you've chosen to leave Cornwall.'

Debra flung round from the window and her tumultuous thoughts were in her eyes, making her look as tormented as she felt.

'Did I startle you?' Jack Salvador stood there in a navy-blue pin-stripe suit and with his lean face shaven and his hair combed he looked the distinguished author whom Debra had admired for a long time.

'Yes.' She forced a smile. 'I was miles away in my thoughts.'

'Having regrets about leaving Lovelis Island?'

'N-no.'

'I believe you are, Miss Hartway. I believe you've fallen for him, haven't you?'

'I'm sure I don't know who you mean!' His words had made her heart turn over.

'I mean young Dean.' His eyes narrowed thoughtfully. 'Who did you think I was referring to?'

And in order to safeguard her feelings for Rodare she snatched at a name. 'Stuart Coltan—he's terrifically handsome, isn't he, and he assumes that every woman wants him.'

'Ah, so Coltan is on the island.' Jack looked cynical. 'A ubiquitous young man who hangs around Zandra and makes use of her. So he failed to impress you, Miss Hartway?'

'I can't stand him!' she rejoined. 'The little boy is a darling, of course.'

'Shall we go to lunch?' Jack held open the door, and held Debra's gaze as she approached him, a man of embittered charm . . . the author she had longed to meet, who from the beginning had been her reason for wanting to work at Abbeywitch.

CHAPTER EIGHT

THEY sat in an alcove of bottle-glass windows and nearby a fire glowed cheerfully in the stone fireplace. A game of darts was going on in the saloon bar and Debra listened to the thud of the darts in the board as her host ordered the meal. They had both chosen the silverside of beef with pease-pudding and vegetables; a good old English lunch to go with the ambience of the oak-panelled dining-room.

'I can understand why you chose to stay here,' Debra remarked.

He glanced at the oak beams and the panelling almost black with age, the floor of foot-worn flagstones and the pair of duelling pistols hanging above the fireplace.

'Because I like things of historical value,' he agreed. 'I have no use for the plastic age; I abhor modern gadgetry up to a point but I have to admit that dictating my work on to cassettes appeals to me. I hope you didn't find listening to the tapes too much of a bore?'

'Far from it,' she assured him. 'You must have been vitally involved with the book because the plot and the characters are so alive.'

'Yet you won't stay to complete work on it.'

He ran his gaze over her face and took in her mist-green, cowl-necked sweater. 'Don't you care for Cornwall, the garden of legend as it's called?'

'Cornwall's a magical place but—' She glanced away from him, seeing a wet and distorted world beyond the bottle-glass windows. 'You could send the tapes to London and let me work on them at the office—won't you do that, Mr Salvador? I'd take every care of them.'

'I'm sure you would, but I just can't take the chance of one of the tapes going astray. I know how egocentric I sound, but if you were a writer yourself, Miss Hartway, you would understand how I feel. A book to an author is like a child.'

Debra looked at him gravely when he said that and something in her eyes must have got under his skin. 'Dammit, what right have you to judge me?' he demanded. 'You're thinking to yourself that a child of flesh and blood is worth far more than a novel about made-up people, even if I happen to know that Dean isn't my son.'

'How can you be so certain—?'

'Certain?' Lines of pain clawed at his face. 'Because I received the information from my own wife, that's why!'

Debra recoiled as if from a slap. 'Oh no!'

'Oh yes, she was quite defiant about it—she

said she was leaving and taking Dean with her, and when I said that only over my dead body would she take him, she flung at me that I had no right to him; that being her husband didn't make me the father of her child. She ran off then to the other end of the yacht where one of Zandra's theatrical friends was doing impersonations. I stood there by the rail listening to the laughter and hearing it as if it came from hell. I told myself she was lying about Dean, but I had never known Pauline to lie about anything. She had an almost childlike candour, quite embarrassing to my mother when Pauline would state in front of rather grand friends of the family that she grew up in the slums of Belfast and wore her sisters' cast-off clothes. She'd talk about how her feet were smaller and the handed-down shoes had to be stuffed with cardboard soles in order to make them fit.'

Jack Salvador sat there in silence, gazing beyond Debra as if he saw the ghost of Pauline, the girl who had danced her way into his heart but had not been able to attune herself to his imaginative mind.

'That was the night she died,' he said quietly. 'How it happened, why it happened, remains a mystery. You are probably thinking, Miss Hartway, that I had every reason for seeing her dead, but I had nothing to do with her death. I believe the inquest verdict was the correct one. She was over-excited and she'd been drinking champagne, and she took with her the name of her lover.'

Debra sadly wished that Pauline's lover had been only a myth, but Mickey Lee had seen them together on the beach. He knew the man's name but some primitive impulse kept him from telling Jack, who had always befriended him. Jack was the same age and he was less intimidating than Rodare . . . Rodare who came every so often from Spain, bringing with him the dark gold look of his mother's people; the smouldering danger and charm of the Latin temperament.

Was it possible, Debra wondered, that Pauline had tempted him and made him betray his strong sense of Spanish morality? Was that why she had glimpsed his likeness in Pauline's little boy?

She sat watching the waiter as he cut appetising slices of spiced beef and laid them on the plates. The pease-pudding was added, then the potatoes, carrots and turnips. It all looked delicious but Debra ate her lunch in an automatic way, feeling it was an effort to get the food past the heaviness in her chest. She swallowed red wine with each mouthful and listened rather inattentively as Jack Salvador talked about Cornwall, which he obviously loved as much as Rodare loved Andalucia.

He talked of the wild coppery moors and the

lonely grandeur and the superstitions that were as firmly rooted in Cornish people as the misty banks of bell-heather, and the old moor-stones that were supposed to be men and maidens who had been petrified for dancing on the Sabbath.

'This magical realm of Morte d'Arthur and the Wizard Merlin.' Jack smiled almost to him-self. 'Land of legendary lovers such as Tristan and Iseult. When Rodare and I were boys we'd join the fire circles on Midsummer Eve and when the flames had died down we'd all clasp hands and leap among the embers to drive away the Devil. Fire is supposed to ward off witches and demons, and sometimes at dusk-fall the moors can be very evocative, and only a fool will glance over his shoulder when crossing Bodmin after dark.'

'I can understand why you've used Cornwall so frequently in your books.' Debra watched him across the rim of her wine-glass and remembered the hours she had spent in the leathered den at Abbeywitch, listening to his voice on tape, her fingers tapping away at the typewriter keys as she transcribed his latest book.

'It has atmosphere and history,' he agreed. 'So you think my new book has been worth-while? Have you no criticisms? Contrary to what people think, authors hunger for an opinion whether it stings or strokes their ego.'

'I can only stroke your ego,' Debra smiled. 'As I said, you must have been deeply involved with your characters.'

'Perhaps so.' He brooded on her words. 'Possibly, do you think, to the detriment of my marriage?'

'I—I can't give you an answer to that question, Mr Salvador. I don't know what makes or breaks a marriage.'

'Of course not, you're just a girl and I put to you a question that wise old men can't answer. The seas of marriage aren't easy to navigate and I suppose mine went on the rocks because Pauline and myself weren't truly compatible. I took her away from the bright lights of show business and brought her to Cornwall because it's where I need to work. It was rather like plucking a southern flower and planting it in soil that changed its character—but, by God, she was pretty! And I swear she was mine—utterly mine in that first year we had together.'

'Then you have something good to remember,' Debra murmured. 'If you realise that she was missing the bright lights and the excitement of show business, can't you forgive her for not being quite an angel?'

His face grew shadowed again and he pushed his plate away from him. 'I wouldn't be fool enough to think any woman an angel, but when Dean was born I believed him to be my son and I loved him so when he was placed in my arms. He wasn't nude-looking like so many babies because he already had dark hair, and there is no feeling in the world such as a man feels when he holds his first child. I worshipped that boy, and then she said he wasn't mine and it was as if a fist reached inside me and tore away part of my heart. I don't feel good remembering that, Miss Hartway.'

'I'm so sorry.' She spoke involuntarily. 'It's naïve and clumsy of me to talk to you about returning to Abbeywitch. Every stick and stone of the place must remind you of details you want to forget.'

'I realise that you have the child's welfare at heart,' Jack's brow was dark and frowning as he studied the dessert list on the menu. 'The steamed jam-roll with custard is nice, or would you prefer strawberries and cream?'

'Oh, I don't know if I can manage a sweet,' she said hesitantly. Her appetite was fickle today and she had decided that she wanted to catch her train as soon as possible . . . she had imposed on Jack Salvador long enough with her idealistic notion that his place was with Dean, even if the child did remind him of Pauline's infidelity.

'We'll both have strawberries,' he said, and beckoned the waiter to their table. The dining-room had filled up with people and the warmth and chatter made it a haven against the rain that was pelting against the windows and splashing from the stone sills to the cobbles of the courtyard.

'I'm sure you like strawberries.' Jack's brow had cleared a little and his eyes, when he looked at her, held no reproach of any sort. 'I'm equally sure that you like little boys and Dean has inherited a great deal of charm from his mother. I expect you look forward to a happy marriage, eh?'

'No—I want to have a career.' She spoke with a fervency which was all part of her flight from Rodare. 'I've always loved books and nothing makes me happier than working among them. I'd like to go on to become a chief editor—I mean it, Mr Salvador, even though you're looking at me as if you think I'm kidding myself and hungering for a great romance.'

'It's perfectly natural for a girl to hunger for romance and I don't see why you should make an exception of yourself.' A smile kindled in his eyes. 'I'm not so soured on romance that I'd warn you off—you might be fortunate enough to find your very own Tristan or Galahad.'

Debra smiled slightly, thinking to herself that instead of meeting a gallant Sir Galahad she had met someone more in the shape of the overpowering Lancelot who had betrayed King Arthur by making love to his wife Guinevere.

'I find the world inside books safer than the

one outside them,' she said. 'I find the people I read about easier to—like.'

'Because the people in the real world are a little too fond of exploiting each other, eh?'

She nodded, and they didn't speak again until the waiter had served their strawberries, large and moistly bright, the cream the true clotted cream of the West Country, blending so temptingly with the strawberries that Debra's appetite forgot to be fickle and it really was a delicious sensation biting into the plump berries, the juice and cream like a sensuous wine.

They were drinking their coffee when Jack said: 'I'd really like you to continue work on my book—won't you reconsider and return to the island? Surely in view of your praise of the book and your ability to lose yourself in an author's make-believe world you can cope with my mother? Won't you give it another try?'

Debra was on the point of regretfully shaking her head when she was struck by an idea, one so simple and yet so difficult to face up to if he should comply with it.

As she sat hesitating and weighing up the consequences of his possible agreement, he leant forward and stilled her drumming fingers with his lean hand. 'You're indecisive, aren't you? Your sense of duty is pulling you in two.'

'Yes,' she admitted, and felt the captivation

of her hand in his. 'Aren't you pulled in two
yourself, Mr Salvador?'

'Back to that, are we?' But he said it without
rancour. 'Come along, what's on your mind?'

'How do you know I have something on my
mind?'

'Your eyes tell me so.'

'I see.' Her lashes flickered and her gaze fell
to his hand covering hers; it was his left hand
and when she saw that it still wore a gold
wedding band she knew she must speak out. If
she didn't do so regret would be her travelling
companion on the train journey back to
London and she would always wonder if he
would have given her a positive answer.

'I'm willing to make a deal with you,' she
said, the pulse in her throat beating like a small
tom-tom.

'What kind of a deal?'

'I'll return to Abbeywitch and finish work on
your book if you'll come with me.'

In the silence that hung between them the
noises in the room seemed to grow louder;
someone dropped a fork and it made a musical
sound as it hit the oak floor, then a woman's
laughter broke off as lightning shimmered in
broken pieces against the windows, followed
by a peal of thunder. 'Storm!' a voice
exclaimed.

'The gods are angry,' Jack murmured.
'They're crossing swords up there—that's

what Rodare and I used to believe as boys.
Rodare has returned to Abbeywitch, hasn't
he?'

'Yes.' When the lightning licked again at the
bottle-glass Debra felt her hand leap in Jack's
like a trapped frog.

'Are you afraid of storms?'

'Not as a rule—no.'

'But right now you're breaking a rule of
your own, eh? You usually mind your own
business?'

She flushed slightly. 'Will it make you any
less happy, Mr Salvador, to be in the same
house with Dean? He's only a baby. He hasn't
done anything wrong and you're punishing
him and yourself. You said you loved him
madly when he was born, and he's still the
same little boy. He still has such a capacity for
affection—perhaps that was his mother's only
fault, that she needed affection and you—you
are a born writer and maybe you gave so much
to your work that she felt left out. Perhaps you
had forgotten to show her that you needed
her—it would be cruel of you to do the same
thing to Dean.'

'Affection and cruelty are provocative
words, Miss Hartway, especially when you
use them in reference to my marriage.'

'I know they are.' Debra felt unsure of the
ground she was treading on, but she had to
proceed. 'I don't pretend to have lived a very

full life so that I'm able to judge men, but I wouldn't like your books so much if they didn't have compassion in them, and yet you deny it to Dean. Surely the love you felt for him when he was born is still there in your heart? Surely love doesn't die so easily?'

'You speak of love, but what do you really know about it?' His eyes searched her face. 'Do you imagine that it's a gentle emotion?'

Debra shook her head. 'I imagine that it's made up of many things and I hope that pride and passion aren't its prime ingredients. I hope it doesn't mean total submissiveness on the part of the woman or total possessiveness on the part of the man. Why should love turn a woman into a slave?'

'Miss Hartway,' he leant back in his chair, releasing her hand from his, 'you've been reading far too many books. Love between real people is one hell of a battle and the injuries inflicted can be as deep as the pleasures.'

'I realise how much you've been hurt,' Debra spoke feelingly, 'but the physical pain of the injury is over and I think you're giving in to pride.'

'We Salvadors are proud, or hadn't you noticed?'

'Oh yes, I've noticed!'

He arched a brow at the intensity with which she answered him, and then for a while he sat in sombre thought leaving Debra to listen to

the thunder as it growled above the rooftops of
Penarth.

She felt astounded by her own temerity in
discussing love with a man who had enjoyed
the sweet and the bitter of it. All she knew of
love was a confused sense of attraction and
doubt centred around his brother, who had
the shape of someone she had sometimes
glimpsed in a dream.

Debra wasn't going to allow a dream to
deceive her. Jack's wife had died among the
rocks of Lovelis Island and when the seabirds
cried it was as if her ghost wailed among them,
calling to someone within the stone walls of
Abbeywitch.

The island and the house beckoned Debra
back to them, but this time she told herself she
was less innocent and she would be able to look
at Rodare with eyes no longer bemused by
him. Now she would see him as a man subject
to dark passions . . . making her wonder what
his thoughts had been when he had stood over
her that day on the beach, seeing her defence-
less at his feet.

Suddenly Jack Salvador spoke and Debra
came out of her thoughts with a visible effort,
the disturbing image of Rodare fading uneasily
in the presence of his brother.

'I think, Miss Hartway, that you have a deal.'

But Debra felt trapped in her own silence . . .
she had flung down the gauntlet and Jack had

picked it up, but now she felt afraid of the challenge.

'I'm holding you to it.' Jack eyed her with a frown. 'You've pleaded your case in Dean's defence and made me feel guilty, and that's what you wanted when you came looking for me. I'm going home and you are going with me—that was the bargain.'

'Yes,' she admitted, and saw in the adamant set of his jaw his likeness to Rodare. It was vagrant that likeness; it came and went and it added to her awareness that she had talked herself into a situation fraught with problems.

'There's no need to worry any more about my mother.' Jack picked up the bill and studied it. 'I shall see to it that she doesn't bother you—did you enjoy your lunch?'

'It was very nice, thank you.'

A glimmer of amusement came into his eyes, which dwelt on her as if he didn't quite know what to make of a secretary who made bargains with him.

He beckoned the waiter and as he took his wallet from his pocket he said casually: 'This storm isn't going to let up for a while and we'd have a wet journey home if we went today. I suggest that you stay overnight in Penarth and we'll arrange to have Mickey Lee pick us up when he comes across for the family mail and the morning newspapers. You could probably book in here at *The Cap And Bells* for the night.'

'All right,' she said, feeling relieved by his suggestion. She was committed to going back with him to Abbeywitch and a few more hours in Penarth would be welcome. She would have time in which to adjust to this turnabout in her plans; time in which to build up the nerve to face Rodare on her return. Dare she ask Jack to ensure that his brother didn't bother her?

Oh lord! Her legs felt trembly as she walked with Jack out of the dining-room. What would be his reaction when he found out the real reason for her flight from the island? Would he understand and believe that Rodare's presence in her bedroom had been entirely innocent?

Could he possibly understand when a suspicion of Rodare ate like a worm at the core of him?

Debra went with him to the reception desk and stood there in a mood of misgivings as he arranged for her to stay overnight at *The Cap And Bells* at his expense. She tried to protest about payment for the room being added to his bill, but he overruled her. She was staying as his guest and he further informed the receptionist that her suitcase was upstairs in his room for the present. They would transfer it to her room later on.

'Let's sit in the lounge.' He led her into a room whose mullioned windows looked out over the drenched beer-garden. They sat in winged chairs at either side of the fire, down whose wide chimney large drops of rain fell spitting among the log flames. Jack lit himself a thin cigar and after taking a few thoughtful draws on it he asked Debra to tell him all about Dean.

She saw that now he had made his decision he looked more relaxed. Hers had been quite a victory, she realised. Dean mattered more than any of them for he couldn't fight his own battles, and a glow of pleasure encircled her heart as she sat answering questions about Pauline's baby.

Yes, he was growing by leaps and bounds and he was a bright and friendly child. Yes, he was still fond of splashing about in his bath and seemed to have an inborn love of water. Yes, he had a number of his milk teeth and already he was starting to pull himself to his feet in his efforts to toddle.

Jack reflectively smiled to himself. 'He's everything I'd want in a son, do you know that, Debra?'

'Don't you think,' Debra said quietly, 'that Pauline may have lied to you? She wanted to leave the island, didn't she, and she knew you'd fight tooth and nail to keep Dean at Abbeywitch? Oh, I know you said she never told lies, but people will go to extremes when they want something badly enough and she had lived among the Salvadors long enough to find out all about their pride. She knew how

you would react if she told you that Dean
belonged to her lover.'

Jack stared across at Debra; the room was
dim from the pelting rain and from the
shadowed panelling of the walls upon which
old faded prints were hung. In the large
winged chair Debra looked the mere girl that
she was, untried in the ways of love but
reaching into her heart for an answer to the
question that haunted him.

'You believe Dean to be a Salvador, don't
you?'

'Yes,' she replied.

'You must also realise how that could have
come about?'

Debra looked away from him into the fire,
and it was then that she decided to tell Jack the
real reason why she had left her job on Lovelis
Island, and so she plunged into it, telling him
all about the party and the after events which
had led to his mother coming to her room and
finding Rodare with her.

'He thought we should get married. He was
terribly concerned about my reputation and
what people would say about me, and of
course he didn't like the tag that people might
hang on him. He said that Spanish rules of
behaviour applied to Abbeywitch and he felt
he owed it to me to tell your mother that he
intended to marry me.'

Debra paused, remembering some of the

scornful things Lenora Salvador had flung at her, implying that she be paid off for any services she might have rendered Rodare.

'Your brother was being gallant, Mr Salvador, but I couldn't let him go through with it—there being no need because we hadn't done anything wrong. I packed my suitcase as soon as it was daylight and I asked Mickey Lee to bring me to the mainland. He thought I needed to collect a pay certificate from you and that's why he brought me to *The Cap And Bells*.'

'Rodare was prepared to marry you?' Jack leant forward in order to search her eyes. 'On the other hand, you weren't prepared to marry him, eh?'

'I—I wouldn't marry anyone for those reasons. I knew he was just being polite and honourable—'

'Honourable?' Jack demanded.

'Yes. He could easily have walked out of my room and left me looking demoralised. Instead he stayed and defended me in the only way he could think of, and obviously he thinks in Spanish rather than English.'

Jack sat there mulling over her words and in a while he shook his head rather like a man emerging from deep water. 'You say it all in those last few words, don't you, Debra? When it comes to contact between men and women Rodare sees that iron grille and doesn't trespass, and I should have seen it where he's concerned!'

He surged to his feet and paced back and forth across the creaking floorboards covered by footworn carpet in which the woven roses had long since faded. The lightning had lost its strength and the thunder had faded into the distance, and within Debra there was a transient kind of peace and she leant back in the wings of her armchair and watched Jack Salvador throw off the burden he had carried ever since Pauline had drowned in the waters surrounding Lovelis Island.

She had made it possible for him to go home and already Debra had an image of him walking into the nursery and taking back into his arms the little boy he had never stopped loving.

'I want to go now!' He made for the door. 'Wait here—I'm going to look for Mickey Lee.'

The lounge door closed behind him and in the silence Debra felt the beating of her heart . . . she needed time, even if only a night, in which to find some courage for when she walked back into Rodare's house. The things she had said to Jack Salvador about his brother were the idealistic things she would like to believe . . . if only she could believe them!

There was more to why he had leapt in with his proposal of marriage, and Debra drew her lip between her teeth as a person does when pain strikes a sensitive place in the body. She didn't doubt that Rodare Salvador did think like a Spaniard in many ways, especially in relation to passion and pain.

For decades the Inquisition had flourished in Spain and it was probably bred in the bones of a Spaniard to seek absolution for the commitment of a sin.

Debra rested her cheek against the wing of her chair and gazed into the hot heart of the fire where the flames had burnt their way through the logs, and she remembered her sense of shock when Lenora Salvador had reminded Rodare that he was committed to make his home at Abbeywitch as a married man.

Quite a punishment, Debra thought, for a man who related to Spain as if it were his own skin. What a way to absolution to tie himself down to a wife and a home he didn't love.

Abruptly the lounge door opened and her nerves quivered. 'I told Mickey to wait about,' Jack said as he entered the room, 'but it seems he won a couple of pounds playing darts and happy as a sandboy he went off home without a care in the world. Anyway, he'll be back in the morning and we'll leave then.'

Debra looked at him dumbly, wondering why she didn't tell him that she didn't want to go.

'It will be all right,' he assured her, catching her look of appeal. 'I'll explain how you feel to

Rodare, and I'll make sure that my mother understands the situation.'

'You must make her understand that my only reason for being at Abbeywitch is to complete work on your book.' Debra spoke with such intensity that her voice shook. 'The very fact that I'm returning in your company will make her dislike me all the more—'

'Dislike is a strong word,' Jack broke in.

'Your mother is a strong woman,' Debra rejoined. 'She isn't afraid to say what she thinks even if she upsets people.'

'And she upset you?'

'Quite a lot.'

'Because you don't care to be thought of as the kind of girl who plays around?'

'I'm not that kind of a girl, Mr Salvador.' Debra gave him an unwavering look. 'I'm not a prig either and I accept that lots of women are as desirous of expressing their freedom as men have always been, but I just haven't the kind of nature that needs the attentions of men all the time. I enjoy my work. It fulfils me, and I don't want involvements that go from white heat to sullen coldness. I am my own person!'

'Indeed you are.' Jack came across to her, took her by the hands and drew her upwards. 'And in your own way, Debra, you are as strong as my mother. I know you think her a snobbish and suspicious woman, but she was the second wife of a man she idolised and I think she knew that she never really replaced the tempestuous Spanish dancer who gave birth to Rodare. Added to which, I could never be the eldest son and heir to the property. These things rankle, so when she found an opportunity to belittle Rodare she took it.'

'Do you mind that you're not the eldest son?' Debra asked him.

'It would be nice to own Abbeywitch,' Jack admitted, 'but I grew up knowing that my brother in Spain would inherit. The property is entailed in his favour, though my mother has always insisted that the form of marriage my father went through with Rodare's mother could be disproved in court. I doubt it!'

'What form of marriage was that?' Debra looked curious.

'She was a Spanish gipsy and they were married in the gipsy way.'

'Bonded by blood,' Debra murmured, seeing in her mind's eye the leaping flames of the camp fires, the silk scarf tying together the bleeding wrists of the couple. The night would have been filled with tempestuous music, and gipsy bride and English husband would have stolen off into the starlit hills to consummate their marriage. The romanticism of it appealed to her and she couldn't help but realise that Rodare had wild strains of passion in him which he couldn't always control.

Passionate impulses at war with a rigid sense

of morality which caused a duality in his nature: the heart of him hot with Spanish fire; the feet of him bound to the rock and stone of Lovelis Island.

'I suppose Rodare's mother couldn't bear to live anywhere else but in Andalucia?'

'That's what broke up their marriage,' Jack agreed. 'Rodare grew up in Spain and I can't imagine him ever wanting to leave—I can't help saying that I still find it strange that he asked you to marry him.'

'Oh, it was only a gesture.' She half-smiled. 'The *sombra y luz* in his nature.'

'The shade and light, eh?' Jack studied her as if he found her unexpected and rather intriguing. 'So you see Rodare as a divided man on account of his parentage? Both my parents were of the same social clique which my father rejoined after he took Soledad and her son home to Spain. Inevitably he grew lonely and married my mother, who got herself pregnant very quickly in order to cement the marriage. I admit that she can be a difficult woman at times, but can any of us help the nature we're born with? Our destinies are in our genes.'

'Not in our stars?' Debra murmured.

'The stars are too far out of reach,' he replied, 'even when we see them in another person's eyes.'

CHAPTER NINE

DEBRA felt as if she had been swimming against the tide and now it was carrying her back to the sands of Lovelis Island. As it came into sight, she felt a wild fluttering inside her . . . within the next fifteen minutes she would be stepping on to the beach where her very first meeting with Rodare had taken place.

She felt a pair of eyes upon her and turned to look at Jack Salvador. It touched her the way his fingers were twined in the string which secured the boxes of toys for Dean. They had gone out in yesterday's rain in order to buy them, and she knew that in his own way Jack was just as strung up as herself.

'He'll love the lion,' she smiled. It was a big woolly creature with wheeled paws so Dean could ride on its back, and the instant they had seen it in the shop they had agreed that it was the ideal present for him. But once in the shop Jack had bought soldiers and farm animals, a Panda police-car and a Paddington Bear, and mechanical toys such as a donkey that kicked its back legs in the air.

'I can hardly wait to see him again.' Jack's eyes were agleam with anticipation. 'I can just imagine how much he's grown—do you think he'll have forgotten me?'

'You'll soon know.' The island drew closer all the time, the snouts of its offshore rocks looming ahead of the motorboat, whose engine throbbed down into low gear as Mickey Lee guided it to the beach.

'You're back home, Mr Jack,' he said, rather hesitantly.

'Home!' Jack leapt ashore and took deep breaths of the island air which after yesterday's storm seemed laden with ozone.

'Mr Jack—' Mickey pulled a face of such agony it was as if he was having a tooth pulled without the aid of ether. 'I didn't like to tell you right away—'

'What the deuce are you on about, Mick?'

'It was the storm—' Mickey glanced at Debra, then again at Jack and it was obvious that he was trying to break some bad news. 'A bolt of lightning struck the west wing and caused a lot of damage, Mr Jack. All the terraces along that side of the house crashed into the sea and the walls and ceilings of the rooms caved in. I—I had to fetch the doctor because Nanny Rose and the babby were buried under the rubble.'

'Buried?' Jack grasped Mickey by the arm and his eyes glazed. 'Oh God, don't tell me Dean's been hurt?'

'The babby's all right,' Mickey said soothingly, 'apart from a scratch or two. They found him underneath his cot, just a bit dazed and the scratches are nothing to worry about, but poor Nanny Rose took a whack on the head that knocked her right out.'

'Ye gods!' Jack flung a look up the cliffside. 'The house seems cursed—but my boy is all right, Mick? You're not holding anything back from me?'

Mickey Lee energetically shook his head and crossed his heart. 'Doc Tregarth went over him from top to toe and called him a tough little tyke like all the Salvadors. But as I say, his nanny is laid up and your Ma is taking care of the little fellow.'

'Let's hurry.' Jack caught Debra by the wrist and flung at Mickey that he bring up the boxes and baggage. When the pair of them reached the top of the cliff steps they were both out of breath but equally anxious to make sure that Dean was safe and well, and that Nanny Rose was recovering from the ordeal.

There was Abbeywitch with the façade of gables and ivy-hung walls at least undamaged, and Debra wondered if it was an omen of bad luck that on the very day she met Jack and persuaded him to return home, the house was struck by lightning. Even as they entered there was a smell of brickdust and plaster lingering in the air, and Debra was gripped by such a feeling of restraint that she hung back and watched Jack go alone up the blackwood staircase.

Dean was with Jack's mother and she had no part to play in their reunion. She stood alone in the hall, beneath the big portrait of the founder of the family, and felt like an intruder and far less welcome this time than she had felt the very first day she entered Abbeywitch. Then she had been gripped by anticipation, eager to begin work and never dreaming that here she would meet a man who would trouble her heart and disrupt her life.

She was back on his territory and every nerve in her system was warning her of his presence. He might at any moment appear in the hall, and Debra was certain that when she saw him she would feel again the thrill and the fear that nobody else could evoke. He shattered her romantic dreams and rebuilt them not of rainbows but of storms.

A movement at the top of the stairs caught her attention, where they branched left and right and formed a gallery that overlooked the hall. Her heart lurched as she saw standing there the man who at this moment filled her thoughts to the exclusion of everything else.

She wanted to turn and flee from his house, but like someone in a dream she couldn't break the spell that held her there as he came down the stairs at his leisure, as if he had all day in which to approach her across the hall. Beneath the black brows his eyes had the intensity of ebony and though she tried to read them, their language was beyond her.

'I understand that you came back with my brother.'

'Yes.' She gave him a look which she hoped was remote. 'I hope his little boy is all right after that terrible incident yesterday? Mickey Lee told us about it—he said Nanny Rose was hurt.'

'She has signs of concussion and is being nursed by Mrs Lee.' His eyes swept Debra up and down. 'Jack's return with you in tow is another bolt out of the blue.'

'I expect it is.' Her body was rigid with tension. 'I've come back to complete work on his book—I haven't returned for any other reason.'

'What reason could that be?' he drawled.

'Y-you know—'

'Ah, could you be referring to our engagement?'

'We aren't engaged, so please stop pretending we are.' She met his eyes with a show of bravery, but could feel how her body betrayed her resolution as he suddenly stepped close to her and placed his hands on her shoulders.

'You're shaking,' he said.

'I—it was a shock, hearing that the nursery wing had been struck by lightning—'

'Your room suffered as well. The bolt struck around tea-time and there is every possibility

that you might have been upstairs at the time.'
With eyes and hands he held her immobile.
'Fate plays strange tricks, does it not?'

She nodded, and said with urgency: 'I won't
be held to that impossible proposal, *señor*. I
have no intention of—of marrying a man with
whom I share no love.' The word alone, and
saying it to him, made her lips feel as if they
were burning.

'No love?' He gave her a look of mock
despair.

'None,' she asserted, hating that he should
mock her. 'I consider that love should mean
fidelity, friendship and fun, and there isn't
likely to be much of those in a marriage of
obligation.'

'What,' he asked, 'if I refuse to retract? What
if it suits me to make what you call a marriage
of obligation?'

'Suit yourself of all you want, *señor*, but don't
drag me in.' Having taken her stand, Debra
was determined to show him that she meant
every word, and in the strangest way she did
despite his physical effect upon her. Even if her
knees were quivering, her chin was in the air
and there was a fighting light in her eyes.

'You aren't concerned to be thought of as the
kind of girl whom a man feels free to visit in the
night?' He watched her intently, as if waiting
to see in her eyes some giveaway sign of what
she was really thinking.

'I'm true to myself,' she said, 'no matter what others might believe of me.'

'And yet that night there was in your eyes a "please protect me" look, are you aware of that?' he asked.

'Whatever my look, you misconstrued it, *señor*.' Debra felt as if the pair of them were fencing, that each time a thrust of his drove her backwards she had to find some way to deflect his attack. 'I'm fully able to take care of myself, and I feel sure that now your stepmother has the little boy in her care she'll lose interest in me. You very well know that your proposal of marriage didn't fool her in the slightest—and quite frankly I don't think you made it out of any real concern for my reputation.'

'Is that so?' His eyes narrowed to a gemlike hardness. 'You seem to have returned to Abbeywitch with a determination to make an enemy of me—may I remind you, *señorita*, that I am the master here and if I so wished I could tell you to remove your presence.'

'Then do it,' she challenged him. 'I only returned for your brother's sake, but I'm quite prepared to leave again—'

'Of course you aren't leaving,' he interrupted. 'I'm quite impressed by your cunning in getting out of Mickey Lee my brother's whereabouts. Mickey is a loyal creature, especially to Jack because they grew up together while I came only on summer visits to the island. Mickey is a true Celt and he mistrusts anyone whom he regards as foreign. I am foreign to him, but he obviously sees in you a kindred spirit.'

Suddenly Rodare's hands left her shoulders and had hold of her face, his thumbs stroking the fine texture of her skin. 'With those sea-green eyes you could be a Celt yourself. Are you one?'

'Partially,' she admitted, 'on my mother's side.'

'Hence the air of mystery,' he murmured. 'So you don't wish to become my wife?'

'No more than you wish to become my husband,' she rejoined. 'Love and marriage aren't fuel for farce.'

'A farce, eh?' And as he spoke he thrust his fingers up into her hair and gripped her skull between the palms of his hands. 'Be careful, Miss Hartway, now you are back in my house. Don't think you will become a shadow again who flits in and out of that den where you work on Jack's book. You have inside this head covered in horse-chestnut hair a mind whose workings intrigue me and so when I ask you to walk with me, you will walk, and when I ask you to ride with me, you will ride.'

He tilted her face as if it were a kind of offering and he brought his lips dangerously close to her mouth. 'Do you hear me, Miss Hartway? If you wish to be employed in my house you will do as I demand.'

'And if I don't do as you demand?' she fought back.

'Then I shall prove to you that I'm not a man to be provoked.' His breath stirred warm against her mouth and she was reminded too vividly of their encounter in the conservatory, and deep inside her secret self she wanted just once more the hard possessiveness of his arms holding her to the power of his body as he took his fill of kissing.

Oh God, her heart had been unwarned that infatuation for a man could invade so deeply, so at the centre of her innermost self. She didn't want such yearning for this man whom she had just refused to marry and in a fury with her own feelings she found strength to wrench herself away from him.

'You—you're like a big cat who needs a mouse to play with,' she panted. 'I think I'd better leave—I don't think I could stand it here, never knowing when you were going to pounce on me!'

'Pounce?' he breathed. 'I don't like the word, Miss Hartway.'

'Why, does it hit too close to the truth, *señor*?'

His eyes flickered with a warning fire and Debra cried out as he caught hold of her and forced her across the hall into the very same alcove where Stuart Coltan had kissed her the evening of the party. She was pushed against the wall, held there with one hand while he wrenched open her jacket so he could bring himself hard against her writhing body that was rejecting him and wanting him in equal measure.

Twist and turn her head as she might, he captured her mouth and kissed her with a savagery that took no heed of time or place. He thrust a hand inside her blouse and filled it with her straining breast, and with hip and thigh he trapped her slender body to his body, stroking fire into her blood until she felt she was going crazy. Then at the very pitch of sensuous tension, he released her, pulling away and leaving her with lips apart and eyes dazed.

They faced each other in a panting awareness of what each had felt in the heat of mouth upon lips . . . of unsparing fingers upon supple flesh.

'You brute,' she whispered, and with head lowered she rebuttoned her jacket and felt she would fall to her knees if she tried to run from the very sight of him.

'You enjoyed it!' His eyes blazed darkly into hers, then he spun on his heel and strode off out of the house, leaving her mortified and unable to deny the flame-like thrills he had induced when he touched her. She felt sensitised to the very centre of her being and she stared blindly at the door out of which he had walked with his head held so high, and she despised herself as much as she despised him for the emotions he had aroused.

Desires which had been lurking in both of them ever since their first encounter on the beach . . . urgent, dark desires.

Debra wildly told herself that she couldn't stay in this house, but even as she emerged a little tidier from the alcove, she saw Jack Salvador coming downstairs with young Dean clasped in his arms. 'Come and say hello to my son,' he called out to her.

What else could she do but force a smile to her lips and silently implore her knees to hold firm as she walked towards Jack and the boy.

'Dibby!' He knew her and started jigging up and down in Jack's arms and as if seeking some of Jack's protection of the child Debra drew close to both of them and kissed Dean with an aching kind of tenderness. She kissed the bruise on his chin and bent her head and kissed the scratches on his plump legs.

'Poor little darling,' she crooned. 'You must have been so scared by the storm, but now your Papa's here and you're safe and loved.'

'I can see you're fond of children,' Jack smiled.

'Dean is someone special,' she quickly replied. 'I'm really a career-girl at heart.'

'I wonder.' Jack looked quizzical. 'You have a caring heart, Debra, and it will govern you.'

'No,' she argued. 'I intend to guard it for all

I'm worth—I don't want my heart leading me astray.'

'We all say that when we're young, Debra. We're all so certain that we make our own destiny and do our own choosing, but there's some devil inside us that upsets the apple-cart and hands us the fruit that looks so sweet and sometimes turns out to be so bitter.'

'You don't need to be bitter any more.' Debra held Dean's little hand and tickled his palm. 'Look who came out of the apple seeds.'

'Yes, just look.' Jack eyed the boy with a kind of wonderment, and then with a flash of pain. 'I could so easily have lost him again and I daren't think what that would have done to me—driven me mad I believe. The nursery and your previous room are a shambles so you'll be located in the east turret this time . . . like Rapunzel of the flowing hair which she braided into a rope so her lover could climb up to her.'

'I have no lover.' Debra spoke with quiet control.

'That business with Rodare has to be sorted out.'

'I—I've seen him,' she replied, keeping her gaze on Dean in case some revelation of her churned up feelings showed in her eyes. 'I believe I've made him understand that his proposal of marriage was unnecessary—with his flair for drama he should have been an actor or a writer.'

Jack gave a laugh. 'It's in the blood, and rather in the atmosphere of this old house on an island. Islands are rather cut off from civilisation and surrounded as they are by the sea they tend to intensify the emotions of those who live on them. The sea, after all, is the most elemental of all the elements so can it be wondered at that we Salvadors tend to have emotions that match those high waves and those low troughs.'

'And those dangerous undercurrents,' she murmured.

'Ah yes, those undercurrents.' He quizzed her thoughtfully. 'So you've confronted Rodare and made him understand that you are here at my bidding?'

She nodded and watched Dean nod off slumberously against Jack's shoulder . . . oh yes, whatever the outcome, it had been worth her while to seek out Jack Salvador and put at rest his doubts and fears regarding Dean. If deep within herself she harboured her own fears, they didn't matter so long as Jack believed he had sired Pauline's baby.

There was sudden activity in the porchway and Rodare strode back into the house followed by Mickey Lee and both of them were laden with suitcases and boxes.

'Mickey tells me this is yours.' Rodare exhibited Debra's suitcase, very much a poor relation compared with Jack's pigskin baggage. 'He said he collected it from Jack's room at *The Cap And Bells*.'

'Yes, it's mine.' She flushed vividly despite the innocuous reason why it had been in Jack's room. He had suggested that she leave it with his baggage while they ate breakfast down in the dining-room. Mickey had arrived while they had been eating eggs and bacon, ambling in from the newsagents where Jack had left a message for him, a great grin on his face when Jack told him to fetch the baggage because they were going home with him to Abbeywitch.

And here in the hall of Abbeywitch Debra was made uneasy by the way Rodare was regarding her . . . what on earth did he imagine, that she had used actions rather than words in order to persuade his brother to return home?

'Has it been decided where you will sleep?' he demanded.

'I'm not sure that I—'

Jack overrode her tentative words. 'I thought Debra would be comfortable in the east turret, in the Sky Room.'

'There?' Rodare frowned at Jack.

'Yes, I know it used to be Pauline's hide-away, but I think Debra will appreciate the quietness and the view.'

'If you say so.' Rodare glanced at Debra as if curious about her reaction to his brother's words. She had reacted when Jack mentioned

Pauline but she strove to hide it, especially from Rodare.

'If you will come with me,' his voice was as smooth as silk, 'I'll lead you to the Sky Room.'

But hesitation held her in its grip and Jack said encouragingly: 'You'll be comfortable there and I'll see you in the den later on. I want to see how far the manuscript has progressed.'

It was now or never Debra told herself. She either took her suitcase from Rodare and walked out of Abbeywitch or she followed him to Pauline's hideaway, as Jack had called the room.

'Are you afraid the room is haunted?' Rodare taunted.

'Not in the slightest—a ghost is the least of my worries.'

'You are more scared of the living, eh?'

'Without a shadow of a doubt, *señor*.'

'The Salvadors in particular?'

'Yes.'

'Yet you returned.'

'I—I have work to finish.'

'Then you had better not waste any more time dithering.' He marched to the stairs and Debra reluctantly followed, keeping one tread lower than he as he mounted to the topmost gallery and turned left, leading her along a passage to a door that gave access to the steps of her new domain.

They spiralled upwards with little windows

deep in the stonework and Debra had an image in her mind of Pauline coming here to hide from her mother-in-law.

Debra had always been curious about the turrets but had been told by Nanny Rose that they were never used. She expected signs of neglect but when Rodare unlocked the door and stood aside for her to enter, a shock of delight ran all through her.

She couldn't contain a little gasp of surprise and pleasure and felt Rodare pierce her with a look as he carried her suitcase across the room and placed it on a cane-backed seat at the foot of the bed.

'You don't have to sleep here if you don't want to,' he said.

'I want to very much.' She walked to one of the windows and gazed down at the flickering sea, excited by the thought of how self-contained she would be in the turret, almost in seclusion from the family. She also liked knowing that the door could be securely locked.

As these thoughts went through her head she felt Rodare watching her . . . they were very alone up here and she was still feeling the after-effects of the way he had kissed her. She still felt threatened by him, animal still, his shirt open against the dark-gold skin that was never cold to the touch.

Such thoughts had to be overcome and she proceeded to examine the room, going from one piece of furniture to another and opening drawers and cupboards.

Over the floor lay a round carpet with a pagoda design and the furniture was in pale bamboo so the effect was slightly exotic. The bedcover and curtains had a bamboo design on them and were silky to the touch, and Debra noticed vanity items still in place on the vanity-table.

Debra's heart gave a sudden throb . . . had Rodare ever been alone here with Pauline? The thought was a tormenting one that drove her to the door which she held open in readiness for him to go.

'Do you mind?' she asked. 'I'd like to unpack my things.'

Instead of going, he wandered to the vanity-table where he withdrew the stopper of a swan-necked scent bottle and sniffed at the scent applicator. 'Tell me something—are you planning to replace Pauline?' he asked.

That he should ask such a thing made Debra feel furious. 'I suppose that's going to be your strategy, to be as hateful as you can? Such a thing never entered my head!'

'Come,' he swung round to face her, 'Jack is your ideal, is he not? Isn't that why you came to work for him, because you are fascinated by his novels, and isn't it true to say that a writer is reflected by his writing? Surely the very romance of it appeals to you, a widower with a baby son on his hands, who is so grateful to you for making him see the error of his absence.'

Temper flared into a flame that Debra couldn't control. 'I'm beginning to hate you—'

'Only beginning, Debra?' He began to approach her. 'Haven't I been a thorn in your flesh since the day we met?'

'Yes,' she recklessly agreed. 'This job started to go wrong for me when you came back to Abbeywitch. You resent the island because it isn't your precious Andalucia . . . you regard it as a kind of burden, and so you start to look for a distraction and this time you settled on me to provide you with amusement. No one very special, only the girl working on your brother's book, a bit of a mouse who might take a nibble at a few crumbs of attention.'

Debra regarded him, her eyes pure green. 'I don't want your attentions, Señor Salvador. My head isn't turned by your machismo!'

'Your head might not be turned, m'dear,' he mocked, 'but if I chose to kiss you right now, if I chose to touch you, the rest of you would melt to jelly in my hands. *Gran Dios*, do you imagine I don't know when I arouse a woman?'

As his gaze went over her, a hot flame of memory licked her skin. She could hardly bear to remember the dark desires he had set aflame between them so that every particle of her body had wanted to be consumed by his touch.

'I daresay you've had lots of women,' she

said icily. 'Women are just toys to you—the playthings you discovered a long time ago. I don't think you ever had any conscience about any of them until—' There she broke off, as if a hand clamped itself around her throat. To mention Pauline would be going too far, and that poor dead girl deserved to rest in peace.

'Do go on.' With voice and eyes he menaced her. 'When did I suddenly develop a conscience—when I met you?'

Debra caught her breath sharply, like someone who had come close to being burnt. 'I—I don't want to discuss it any more. I came back to continue with my work a-and if you have any feeling for your brother you'll allow me to work in peace with him.'

'I wouldn't dream of intruding upon such an idyllic partnership.' He drew level with her and she had to fight her inclination to shrink away from him in case they made contact. Gleams of mockery danced in his eyes as he stood over her.

'Do you imagine that you and I can live beneath the same roof and behave like polite strangers?' he asked. 'It just isn't possible.'

'It has to be,' she breathed.

He shook his head at her. 'Between us, *señorita*, there is an affinity, deny it though you will. It may be one or the other of the two most powerful emotions in the world and until we have resolved the question we can't help but be aware of each other. But for now, you will be glad to learn that I have business on the mainland which will keep me absent from Abbeywitch for a day or two. Do keep busy, won't you?'

After he had gone she leant against the solid support of the door and slowly her heart quietened down. If only he were returning to Andalucia, then she would be free of his dark bedevilment!

By the time she went downstairs he had departed for the mainland and the house was quiet. Debra guessed that Zandra and her group would reappear later in the day, but right now she could relax a little and enjoy discussing Jack's book. He was in the den when she entered, at his ease on the window ledge. He smiled through the smoke of his cigarette as if he liked the light linen dress into which she had changed.

'It feels good to be home,' he said warmly.

'You seem to be very much a part of Abbeywitch.' Debra felt a warm sense of ease in this man's presence, so unrelated to the emotional turmoil she felt when Rodare came anywhere near her. 'You fit into its ambience.'

'More so than Rodare, I think you imply?' He quirked an eyebrow at her. 'As the pair of you are so obviously cat and dog I can take it as read that you are free of any entanglement?'

'Oh yes,' she said emphatically.

He smiled and came to the desk where he picked up the sheaf of typed manuscript. 'I've been going through this and you've done a good job, but I've decided that I want to change certain parts of the first chapter—do you mind?'

'It isn't for me to mind, Mr Salvador.' She accepted what he said, but to her way of thinking the first chapter seemed perfect.

'I'd like you to call me Jack.'

Her eyes widened upon his face but she didn't argue with him. If it flickered through her mind that Rodare would be ironically amused by the familiarity she strove to stay composed. His hint that Jack was developing an interest in her had to be ignored.

'Do you want to dictate?' she asked him, preparing to pick up pen and notebook.

'Tomorrow will do,' he murmured, his eyes upon her face. 'You have done me a great service, Debra, and you are so unassuming that you don't seem to realise your own capacity for feeling the aches and despairs of other people. Who made you so wise, you who look so young?'

'It must have been my parents,' she smiled, warmed by his approval yet able to retain her composure.

'Are they both still living?'

She told him a little of her situation. 'My mother deserves every bit of happiness she's now enjoying. She worked so hard after my father died and she held a lot of sadness in her heart until Ben Langham came along and fell in love with her.'

'Love is important to you, isn't it, Debra?'

This time she was disconcerted by Jack Salvador, and this time it showed, and he stepped a little nearer to her so she became aware of his lean height and the way his weeks of solitude had worn hollows into his face and silvered the hair above his brow.

'Love in the truest context of the word,' he added. 'Love that doesn't come to all who bend the knee and have faith that it won't be a moth the flame will destroy.'

'Do you read Eric Mackay?' she asked, slender in her lemon-coloured dress, the afternoon sunlight in the gloss of her hair.

'Romantic as Byron,' Jack murmured. 'A great shame his more celebrated sister outshone him—have you ever read the Corelli melodrama?'

Debra shook her head. 'I prefer your books.'

'You flatter me, young woman.'

'Oh, you know they're good.'

He laughed. 'I regret the loss of Miss Tucker, but you are going to suit me fine. Shall I suit you, do you think?'

'I think so,' she replied sedately.

He raised his cigarette to his lips and drew on it, his eyes holding her gaze through the screen of smoke. 'No more tremors of apprehension regarding my mother?'

'I can't be sure—' Debra heard birds twittering in the courtyard beyond the window and a kind of peacefulness brooded over the day. The trees and flowers had recovered their glory and weren't bowed down as they had been by yesterday's storm, but the storm had left its reminder in the heap of rubble that lay at the foot of the west-side cliffs; chunks of stone split by the lightning and hurled down upon the beach, and Debra remembered what Jack had said about the house being cursed.

Had the long-ago abduction on the beach left a kind of curse upon Abbeywitch?

She gave a slight shiver which Jack misinterpreted.

'Mama will have me to deal with if she starts on you again.'

'She must have been delighted that you've come home?'

He nodded. 'We call it home, this house and island that belongs to my half-brother. He could throw us all out if he felt so inclined, and I believe he almost did when—'

Jack broke off, but Debra knew instinctively what he had left unsaid. He had been about to say: 'When Pauline was drowned!'

'If you don't want to do any work right now I'll look in on Nanny Rose,' she said breathlessly. 'I ran into Mrs Lee as I was on my way down to the den and she said Nanny Rose was sleeping. She might now be awake.'

'I'll come with you,' he said, stubbing out his cigarette. 'She seems to have taken quite a battering and I'm infernally thankful that Dean was in his cot. As it overturned the covers sheltered him, but his nanny was in the rocker, it seems, sewing by the window.'

When they entered the bedroom where Nanny Rose was recovering they found her propped up by pillows, enjoying a cup of tea. Her poor head was bandaged and there was a large dressing on the side of her neck, but the instant she saw Jack Salvador she summoned a smile.

'So it's true,' she said, 'you're back home, Mr Jack.'

'Yes, I've come home, Nanny.' He strode to her bedside and bending down to her gently kissed her cheek.

'And not before your time,' she chided him. 'The little lad needs to have his father with him, especially the way things are. I hope you intend to stay?'

'I fully intend to stay, Nanny Rose.' Jack beckoned Debra to the bedside. 'I think you know this young lady, eh?'

For moments that stretched almost to a minute Nanny Rose and Debra looked at each other and both of them were remembering the things they had said to each other the morning

Debra had fled the island.

'So you didn't get to London?'

'It seems not.' Debra reached for Nanny Rose's hand. 'I expect Abbeywitch has cast its spell over me.'

'Humph!' Nanny Rose looked as if she was thinking that it was more than a house which had cast its spell over Debra.

'Are you in pain, Nanny?' Jack looked concerned.

'My cuts and bumps will mend,' she said. 'Hurts to the body do mend if they aren't mortal, not like some of the hurts we inflict on our feelings.'

Though her eyes were still shadowed by pain and shock the old light of wisdom was creeping back, there in the glance which went back and forth from Jack to Debra.

'You're looking more yourself, Mr Jack,' she finally said.

'I'm feeling more myself, Nanny.'

'Starting to put the sadness behind you, is that it?'

He inclined his head. 'I had no right to run out on my responsibilities to Dean, and it's something I shall never do again. You've looked after him well, Nanny. He's a splendid boy and I'm proud of him.'

'You've every right to be proud,' she agreed. 'He's bright as a lark from morning till eve, and by the time I'm out of this bed his grandmother will be glad to hand him back to me.'

A glimmer of amusement lit Jack's eyes. 'You think he'll wear her out, eh?'

'He's growing fast, Mr Jack, and he's in to everything.'

'Well, I'm here to share him with Mama, and Debra's here to do my other work, so we'll manage. All you've to worry about, Nanny, is getting back on your feet. The storm has passed us by and now we're into calmer seas.'

'It never does to anticipate, Mr Jack,' she warned.

Her words brought a frown to his brow. 'I don't see why we shouldn't look forward to some halcyon days—haven't we earned them?'

At that point Debra decided to intervene. Nanny Rose looked very frail and she wasn't a young woman who would bounce back to health without a struggle.

'You must get your rest.' She raised Nanny Rose while she removed one of her pillows so she could recline more comfortably. 'There, how does that feel?'

'You're a kind, good girl.' Nanny Rose gave a sigh of satisfaction. 'The pain-killers make me feel drowsy—'

'Sleep and don't worry any more,' Debra murmured. 'Dean is safe and sound as a chapel bell.'

A smile flitted across his nanny's face. 'He

sang in the choir did David *bach*; clear as a bell he sang.' With another sigh she turned her face into the pillow and fell quietly asleep.

'Who was David?' Jack gave Debra an enquiring look.

'Nanny used to know him when she was only a girl. He worked as a coal miner and died in an explosion with the pit ponies.'

'I see.' Jack gazed down at her in a concerned way; it somehow wasn't noticeable when she was about her duties that she was such a slight woman. 'I hope she's going to be all right?'

'She has a tenacious will,' Debra smiled, and they walked quietly from the room and left Nanny Rose to dream of the gallant young man who wouldn't leave the ponies to perish alone.

'Dammit,' Jack growled, 'it always seems to be the nice people who bear the burdens and carry the crosses! The self-loving never seem to suffer much!'

'The way of the world,' Debra reminded him. 'The path to damnation has always been the smooth one, but would you want to take it?'

'I suppose not.' He gave a brief laugh and caught Debra by the hand. 'Come and take a stroll with me in the garden, the rhododendrons grow there like young trees and they are one of the reasons why I love Abbeywitch. Later on, you and I will have tea with my son.'

'Your mother will be there,' Debra reminded him. 'It's kind of you, but let me settle in—don't foist me on her.'

Jack's fingers tightened on hers, then relaxed. 'If that's what you want, Debra, but come and see the rhododendrons with me.'

They were huge, so bursting with scarlet and mauve that they seemed unreal, almost theatrical . . . in keeping, Debra thought, with the atmosphere of Abbeywitch. As she strolled the winding paths with Jack it was like being in the woods of an enchanted castle, and she wondered at the trick of fate that made this place the inheritance of the wrong man.

Jack had his roots here, but Rodare's were in the stonier soil of faraway Spain. He was the master of the property by birthright, but Jack seemed to love every aspect of the place and it struck her rather painfully when he paused to cup one of the huge flower heads in his hands.

'They're like bewitched court ladies,' he said, 'but soon their day of glory will be over and it will be Midsummer.'

He let go the flower and swung to face Debra on the sun-dappled path. 'Thank heaven you came and found me—I was going to damnation before you came and that's the truth! Dear God, but it's good to be back!'

For him it was good, she thought, but for herself it was a path strewn with obstacles and one of them stood six-foot tall.

CHAPTER TEN

IT wasn't long before workmen from the mainland had attended to the storm damage. They dumped the rubble and stone into the sea and when they departed the only outward sign that lightning had struck the house was the blank wall where the terraces had been.

It was good to hear again the sounds of sea and birds, but working as she did in the den, Debra hadn't been too aware of the noise in the west wing as the rooms were repaired . . . she was far more aware of the arrival by launch of a pair of house guests whose presence didn't really surprise her.

The workings of Lenora Salvador's mind were transparent; her son Jack was home and if there was any chance that he was going to miss having a wife then his mother duly presented Sharon Chandler to him by inviting her and her mother to the island. Complete with their personal maids and a curly-coated French poodle, they settled in.

Debra had re-established her working routine, but she couldn't help but miss her morning visits to the nursery and the company of Nanny Rose at mealtimes.

Dean's nanny was still in the throes of her recovery, and Lenora was still firmly in charge of her grandson, so Debra saw Dean only when Jack brought him to the den. He was growing by leaps and tumbles, but he and Jack were now firmly bonded and this for Debra was a source of real pleasure. Less so was her constant awareness that Rodare was still in residence and hadn't yet felt the sudden urge to pack his bags and go flying back to Spain.

When alone at night she would forcibly brush her hair in an attempt to brush him out of her mind. But with her windows open, she often caught the sound of laughter and sometimes the sound of music, and knew that down in the drawing-room the Salvadors were entertaining Sharon and her mother.

Debra wondered as she sat there by the window, the night air blowing cool against her face, what it felt like to be the kind of girl whose wealthy parents made it possible for her to pursue a life of ease and pleasure.

A girl who had time on her hands to learn the art of being lovely and charming, her sole aim in life being that of a social butterfly whose mind didn't need to dwell on the serious business of earning a living.

An image of her with the Salvador brothers would steal into Debra's mind, charmingly dressed, always ready with the amusing quip and practised in the art of making men feel as if they could rule the world.

The drifting sound of dance music couldn't help but awaken in Debra the memory of the way she had danced with Rodare, following his steps so easily as if a kind of magic led her through the movements of the dance. Remembering the pliancy and strength of his body, she covered the burning warmth of her cheeks with her hands . . . it was useless to deny the power of his physical ascendancy over her. It was a spell that wouldn't be broken until she saw him no more.

In a kind of trepidation she waited for him to leave Abbeywitch, and at the start of each day she wondered if in the midst of her work he would open the door of the den and stand there tall and dark, looking in upon her, making good his warning that he wasn't going to allow her to be just a shadow in his house, flitting between turret room and den.

Work was her distraction and soon she became absorbed in her editorial task, only breaking off when the maid arrived with her morning or afternoon refreshment on a tray. Then, inevitably, her mind would fly back to that first time Rodare had ordered wine and biscuits to be brought to her.

Always in the morning it was wine and biscuits. In the afternoon it was a pot of tea and a slice of fruit cake, and because Debra wasn't

partial to cake she would rather guiltily feed it
to the birds from the window. The tea she
enjoyed with relish, seated on the wide ledge
of the window, alone and yet not really lonely.
It wasn't in her nature to be gregarious and
now the Chandlers were guests in the house,
she was glad to be isolated in the den.

And relieved that Stuart Coltan stayed away
from her. Whenever she did see him he would
give her a rather brazen stare but pass her by
without comment.

She was aware, however, from remarks
made by Jack, that Coltan had charmed Lenora
into accepting him. According to Jack his
mother found Stuart attractive, amusing and
attentive. The indications were that she might
find him an acceptable son-in-law, and Jack's
tone of irony made Debra realise what was
going through his mind. Had his mother been
more approving of the show business girl he
had chosen to marry then his marriage might
not have suffered such trauma and Pauline
might still be alive.

Debra thought he had been unwise to try
and love wife and mother under the same roof,
but at the same time she understood how
much he relied on the atmosphere of the island
to inspire his work. His fiction teemed with
drama and suspense, and Debra sensed
strongly that he drew inspiration and ideas
from the atmosphere of Abbeywitch; his roots

as a writer would be torn from their bedrock if he didn't breathe the air of Lovelis Island, if he didn't listen to the voices of his imagination in the thunder of the waves, if he didn't see the sun go down in glorious flame at the end of the day.

As she grew to know him, Debra realised that Jack Salvador was more akin to the island than Rodare would ever be. His nature was that of a Celt while in Rodare lay impulses that were purely of Andalucia where for generations the fierce and possessive Moors had ruled, dark-skinned and autocratic and, as Rodare had said himself, jealous guardians of their women.

Disturbing thoughts to be having while she drank her tea and listened to the birds squabbling over the cake crumbs, but Debra couldn't shake free of them. The courtyard beyond the window was somehow Moorish in its arrangement of archways, with a fountain jetting into the sunlight and making a rainbow across the wide stone basins. Had the stonework of the court been white instead of grey then she could almost have fancied herself in Spain.

A train of thought that was abruptly halted as the door of the den opened to admit the one man in the world with whom she didn't want to be alone.

Lithe and tall, strikingly dark in beige linen

trousers and a black silk shirt. The height and
stance of him suggested castle doorways . . .
great Moorish castles studded with iron. He
smiled and she saw the menace in it; he seemed
to sense that he wasn't welcome.

'Good, I catch you in the midst of your
tea-break. I wouldn't want to interrupt your
work because I know how much it means to
you.'

Debra chose to ignore the tinge of sarcasm in
his words. 'I'm about to start again,' she said,
'so if you were looking for Jack—'

'Jack?' he broke in. 'That was never the way
Miss Tucker referred to him; that good lady
was always very formal.'

Debra flushed slightly and her mood of re-
laxation was quite dispelled. 'I use your
brother's first name at his request,' she said
defensively. 'Were you looking for him, *señor*?'

'No, I came on purpose to see you.'

'Oh—what about?' Her pulses hammered as
he crossed the room in a leisurely fashion and
when he reached her, where she still sat in the
windowseat, he handed her a small box
stamped with the name of a Penarth jeweller.

'It's all right,' he mocked, 'I'm not giving you
an engagement ring.'

She opened the box and felt a quick stab of
joy at seeing her pearl pendant and chain
which Rodare had promised to have repaired.
She examined the little pear and the fitment

and found they were as good as new and glossy from a careful polishing.

'I am grateful to you.' She met his eyes confusedly. 'You must tell me how much I owe you.'

Instantly his eyes had a deadly sheen. 'Very well, if you wish to pay me, *señorita*, then pay me with a kiss.'

'Please—' She bit her lip. 'Be serious—'

'Isn't a kiss a serious business?'

'I think so, *señor*, but I'm not so sure that you do. Let me pay for the repair.'

'I've told you the price.' His entire air was inexorable as he stood over her and she knew he would stand there the rest of the day if she didn't do as he asked. She raised her face and offered her lips, and then gave a startled cry as he pulled her upright and made her yield to him.

Why pretend that she hadn't longed for the heat of his skin against hers . . . why deny that it wasn't a pleasure to feel his lips devouring hers . . . why fight when she longed to surrender?

Yet fight him she did, wrenching aside her head so his lips slid against her neck. 'What a little vixen you are.' Yet he was almost smiling as he looked down into her eyes. 'What are you going to be like, I wonder, when a man really has you at his mercy?'

'I'll see that I don't get caught,' she retorted.

'Aren't you caught right now?' he mocked. 'You are still in my arms and I am quite strong. I think I have you cornered, vixen.'

'To my way of thinking, *señor*, you seem to be breaking a rule of your house.' It took every ounce of nerve for Debra to defy his eyes. 'Didn't you say that while I'm employed here I'm safe under your roof?'

'So you don't consider yourself safe in my arms?'

'I've never felt so unsafe.'

'Do you mean to flatter or offend me?'

'Take your pick, *señor*.'

'By the devil, you're a cool young woman.' He released her, holding wide his arms so she could make her retreat, which she safely did to the other side of the desk.

'I—I'm pleased to have back my pearl and chain,' she said. 'I value them very much—thank you.'

'They become you.' He took out his cheroot case and casually lit one. 'Wear the pendant tomorrow evening—Midsummer Eve is quite an event in this part of the country and after we've dined a fire is being lit on the headland in order to drive evil spirits away from the house. The event should appeal to you. I feel sure you believe in things supernatural.'

She wanted to laugh in a cool way and deny his assertion, but the thought of a huge bonfire flaming on the headland and throwing big sparks into the sky made her eyes glisten with fascination. She knew it to be a pagan custom and when the fire died down people leapt the embers in order to show the Devil a quick pair of heels.

'I should like to see the bonfire,' she admitted.

'And see it you shall.' He drew on his cheroot. 'The signal fire for all the other fires is lit on Carn Brea and the chain extends from Land's End to the Tamar. In some regions the bonfire is crowned with a broomstick for the belief is that the flames drive the witches and devils into hiding.'

A smile brushed Debra's mouth. 'Will it be wise, *señor*, for you to attend the ceremony?'

'So I'm a devil in your eyes, eh?' He spoke sardonically as if never for a moment had he thought himself a saint. 'Will it please you if I evaporate in a cloud of smoke on Midsummer Eve? Will you then feel free of me?'

She lowered her gaze to the pearl and chain glistening in her fingers. 'I'm not bound to you, am I? I thought we had settled the matter, that we are free of each other and there never was any foundation for your proposal. It was a piece of theatre, wasn't it? I think all the Salvadors are fond of drama, that's why Zandra sent her mother to my bedroom in order to create a scene.'

Debra raised her gaze once more to his face,

gone a little brooding through the smoke of his cheroot. 'I survived that scene, but I wouldn't want to face another like it, so please—'

'Please?' he interjected.

'Y-you know what I'm trying to say, *señor*.'

'You don't want me near you, is that it?'

She nodded, for if she actually spoke the words they might choke her with their dishonesty. To look at Rodare was to see the dark fires smouldering in him, beckoning the palpitating moth to scorch body and soul in his flame. There might be ecstasy in his arms, but of the kind that burnt fiercely and then left ashes . . . ashes scattered to the wind from the high cliffs.

'Who do you want near you?'

She gave him a startled look. 'I don't want—'

'Don't lie to me or yourself.' He swept his eyes around the den as if visualising her alone in here with Jack, the two of them deep in discussion and very much a part of the world of books. 'My brother and Pauline were a misalliance from the start, two people from different worlds who didn't know what to talk about when the kissing stopped. But with you it's different, is it not? He's never lost for words when he's with you—you've crept under his skin, haven't you?'

'I—I don't know what you mean—'

'Don't pretend to be dumb.' As he gestured, ash spilled down on some of the typed sheets of Jack's book, and when she reached forward to shake off the ash Rodare gripped her by the wrist. 'I could shake you,' he breathed.

'Let go of me—' She tried with her free hand to unlock his fingers, but he had suddenly thrown away the key of his temper and he remorselessly held her where she was.

'Do you think I can't read you?' he jeered. 'You're transparent through and through. You see Jack as a tragic hero who needs a shoulder to rest on. He doesn't realise how tender, does he? Silky smooth to the touch, sloping beneath the hand and leading to even more pleasant places—ah, how I can touch you on a nerve, *pequeña*. Can my brother do to you what I do—I think not!'

'Your brother respects me,' she shot back at him. 'When I'm alone in this room with him I—I don't need to be all on edge, wondering if he's going to grab hold of me. Why don't you play your game of cat and mouse with Miss Chandler?'

'With her a game such as this wouldn't be quite so entertaining,' he said shamelessly. 'You react, Miss Hartway. Just a word or a look from me and you are ready to dash into your mousehole—I just can't resist pursuing you.'

'Oh, let me go!' She struggled valiantly and knew that when she was close to him she had two enemies, and one was herself. A traitorous part of her wanted his closeness . . . wanted the sensual awareness of his dark-gold skin over pliant flesh and firm bone . . . wanted the warmth and weakness that enveloped her when he touched her.

'What if I know what you are thinking,' he said softly. 'What if I can read those large imploring eyes of yours?'

'Y-you obviously think you can read every woman,' she retaliated, her heartbeat unnervingly quickened by his insinuation.

'I don't wish to read the eyes of every woman, but yours are a book that titillates me.'

'Titillate?' she took him up. 'What do you mean?'

'You know well enough.' His eyes ran over her, knowing her beneath the neat dress in a delicate shade of green. 'To all outward appearance you are the demure and dutiful editor of my brother's book, but there are depths to you, little madam, which I'm aware of, and it's my awareness which you resent and which you fight. You prefer to hide your secret self.'

'Don't you as well?' She flung a defiant look at him. 'I don't think you'd want anyone delving into your personality to see what you've got hidden away. You think because you walk tall and look over their heads you have people at a disadvantage, but I may not be fooled by your haughtiness.'

'The thought makes me tremble,' he

mocked, but his eyes glittered as they swept her face. 'I guard my secrets well, *señorita*, and you are a little too young and guileless to be good at divining the male of the species, least of all a Spaniard. How many Spaniards have you known?'

'Only you,' she admitted.

'In fact,' he drawled, 'how many men have you known?'

'Very few, *señor*.'

'And I believe you, *señorita*.'

'You didn't when we first met.'

'You believe I took you for a seductress?' Tiny specks of flame seemed to burn and dance in his dark eyes.

'I—I don't think you were too sure of me.' His amusement made her flush; he made her feel a naïve plaything in his hands and she longed to show him that she wasn't a puppet he could pull in and out of his arms on emotional strings. 'I think we know each other a little better, don't you, *señor*? First impressions are never reliable, are they?'

'So you don't intend to rely on your first impression of me?' His eyes quizzed her face, alert and just a little dangerous. 'You thought I might be an actor, didn't you?'

'Yes.' How vividly she remembered that first moment when she had looked into his eyes, and then, as now, they had captivated her against her will.

'And now you know me a little better, I wonder what you think?'

'I think you're self-willed.'

'True enough.'

'As ruthless with yourself as you are with others.'

'Ah, there you make an interesting observation.'

'A valid one, *señor*.' Debra ran her gaze over his face, seeing the power of his features and the passion brooding in his eyes. He was of his mother's people and hot blood ran in his veins, and Debra felt sure that if desire had carried him beyond restraint with his brother's wife, then somewhere deep inside he burnt with guilt. He stared down at her and then, as if glimpsing in her look a question in fear of an answer, he let go of her and turned away so he was looking out of the window.

Debra rubbed her wrist where his fingers had gripped, then seating herself at the typewriter she put on her spectacles and fed a sheet of manuscript paper into the machine. She felt him stir and from her nape downwards she was conscious of him behind her chair, brimming with the power to disquiet her as no one else ever had. His very silence sent a thrill of emotion through her flesh to the bone . . . it was a silence heavy with the thoughts of a man who didn't share his troubles very easily, and if the source of that trouble was Pauline, then

Debra didn't want to know.

Her nerves jarred when the door of the den opened to admit Jack, who broke off in mid-speech as he noticed Rodare by the window. 'I hope you aren't disturbing Debra,' he said brusquely.

'As if I would disturb this jewel of efficiency.' Rodare spoke with irony. 'Knowing this to be the inner sanctum where the two of you confer on the great book, I merely strolled in to get a whiff of the magical air. I haven't disturbed you, have I, Miss Hartway?'

'Not in the least.' She managed to sound composed but didn't know how she achieved it. 'When I'm absorbed in my work I'm unaware of minor interruptions.'

Jack gave a laugh and shot an approving look at her. 'That puts you in your place, brother.'

'Ah, yes, Miss Hartway is the embodiment of the cool career girl, always neat as a pin and just as sharp when she feels like it. You are so lucky to have her working for you, and isn't this den the perfect place for the high priest of fiction and his acolyte.'

Jack's amusement abruptly faded. 'When you use that tone of voice, Rodare, I get a whiff of mischief. Is there something on your mind that you want to air?'

'Should there be, *hermano*?' He used the Spanish term for brother.

'Several things.' Jack stood frowning in a ray

of sunlight which picked out and set glimmering the silver in his hair. When together, Debra noticed, the two men were as different as a rapier and a lance, each in his own way a man to be reckoned with and not always in tune. Right now they were eyeing each other like opponents, as if Jack still harboured a very personal grudge against Rodare, who knew of it and had to be on the defensive.

'Name one,' Rodare challenged.

'The girl at that desk,' Jack said deliberately. 'I hope she's made it clear to you that she doesn't consider herself under any kind of matrimonial obligation? She ran away from the very notion of it!'

'And she returned,' Rodare drawled.

'In my company,' Jack rejoined. 'I've told Mama, and I'm telling you, Debra is under my protection.'

'How gallant, Jack, and how that must put to rest Miss Hartway's girlish fears that I shall cause her to take fright again. I wonder what it is about me that gives her nervous palpitations? The fact that I resemble our esteemed ancestor who plucked himself a piece of girlish booty and took to sea with her?'

He abruptly swung a look at Debra and caught her staring wide-eyed at him through the tortoiseshell rims of her glasses. They gave to her face, those rims, a vulnerable look, intensifying its heart shape.

'Afraid I shall repeat his performance, *señorita*?'

'You look capable of it.' She had made her reply out of pure defensiveness rather than spite, but she knew how he would take it.

'If you know that,' he said, his voice edged with meaning, 'then next time you're alone on the beach you had better take care or history might repeat itself.'

'You lay a finger—' Jack started to say, but Rodare was on his way to the door.

'Will it be swords at dawn, *hermano*?' The words were flung over Rodare's shoulder as he walked out of the den and slammed the door behind him.

Debra looked at Jack and saw him gritting his teeth. 'I wish the devil would go back to Spain and stay there! I don't know what gets into him, but I can understand your reaction to him, Debra.'

'My reaction—?' She gave Jack an anxious look; she didn't want anyone to guess how she reacted to Rodare and she had hoped that she kept her feelings concealed and under control . . . those turbulent feelings that were her awakening to the urgings of the body rather than the heart.

'You're a sensitive girl,' Jack said, and he came round to her side of the desk and laid a hand upon her shoulder, 'and Rodare's buccaneer manner must alarm you. I can just

imagine how he must have overpowered you
with his arrogance the night he proposed to
you—anyway, I think it's now been made
plain to him that he isn't your type of man,
though I can quite understand why he should
want you.'

Debra caught her breath and gave Jack a
startled look. He smiled down at her.

'Modest as well, aren't you, child?' He ran
his gaze over her hair, so neat at her nape, yet
its colour took fire against her skin. 'Despite
Rodare, are you glad to be back at
Abbeywitch?'

'It's a wonderful house,' she replied, sitting there carefully with his hand upon her
shoulder, remembering what Rodare had said
about how she regarded Jack . . . a tragic
hero who needed a tender shoulder to lean
on.

'Are you glad that we're now working
together?'

'Yes, the book is really coming along and
should be ready on schedule.'

'All the same,' Jack's hand moved and
seemed to hover above her hair, 'all work and
no play isn't fair on a young woman. Each
evening you seem to vanish into your turret,
but I think you should let your hair down for
Midsummer Eve and I'd like you to dine downstairs and take part in the festivity. This evening Mick, my brother and myself are going to

build the bonfire and when it's set alight tomorrow evening it will be a beacon that will be seen across the water. It's quite a sight!'

'Your brother mentioned the bonfire and I would like to see it,' she said, and added warily: 'But I won't dine at the family table—I much prefer to take my meals alone.'

'Because of my mother?' Jack exclaimed.

'Yes—you know how she feels about me, and you have guests in the house.'

'Sharon will be delighted to get acquainted with you,' he said at once. 'She's a bright and friendly girl and not in the least uppish.'

'I'm sure she looks very nice, but my last attempt at socialising with your family and friends was a disaster.' Debra raised an imploring face to Jack. 'I'm here to work for you and it's better that I hover in the background—'

'Just because you're self-conscious about that business with Rodare?' Jack looked obstinate. 'Don't think I'm unaware of your feelings, but as well as being my secretarial editor you are also my friend—at least, Debra, I hope you are?'

'I—I'm pleased to be anybody's friend—'

'Right, and I'm as entitled to have a friend of mine at the family table as Zandra is to have hers.'

'Your mother likes Stuart, but she regards me as only a notch above the housemaids—oh, how can you know how humiliating it was that night, to have her thinking that I was about to get into bed with your brother! She said such things—that was why Rodare sprang his proposal.'

All at once, overcome by a mixture of emotions, Debra sank her face into her hands and let the wave sweep over her. Since her return to Abbeywitch she had suppressed emotion as much as she could, but suddenly it overwhelmed her. It wasn't so much that she felt like weeping, it was that she felt like crying out in distress.

'Child, don't do that!' Jack gathered her upright into his arms, and this time he didn't hesitate to fondle her hair. 'You're always such a composed girl and it worries me to see you like this—it was Rodare coming in here, wasn't it? What did he say to upset you so, damn him?'

'No,' she shook her head against Jack, 'it isn't anything he said. It's just that I don't want to get into another situation like the last one and I—I feel better about working here if I'm left to myself when I leave off work. I want to be—'

'Alone and preferably invisible,' he broke in, his fingers gently stroking her hair. 'I do assure you, Debra, that my mother has calmed down considerably now I'm back at Abbeywitch. She realises that she made a mistake where you're concerned—won't you try and forgive her, for my sake?'

Debra didn't know how to reply to him. The way he touched her hair, the way he spoke to her, soothed and reassured her, but could she really find the boldness to face Lenora Salvador again? Since her return to the island she had taken pains to avoid Jack's mother, and now he asked her to sit at the same table.

'If you go on hiding yourself away,' he said, 'everyone will think you have something to hide.'

'You know I haven't—'

'I want the others to know it as well.'

'But,' she drew back and gave him a perplexed look, 'why should it matter to you what your family thinks of me?'

'It does happen to matter.' His jaw was set. 'I don't intend to say more than that at the present time, but it does matter. I want the rift closed between you and Mama and I'm more or less ordering you to join us tomorrow evening.'

'I see.' Debra raised her chin and gave the rim of her glasses a little shove. 'You're exerting your authority over me?'

'Yes, if you like to put it that way.'

'Will you send me packing if I refuse to obey you?'

'No.' He shook his head. 'But I shall be disappointed in the girl who came so spiritedly to *The Cap And Bells* and showed me where my duty lay. Such spirit, matching that wonderful hair of yours.'

She flushed vividly at the compliment and it was nerves rather than vanity that moved her to take off her glasses and fiddle with them.

'Y-you make it difficult for me to refuse you,' she said, confused by this new side he was showing her . . . mastering her and telling her openly that he admired her hair.

'I wanted to make it difficult,' he rejoined. 'You're a girl to hold your head up anywhere and I expect you to do so tomorrow evening, but if you lose your nerve I shall understand. I won't hold it against you but I shall feel let down.'

They left it at that and resumed work, but something new had crept into the atmosphere between them . . . Debra knew that they had become aware of each other as man and woman.

CHAPTER ELEVEN

FROM a fascinating old book which Debra found on the shelves of the den she learnt that the Midsummer festival of fire was a custom dating back to pagan times before becoming blessed by the church as the Eve of St John.

In each locality the fire was blessed by a priest who spoke his words in the old Cornish dialect, then wild flowers and herbs were flung among the flames and when the fire had burnt down low, those who were still agile joined hands and leapt the embers, laughing and chanting to chase away evil spirits from their homes.

This was linked to the old pagan belief that the fires helped to warm the sun, always a source of worship, and a sun that shone all through the summer helped their crops to flourish and their children to grow. The sun was venerated and devils and witches had to be warded off which was the reason why broomsticks were burnt on some of the fires.

Debra was enthralled by all this old Cornish lore and the meaning of old Celtic words such as Bodmin, which meant house of the monks.

The Cornish, she read, were an unconquered people, tough and durable as the granite cliffs, and deep-natured as the mine shafts which penetrated beneath the sea.

As she laid aside the book, she pondered the strains of Celt and Latin in the Salvador clan . . . in Rodare those strains were intermingled like serpentine rock. The *sombra y luz*, as she had termed it, the light and shade in layers through his personality until it became hard to tell when the lighter side of him would be overshadowed by the dark, almost devilish side.

Whenever she was alone with him Debra was aware of how swiftly he could shift his mood, rather like a tiger whose purr was only a concealment for a sudden attack. Big, tawny, menacing like one of those great cats that prowled in a cage. Abbeywitch, for all its gothic beauty high on the cliffs, was Rodare's cage, and Debra reflected what a shame it was that Jack wasn't the eldest brother. Unlike Rodare he wasn't divided by a love of Spain and an obligation to settle here on Lovelis Island if ever he married.

Rodare had used those very words, a marriage of obligation, as if he had already decided that he could never find happiness anywhere but in his beloved Spain.

She wondered what his reaction would be if she did fall in with Jack's wish that she dine downstairs tomorrow evening. She tried to imagine herself walking into the drawing-room where drinks were served before the family went in to dine, facing up to Rodare's irony, the curiosity of the Chandlers, and most daunting of all the condescension of Lenora Salvador.

Heaven forbid! Snatching a woolly jacket from the closet Debra flung it around her shoulders and decided that she needed a breath of air. She wanted to walk in the moon-light above the cool sea.

As she passed the tall clock on the gallery it chimed eight, the silvery chimes following her down the stairs. The family and their guests were at dinner right now, their ease with each other excluding her.

Silent as a shadow she crossed the hall and slipped out of the side door into the courtyard which extended to archways leading in various directions.

She went in the direction of the headland, along a pathway bowered in trumpet-vine, quince and firethorn. The air was alive with moths like pale floating feathers, and some-where among the trees a rook croaked, for black as the Devil they nested here, craftily aware that later in the year the oaks would shed acorns for them to feed on.

Being a city girl Debra had been wary of the island's wild life, especially the hawks who swooped upon smaller birds in mid-air and fed upon them to the last feather. The seals she loved, especially when they waddled out of the water and perched on the ebony boulders along the shore. Their doglike heads and huge shining eyes had such appeal as they sunned themselves among the sandpipers and the puffins.

She strolled along in the moonlight, breathing the salty air and feeling its cool touch in her hair, which she had let down from its knot. Her eyes glimmered at the mystery and enticement of the sea, splashing in upon the rocks, gentle enough at the moment but when the tide arose the powerful motion of the sea made a bellowing sound in a blow-hole below the headland where Debra walked.

Just ahead of her it jutted out above the beach, forming a kind of plateau, and she was unsurprised to see that work on the bonfire had already begun. It was already half built, perhaps by Mickey Lee who was probably having his own evening meal, for he was nowhere to be seen. A cart filled with logs and boughs and bundles of loose kindling stood with its shafts empty and Debra guessed that Mickey had taken the horse to the stable for its meal of oats.

Was it from here, Debra wondered, that Jack had scattered his young wife's ashes, seeing them waft out over the water and then settle on the crest of the waves . . . rejoining her spirit where she had died?

Debra glanced about her, pulling her jacket closer around her shoulders as a pale image was evoked. Her glance was caught by some wild flowers growing at the edge of the cliff, the moonlight on their petals. She knelt down and was touching the flowers, so soft and cool to her fingers, when a voice spoke above her head:

'Don't pluck blue scabius or the Devil will come to your bedside.'

She went very still, rather like a wild creature who hopes its stillness will fool the hunter.

'Come to your feet and step away from that edge,' the voice commanded.

'I'm all right—'

'You're a little fool.'

'I expect I am.' And defiantly she plucked a single flower and then rose to her feet. As she turned to face her intruder the tide wind caught at her hair and blew it into a coppery pennon, and the moonglow made her skin pearly pale as she stood there indecisive, wanting to pass by him but afraid he would touch her.

'Do you want the Devil at your bedside?' he mocked, long-legged in black trousers, wearing a dress-shirt open against his throat. He looked like a freebooter there in the moonlight, filling Debra with a mixture of feelings.

'I—I've had him there,' she retorted, some-how driven to recklessness, perhaps by the mad moon of Midsummer.

A smile curled his lip and he cast up at the moon a glance which seemed to share her thought. 'The moon is said to incite primitive responses in a woman, and strangely enough when your hair is set free you seem more of a woman and less of an efficient little robot who obeys her master with such quiet dignity.'

'I haven't a master,' she argued, seeing the moonlight like fire in his eyes.

'And don't want one, eh?'

'Indeed not.' She flung up her chin, the blue scabious flower clenched in her hand. 'I wouldn't tolerate one.'

'So you are a free soul, *señorita*?'

'Yes I am, *señor*.'

'With no wish to be the *adorada* of a man who will jealously guard you and make of you his very own possession?'

'How claustrophobic!'

'You believe so, eh?'

'I know so.'

'You know!' He took a step closer to her, his eyes flashing with scorn. 'What can you know of the emotions, straight out of the schoolroom and into an office to work upon other people's imaginings on sheets of paper. You know very little of real life there behind your prickly hedge that keeps men at a distance.'

'Y-you haven't always kept your distance,' she reminded him.

'Perhaps because my hide is so tanned it has become tough as leather—isn't that what you are thinking?'

'Yes.' Her eyes were upon his tanned throat in the opening of his shirt and there was something else on her mind . . . she was quite alone with Rodare up here on the headland, the boom of the tide like a pagan drum, the surging sea lit by the radiance of the huge tawny moon. There was a barbarous splendour to the night as if some of the Midsummer magic and madness was in the air.

'We say in Spain, *señorita*, that when a woman argues with a man she is entering the arena with the bull.'

'I don't quite see you as a bull, *señor*.'

'You don't?' He slowly raised an eyebrow. 'How do you see me?'

'As the matador, with your cape hiding the sword.'

His eyelids narrowed and for long seconds the silence between them was filled with the boom of the sea, echoing up the cliffside and filling the air with the tang of wreck and beaten sand and secret gardens on the bed of the ocean. Debra breathed it in and felt a cool moisture on her skin as she stood there with her hair blowing about her brow.

'I wonder,' he said at last, 'if you realise what you've said?'

Her eyes widened upon his face, so very Spanish with those shaded depressions below his strong cheekbones, the dominant nose and lean, swarthy jawline. 'I thought I was stating a fact, *señor*. Doesn't the bullfighter conceal his sword before dealing the fatal stroke?'

Rodare inclined his head in agreement, but glimmering in his eyes was the smile of a man enjoying a private joke. Held by his gaze, Debra didn't realise that he had moved until his hands closed upon her waist and made a captive of her.

'Don't—please—'

'Don't do what, *santa pequeña*?'

'This—what you're doing—' She strained away from him, but it took no more than a little additional pressure for him to have her pressed against his pliant warmth. He lowered his head and his mouth vibrated against her skin, sending little waves of sensation to the very centre of her body.

'I like to make you suffer, little saint. You put on such airs of demure self-containment, and then I touch you and you are like a moth twisting and turning in the flame, wanting the ecstasy even as it burns your angelic wings. Come, confess it to me! Be a woman for once and emerge from that prim cocoon in which

you keep yourself bound up . . . be again
the girl who danced with me and forgot her
inhibitions.'

'I—I'll never be that girl again,' she panted.
'That girl makes trouble for me—you make
trouble for me! It doesn't affect you if I'm seen
in a bad light by your family a-and you ruin a
job which I've grown to love.'

'Does love of the job include my esteemed
brother?' He spoke the words against the side
of her neck where the soft column had picked
up a distress signal from her heart.

'I—I don't intend to discuss my private business with you,' she said, her voice as rigid as
she tried to keep her body. 'I'm well aware that
you're the master of Abbeywitch, but that
doesn't give you any rights over me. Whatever
your Spanish ways, they don't apply in this
country.'

'It's a pity they don't,' he drawled, his warm
breath fanning her skin. 'In Spain a girl is
dishonoured for life if found with a man in her
room. To the Spanish mind there could be only
one reason for such an encounter and that
reason couldn't possibly be innocent.'

'In our case, you very well know it was.'
Debra found herself fighting him again. 'Let
me go—your brother and Mickey will come
soon and I don't—'

'Don't want Jack to see you in my arms, eh?'

'Of course I don't—he'd think—'

'That you might enjoy having my arms around you?'

'I enjoy it about as much as I'd enjoy having the coils of a snake around me!' The more she struggled the closer he seemed to hold her, those saddle-strong legs of his planted firm on the ground as she swayed in his arms in the tide wind and the moonlight. The image of the two of them was vivid in Debra's mind, etched there in detail against the sky.

'You—you want your brother to find us together, don't you?' she accused.

'The thought never entered my head.'

'Liar!'

'That's no way for a little saint to speak.'

'I've never pretended to be a saint.'

'Then why all this show of resistance?'

'Y-you know why.'

'Not completely, but I'm prepared to listen.'

'I don't play around with men, but you've got it into your head that because I'm a single woman in my twenties who happens to be English I'm available for your attentions. How many times do I have to say that I'm neither available, nor am I dishonoured, as you call it, just because you were caught in my room. In short, Señor Salvador, I'm not your toy!'

Her eyes blazed in the moonlight, fired by temper and a desperate need to be free of Rodare's arms before Jack arrived on the scene.

'You're no better than Stuart Coltan,' she

added. 'You're a whole lot worse because you make out to be the gentleman of honour. I don't find you very honourable!'

Even as she spoke the word she cried out as she felt the ground slipping from beneath her feet . . . as effortlessly as if he handled a toy, Rodare swung her over his shoulder and began to march along the headland with her, making for a wild area of butcher's-broom, tall grass and gorse and the strong tang of sweet-briar. He thrust his way among a tangle of shrub until they were out of range of all eyes, even the tawny eye of the moon.

'You Spanish devil, let me down!' Debra struck with her fist at his back muscles, but they were firm as leather and she caused herself more pain than she caused him.

'When I'm ready, you long-haired vixen.' In retaliation he swung a slap at her backside. 'The time has come, *mujer*, to finish what started between us the day we met.'

'Why didn't you do it then?' She gave him a punch for each word. 'Why didn't you rape me then to get it over with?'

'So you think it's going to be rape, do you?' As he swung her to her feet her hair was a flying scarf of silk which he took in his grip, forcing her head backwards until her slim neck was exposed to where her blouse strained across her breast. His eyes raked over her, a prelude to his touch.

'I like to feel you struggling in my arms,' he said. 'I like it when my fingers climb so smooth a slope to the peak of your breast.'

'Damned devil!' She felt herself shudder as he suited action to his words . . . and what she found unforgivable in herself was that her shudder wasn't one of repulsion. Her eyelids closed heavily while her lips parted . . . parted to receive his lips as his fingers went on caressing her through the fabric of blouse and brassiere.

'Don't—' The word blurred against his mouth. She made her protest, but couldn't stop his fingers from travelling from one button to another until her blouse slid from her shoulders. His hand slid around her and found the tiny hooks that released her breasts from the cups of silk. She cried out, but it was barely a cry as Rodare lowered her to the fragrant grass and the wild clover, his lips pausing for tantalising moments before they began to explore the warm valley that led to the peaks of her breasts. Her limbs grew heavy as sensual little waves began to beat through her bloodstream, her arms tightened around him and her response made him gasp her name . . . gasp as if he were suddenly drowning.

Their lips clung hotly, their breath mingled, then, as his hands began to coax her towards the ultimate closeness, she found the will to refuse him.

'Is this,' she broke his hold on her clamouring senses, 'is this what you did with Pauline?'

Her words were followed by utter stillness, so that in the distance she heard the sound of a voice calling his name, then with the lithe grace he could never lose in any situation, he rose from the grass to his feet, half-turning away from her as he regained his control and thrust a hand through his disordered hair. 'So that's it,' he said harshly.

'Go away.' Debra rolled over so the front of her was hidden from his gaze. 'Go and help with the bonfire a-and tomorrow night—throw yourself on it!'

He made no rejoinder and she lay utterly still, waiting until she couldn't hear him any more, thrusting his way back to the headland where Jack had called his name. She fumbled with tiny hooks and blouse buttons, then made her way to the house through the woodland that merged with the garden. The moonlight on the flowers made them unearthly in their loveliness, and all at once she felt such a reaction against Rodare that she sank down on one of the rustic seats and burst into tears.

She howled inside though her outward weeping was stifled by her hands over her face. The painful tears seeped between her fingers and her weeping was like a grieving over something lost that she would never find again.

Dreams . . . illusions of a love so precious
that it would light up her life as the stars lit the
sky. She had dreamt of romantic splendour,
but now all her doubts and fears were confirmed. It meant no more than two bodies
finding their satisfaction . . . hot lips on palpitating flesh . . . a wild, delirious urging to
give and be taken . . . taken until pain was
pleasure, and pleasure was pain.

'I hate him . . . hate him,' she whispered,
over and over. If she kept saying she hated him
then perhaps in time she would start to believe
it. She would be able to look at him, big,
powerful, beckoning, and nothing would happen inside her. She wouldn't feel as if her heart
was suspended on a tightrope above a steep
drop. She would be still and cold and empty
inside, and safe from any more tumults of
feeling when he laid hands upon her.

It was some time before she felt ready to
enter the house . . . his house where the dark
and glossy furniture was of Spanish design,
intricately carved like the black oak table at the
centre of the hall on which stood the wide
silver salvers always piled with fruit. Tonight
black grapes, peaches and egg-shaped plums.

Debra came to a hesitant halt, for standing
beside the table was a slender figure in sugar-
ice silk crêpe, which was pleated beautifully
and calf-length. A long strand of pearls was
around her neck and she wore pink shoes with

high narrow heels. She stood there as if trying to decide between a peach and a plum, and then from the corner of her eye she must have caught sight of Debra.

'Hello!' She swung round to face her. 'You're Jack's secretary, aren't you?'

'Yes, Miss Chandler.' Debra's heart pounded beneath her blouse . . . did she look very dishevelled and weepy? Did it show that she had been partially stripped by Jack's brother and still felt where his lips and hands had been? By comparison to the immaculate Sharon, she felt degraded.

'We've never been introduced, but I remember you from Rodare's party—how sensationally the two of you danced together. You didn't look much like a secretary to me, the way you turned about in his arms like a real professional. I can never achieve that sinuous movement, though Rodare has promised to teach me.'

Beneath the survey of those blue and rather inquisitive eyes, Debra flushed to the roots of her hair. She felt shabby, used, and wanted to stand under the shower in her bathroom until she felt clean again.

She couldn't help but notice the fresh pink of Sharon's lips. Her brows with a curving prettiness to them, the soft mauve shadowing of her eyelids and the way her hair glistened like a halo. She looked like a beautiful doll straight out of a lace-edged box, with not a fingermark on her.

Tears brimmed in Debra's eyes and suddenly she was dashing past Sharon towards the stairs. 'I—I have the most awful headache, Miss Chandler! Please forgive me—'

Up the stairs she sped, making for her turret where she could be alone to break her heart in peace.

A sustained shower helped and she stepped from beneath the water feeling refreshed in body though her thoughts were still shadowed by the incident with Rodare. There was nothing profound in whatever the feeling was that he had for her, and she wasn't sorry that she had flung Pauline's name in his face.

The name had struck home because instantly she had felt desire go out like a flame in a gust of cold wind. He had spoken only three words, 'So that's it,' and he had spoken them through lips with a locked-in, swearing look.

Debra wrapped her towelling robe tightly about her, her damp and glistening hair caping it. She sat down in one of the cane chairs and tried to read a book, but the print ran together in a jumble and with a sigh she took off her spectacles and rested her head against the cushion.

Sharon Chandler was very pretty and she did seem as friendly as Jack had said she was. Debra didn't envy the prettiness or the wealth that made the girl's life so easy that her problems were reduced to a debate between a peach and a plum. Debra idly wondered if that was how Sharon regarded the Salvador brothers. Was she here on the island to try and make up her mind between them? Surely neither of them would be able to resist if she laid her hand with its pink fingernails upon one sleeve or the other and said, in her well-modulated voice, that she thought marriage would be a good idea and why not try it with her.

Debra had fallen into a quiet mood of retrospection when all at once she was stirred to her feet by a rap on her door. She stood there staring at the door, her left hand clutching her robe against her body. Not Rodare! She couldn't bear to have him anywhere near her! 'Go away,' she prayed. 'Go away!'

Suddenly the doorknob started to turn and Debra was getting ready to tell Rodare to go to the devil when Jack poked his head round the door. 'You all right?' he asked, his eyes fixed upon her face which seemed drained of colour except for the blazing green of her eyes.

She gave a shiver of relief. 'It's you,' she said, and she even managed to give him a smile.

'Can I come in or will propriety be offended?'

'I don't quite know—' Her smile quavered. 'You are the apple of your mother's eye and I feel certain she'd pull out my hair if she caught us together.'

His cheek clefted as he entered, carrying in with him a covered tray. 'Strawberries and cream,' he smiled. 'Want to share them with me?—I know you like them and I picked these a while ago in the light of the moon which means, my pretty wench, that they're bewitched.'

As an enticement he threw back the white cloth and showed her the two heaped bowls and the jug of cream. *'Voilà!'*

They did look appetizing and all at once she didn't want to be alone. 'All right, Jack, but could we—could we lock the door?'

'Ah, sin and strawberries?' he murmured.

'No,' she firmly shook her head, 'the cream will be sufficient.'

'As you wish, madame.' He brought the tray to the foot of her bed and set it down. 'Will this do?'

She nodded and brought forward a chair for him while he turned the key in the lock. 'We've built the bonfire and it's a beauty. It will burn for hours and the sparks will be seen way out over the water,' he informed her.

'Good,' she said, a trifle constrainedly. 'What red-looking strawberries.'

'To put some colour in your cheeks.' He sat down in the chair while she perched on the bed and she was aware of his eyes on her face as she poured the cream.

'This is a very luxurious supper.' She bit into

a strawberry and found it deliciously juicy. 'So they grow in the garden?'

'Mmmm, there's a great patch of them down where the two big magnolia trees grow and they are a glorious sight in August, as you will see for yourself.'

'But I shall have finished work on your book before August comes.'

'That doesn't mean you'll be gone.'

Debra gave him a startled look. 'I don't quite—'

'I want you to stay.' He bit deliberately into a large red berry, his eyes upon her face.

'As your editor and secretary?'

'Yes. Now I've lost Miss Tucker I'm going to need someone on a permanent basis, and we get along fine, don't we? You seem to like it here at Abbeywitch—'

'Jack,' she broke in, 'will you give me time to think over your offer?'

'Do you need time to think it over, Debra?'

She hesitated, remembering how she had hoped when she first came here that Jack Salvador would want her to stay on as his regular assistant with his books. What she hadn't bargained for was her strange involvement with Rodare . . . even if he returned to Spain there would come a day when he would reappear at Abbeywitch, and it was no use assuring herself that those feelings he churned into life would die and fade out of her system like autumn leaves when the season of their burgeoning was over.

She spooned cream over a strawberry until it was quite hidden away. 'I do want to rise through the ranks at Columbine,' she said at last. 'I'm very interested in all aspects of publishing and Mr Holt thinks well of me.'

'I think well of you,' Jack said, a winsome note in his voice. 'You came and saved my reason and I want to write more books with you there to help me. You won't suffer financially.'

'I know, but let me think it over.'

'If you insist, Debra.'

She smiled, but it was something of an effort. 'Lovely strawberries and it's kind of you to want to share them with me. About an hour ago I saw Miss Chandler down in the hall and she seemed to be in the mood for some fruit and a companion. She's sensationally pretty, isn't she? It must be pleasant for you to have her staying here.'

'Yes, she's as charming as a Pears Soap advertisement,' he drawled. 'Always was, from a child, and the peach of her mother's eye. Had you been out for a stroll?'

Debra felt a racing of her pulses. 'Yes,' she licked juice from her lip, 'I did go out for a breath of air. What a moon!'

'It will be even more barbaric tomorrow evening, if all is well and we don't get any clouds rolling in. Did you go along the head-land—we were busy with the bonfire so—'

'I did pass by earlier on, while you were all at dinner.'

'I see.' He ate his last strawberry. 'Have you made up your mind about joining us for dinner tomorrow evening?'

'I—don't see how I can, Jack.'

Something stirred in his eyes and when he spoke there was a slight edge to his voice. 'You're being rather elusive tonight, Debra. First you shy away from my suggestion that you stay at Abbeywitch on a permanent basis, and now you're being indecisive about tomor-row's event. We Salvadors are only people, you know, and you have no need to be scared of people—they aren't quite so dangerous as tigers.'

'Some are.' She had said it before she could stop herself.

'Have you a specific person in mind, Debra?'

She lifted her shoulder in a shrug. 'I feel sure the Chandlers aren't in the habit of sitting at dinner with the hired help, as I've been called.'

'Dash your sensitivity!' Jack reached forward and took her firmly by the hand, and he was about to say something more when his atten-tion was caught by the bruising on the back of her hand, quite lividly dark against her white skin. 'How the devil did this happen?'

Her fingers clenched and she tried to pull

free of his hold on her. 'Oh, I knocked myself. It isn't anything to be concerned about.'

'It looks as if it must have hurt.' And to Debra's astonishment he carried her hand to his lips and kissed the bruises which his brother had made during her struggle with him out on the headland. Stark in her mind was the image of herself being flung over Rodare's shoulder, and she couldn't help but wonder how Jack would react if she told him how close she had come to being ravished by Rodare.

No, she could never tell Jack or anyone about that incident and the way it had ended, with Rodare looking as a matador must look when he makes a false move and the horn of the bull tears him open. Shock, followed by pain, and then a kind of fatalistic acceptance. All those emotions had been stark in Rodare's eyes when he had turned and walked away from her.

Uncertain emotions were in Debra's eyes as Jack drew his lips from her hand. Then he smiled slightly. 'A touch of the Latin in me—do you mind being kissed by your boss?'

'I—it was very nice—'

'I'm pleased you think so.' His gaze dwelt upon her lips, moist and bright from the strawberry juice. 'I'm rather out of practice.'

'Oh,' her smile faltered, 'do you plan to practise on me?'

'Would you let me?'

'I—I don't mind kisses on the hand.'

'To be going on with, Debra?'

Her heart had started to pound and her fingers flexed in his of themselves. He was flirting with her, lightly and charmingly, and so in contrast to Rodare's treatment of her that her shaken emotions brought tears to her eyes again.

'Dear girl—I didn't mean to alarm you!' Jack himself looked a touch alarmed by her reaction. 'What a bundle of sensitive, sweet emotions you are, Debra. I've never met a girl quite like you.'

'Oh, I'm just being silly.' She quickly brushed away a tear which had fallen to her cheek.

'Have I upset you?'

'Of course not.'

'Then it's tomorrow evening you're all churned up about?'

'Yes,' it was a good excuse, 'I think I am.'

'Then I'd better not put pressure upon you—you will come to see the bonfire when it's lit? Father Restormel is coming across from the Chapel of the Sacred Sorrows in order to bless the fire—it's one of our pagan customs turned respectable.'

'I'll be there to see the fire,' she promised.

'Then I shall have to be satisfied with that, shan't I?'

'I'm afraid so.'

'I wonder what you are really afraid of?' he said thoughtfully, and his gaze dropped again to her bruised hand. 'If someone was making you miserable here at Abbeywitch would you tell me and let me deal with it?'

'I'm not miserable,' she protested. 'I'm just a woman and we go up and down like a yo-yo.'

'Did you used to have a yo-yo when you were a child?'

She nodded. 'I used to chalk on the sides of it so it made coloured patterns as it went up and down.'

His gaze ran over her, settling on her chestnut hair. 'I bet you were a charming child straight out of a Kate Greenaway illustration.'

'I was leggy and awkward and my mother impressed upon me that my hair was my one claim to beauty.'

'I have to disagree with your mother.' He held Debra's gaze, gone from green to a slightly shadowed grey. 'You have a kind of beauty inside you, Debra, and now and again it's there on the outside and you have a glow about you. Tonight that glow is dimmed. I know you aren't going to tell me why and I shan't pester you, but let me say again that I want you to stay on at Abbeywitch. I think I have need of you.'

'That's kind of you, Jack.'

'No,' he shook his head, glinting with silver here and there in the lamplight. 'I'm probably being selfish, but that's the way of men, not that I think you an expert on men. Ah, something has just struck me! Perhaps there's a young man working at Columbine whom you care for, and here am I suggesting that you stay on the island and work for me?'

For fraught moments Debra was tempted to let him believe that she was attracted to someone at Columbine. It would give her a plausible reason for wanting to leave Abbeywitch when work was completed on Jack's book, but innate honesty prevailed.

'I've always been too wrapped up in work to be bothered with men,' she smiled. 'My mother worked like a slave taking in boarders so I could have a good education and I don't intend to waste all she sacrificed for me. She was only a young woman when my father died and for years she didn't have any fun—'

'What about your fun?' Jack broke in, a slight frown furrowing his brow. 'Your mother did what she did as much to please herself as to ensure your education, parents are like that. If I went broke tomorrow and couldn't write anything saleable I'd go and work on the bins in order to take care of Dean.'

'I know how much you love him.' Debra's face softened into the smile she often smiled when she saw Jack and the child together.

'God, I do!' A tremor of feeling shook Jack's frame. 'It all came rushing back when I saw him again—I grabbed him in my arms and he was flesh of my flesh! I had no more doubts on that score and I owe you a debt of gratitude that can never be fully repaid.'

'I don't want to be repaid,' she assured him. 'Seeing you with Dean is payment in full.'

'You really mean that, don't you, my wench?'

'Absolutely.' Her eyes silvered as they met his. 'I think it was a stroke of fate that I decided to leave Abbeywitch that morning, and directly I cottoned on to the fact that Mickey knew your whereabouts I decided to gull him into taking me to you. It isn't something I'd do unless driven to it because Mickey is so trusting, but it seemed worthwhile, and as things turned out it was worthwhile.'

'You're a young woman of spirit, as I said.' Jack held her gaze and a forcefulness crept into his eyes. 'Yet the spirit drains out of you when I ask you to become friends with my mother and sister. They won't eat you, you know. Mama has me back in the fold, and Zandra is so smitten with her handsome boy-friend she looks almost like a tabby cat these days, with cream all round her mouth.'

'Do you think they will marry?' Debra wanted to steer him away from that dining-table, where she had no intention of sitting under the dark gaze of his half-brother.

'It's a possibility.' Jack shrugged. 'Zandra

made one bed for herself that turned out to be lumpy, and if she plans to make another then she has to lie on it. Coltan's looks have her in thrall and she can't see beyond them.'

'They're both very handsome,' Debra murmured. 'They do look well together and they have the theatre in common.'

'Having things in common is important,' Jack agreed, and a shadow passed over his lean face. 'My marriage to Pauline failed because she took no interest in my work and I didn't realise how much she needed excitement. I thought having a baby would calm her down, but instead her pregnancy turned out to be hateful to her. When she saw herself losing her slim figure she went crazy and I took no notice of the wild things she said.'

He drew a deep and painful sigh as the memories ran through his mind like hot wires.

'Poor little Pauline . . . she went to my head like a bubbly champagne, but when I became sober again I just didn't know what to say or do to bring back the sparkle into our marriage. It just fizzled out and a kind of sourness replaced the honeymoon sweetness. I know she only wanted to take Dean with her in order to punish me—she never loved him as I did—'

Jack broke off and bowed his head as the painful memories overcame him. Compassion drove Debra to her feet and she went to him, and the moment she touched his shoulder he was upon his feet and with the strength of need he pulled her into his arms. His mouth bore down on hers and she didn't resist him . . . she allowed his kisses, on mouth, eyes, and then her throat.

'God, you're sweet, you are so sweet.' He breathed the words against her skin. 'With you it's like being on a summerlit lake, with the singing of birds and the white swans swimming along in all their grace. You are so different from Pauline.'

'Am I, Jack?' And she could only think how different he was from Rodare. 'It's late, you know. You should be going—'

'Must I go?' His eyes implored her to say no.

'Yes, you must go.' She drew herself out of his embrace. 'Thank you for the strawberries.'

'Thank you for not slapping my face.' He pushed a hand through his hair, and for a jaggedly painful moment Debra was so reminded of Rodare that her knees quaked as she went to the door and unlocked it. Jack came across the room towards her and there was a tinge of regret in his smile, deepening as she swung open the door.

'Little saint,' he said as he passed her by and went out of the room. 'I'll see you in the morning—but we don't work tomorrow. Tomorrow is a holiday and we'll go riding instead. Dream sweet dreams, Debra.'

'You too, Jack.' She closed the door behind

him and then allowed herself to sink back weakly against its support. Little saint! His brother's name for her up there on the moon-swept headland, with the air like a wild wine, and the devil let loose in a pair of dark Spanish eyes.

Wearily she pushed her hands through her own hair, then carried the tray with the juice-stained bowls into the bathroom, where she washed them under the tap. Jack's visit to her bedroom was another secret to add to her list . . . not a dark secret like the one she shared with Rodare, but it wouldn't make her stay at Abbeywitch any easier if his mother found out that Jack came late at night to her bedroom, bringing strawberries and cream.

CHAPTER TWELVE

THE palomino's wheaten mane was half over his proud, bright, blue-nosed face and he snickered his pleasure as Debra fed him a quartered carrot which she had brought from the kitchen.

'You're a real beauty, aren't you?' she murmured, for this was the horse which always stood out from the group that galloped along the sands in the morning. High-stepping and somehow joyous, he was exactly the horse she would have loved for her very own; she didn't dare to imagine how much he was worth.

Suddenly she tensed as she caught the sounds of booted feet on the flagstones of the stable yard, then two men and their girlish companion swung into view and Debra felt her heart thud against her chestbone.

'Sharon will be riding Palo.' The words struck loud and clear against Debra's ears. 'I want no damned novice on his back.'

Her hand slid from the satiny neck and she stepped quickly away, her fingers clenching on her riding stick. In her white shirt, corded breeches and boots she looked the proficient rider that she was, and she tried not to show any feeling as she turned to say good-morning to Sharon and the Salvador brothers.

'Hello!' Sharon smiled gaily. 'Are you going riding with us?'

'I invited Debra,' Jack said at once. 'Grand start to the day, isn't it? Just breathe the air!'

'I bet you think Cornish air should be bottled and sold as a balm for the nerves,' Sharon laughed. 'Horses don't make you nervous then, Debra?'

'Not in the slightest, Miss Chandler.'

'I thought they might as you're a Londoner and more accustomed to big red buses, black cabs, and traffic snarl-ups. How do you stand all that clamour?'

'With difficulty.' Debra forced a light note into her voice even though she was desperately aware of Rodare looming over Sharon and herself as they waited for the groom to saddle up the four horses. She didn't dare to look at him directly; already his remark and his tone of voice had told her what to expect if she did look upward into his eyes.

'It must make a marvellous change for you to be working at the seaside and in such surroundings as these,' Sharon continued in her sociable way. She seemed to Debra to be one of those girls to whom the word butterfly truly applied. The kind to be unaware of undercurrents who when the time arrived would make the perfect hostess for a man of means. She

looked stunning in cream shirt and breeches
worn with tan-coloured boots, the epitome of
the type of girl whose photograph often
appeared in *The Tatler* or *Country Life*.

Her self-assurance was so complete that
Debra felt slightly gauche by comparison,
especially as she hadn't taken the trouble to
apply make-up in order to take a gallop. Her
own face felt schoolgirlish and scrubbed, and
her hair was a horsetail secured by an elastic-
band.

'How different you are from Miss Tucker.'
Sharon's inquisitive glance went from Debra to
Jack. 'She was a little dumpling of a woman
and she was scared out of her wits of the
horses.'

'Horses don't frighten me,' Debra rejoined.
'Though I lived in London and went to school
there, my mother has a sister-in-law at
Torquay and I used to go there for summer
holidays. Her children always went riding so I
used to go with them. Devonshire ponies are
very mettlesome and those we rode at the local
stables were moor-bred.'

As Debra revealed this item of information
about her younger days, she felt the look
which Rodare flung at her. She felt it raking
over her, burning her skin to the roots of her
hair. With all her might she refused to look at
him . . . the high-and-mighty *hidalgo* who had
made her feel so low that she could hardly bear

it. She wanted never to look at him or speak to him ever again. She wanted him to feel her contempt and deliberately she turned her back on him and smiled at Jack.

'Which horse am I riding?' she asked him.

'The chestnut, of course.' His eyes were upon her hair and for a brief moment they shared the secret of their midnight feast of strawberries and cream.

The four of them mounted up and as Debra gentled the chestnut she noticed what a picture Sharon made seated in the saddle of the palomino, who was like moonlight beside the strong and satiny black horse that Rodare rode as they cantered out of the stable yard. Jack was on a dappled grey with a swishing black tail, named Motley.

Jack sidled Motley closer to Debra's mount, who had the rather interesting name of Tidy Boy. After being in his saddle only a few minutes she realised why he had the name, he was smooth as silk to ride, with a grace to his movements which were transmitted to Debra. She realised with a sense of thrill that he would be swift as lightning if she let him have his head.

'That glamour-boy is all show.' Jack pointed with his riding stick at the palomino. 'You realise you could beat him on Tidy?'

'Yes.' She gave a sudden laugh, all the hope and beauty in the warmth of the sun dispelling any sense of gloom. All at once the joy in being alive and capable was racing through her veins. 'Yes, Jack, I can feel it.'

They cantered along behind the two riders ahead of them, to the far end of the headland where it sloped naturally to the sands. The tide was far out and the beach lay like a strand of tarnished gold that stretched all the way round the island . . . a perfect track for a race.

'Go on,' Jack encouraged with a laugh. 'Show your paces.'

Debra was tingling with the need to show the *hidalgo* that she was no novice, as he had called her. There was enmity between them and in a strange way it was easier to deal with than those more subtle, more disturbing emotions he had aroused inside her. Now she lived to wrench back from him her sense of being her very own person.

'Dare I?' Already her eagerness was transmitting itself to Tidy, who was tossing his head as if saying to her: 'Let me show that Palo there's more to being a horse than being beautiful.'

Debra smiled at her thoughts. 'I can see why your brother wanted Miss Chandler to ride Palo, they do go well together.'

'Like peaches and cream,' Jack murmured, a slightly teasing note in his voice. 'You didn't like it when Rodare called you a novice rider, did you?'

'I took the remark from whence it came,' she said, her voice and manner cooling. 'What can anyone expect from a man so arrogant he sets himself above the rules of behaviour he makes for others?'

'Wow!' Jack gave her a look that was slightly suspicious. 'You've a touch of the devil in yourself this morning.'

'True,' she agreed, and her eyes were bright green as they dwelt on the broad-shouldered figure who rode ahead with Sharon. 'He wanted to make me feel small in front of Miss Chandler; he hoped I'd crawl away, back into the den where I belong, but you invited me to ride, you said this was a holiday and you are my boss.'

'Ah, the Hartway spirit is rebounding,' Jack said, with approval. 'Any more surprises for me?'

'Yes.' Quite suddenly, with the vibrant sea air blowing her cares away, she made up her mind. 'I'll dine at your table tonight, Jack. I'll put on my best bib and tucker and I won't give a damn!'

'My dear,' Jack's eyes crinkled in a delighted smile, 'what brought this on—dare I make a guess?'

'Guessing games can be dangerous.' And so saying she dug in her heels and set Tidy at a gallop, crying out as she reached Sharon: 'Race you!'

Sharon at once took up the challenge and, as if by mutual, unspoken consent the two men fell into a canter side by side while the two girls raced their mounts along the beach.

The thrill of the race lit a green fire in Debra's eyes, for Tidy was so fleet on his legs he was like silk streaming through the sunlit air. She could hear the pounding of the palomino and that meant he was in pursuit rather than leading, and with all her heart she wanted to be the winner.

She wanted that word 'novice' hurled back in Rodare's arrogant face. And she also wanted to show these people that even if she was a working-girl she could match their skill when it came to the activities they regarded as their privilege as landed gentry.

The rush of air had loosened her hair from its band and it blew like a pennon as she rode. How alive and renewed she felt this morning, so different from the sad creature who had wept upon the black-oak monk seat in the garden last night. A kind of energy poured through her system . . . the energy of the soldier going into battle she supposed it was, and a laugh broke from her as she realised that Sharon on the palomino had fallen well behind and that she and Tidy were still going strong.

Going too strong . . . the realisation hit her all at once. She tried to slow him down but his own speed had gone to his head and he was eating the air, churning the sand, the Arab strain let loose in him.

'Whoa, Tidy!' she yelled, but he knew her to be a mere girl on his back, light in the saddle and barely a burden for him. That he was out of control didn't frighten Debra, and with tightly gripped knees she strove to get the upper hand, using every atom of her skill from those long-ago summers when she had learnt to ride those big, pinky-white Devonshire ponies who had strong wills of their own.

The wind sang past her ears, bringing all at once the thud of hoofbeats bearing down strongly on her and the runaway chestnut. She cast a look behind her and saw Rodare's black mount streaking along in the tracks made by Tidy, Rodare himself low in the saddle, as she had seen the tough-legged Devonshire lads ride the moor ponies barebacked.

Quite suddenly the powerful black horse surged alongside the chestnut. 'Swing him towards the ocean,' Rodare shouted at her. 'Get him into the water and he'll slow down!'

As much as she wanted to defy Rodare, her common sense told her to obey him. Hauling on the reigns she managed to turn Tidy's head towards the sea and directly he found himself plunging up to his hocks in the water, he slowed his pace and she was in control again. A minute or so later Tidy was standing still and puffing his own foam from his nose.

'You Arab devil!' Debra gave his neck a slap, then tensed in the saddle as Rodare's mount splashed his way to her side. She expected a reprimand and there was defiance in the look she flung at Rodare, her hair wildly tangled about her brilliant green eyes.

'That was good horsemanship,' he said curtly, 'even though you could have broken your neck.'

'As if you'd care.' She pushed the hair back from her damp brow.

'I'd care if you broke the horse's neck,' he rejoined. 'I had no idea you could ride like that.'

'I know you didn't.' She stared at the sea, crawling and winking in the sun. She refused to look at him again, though she was acutely aware of his scrutiny of her on the back of Tidy, who now managed to look as if he were meek and mild.

'Allow me to apologise for calling you a novice.'

'I'm only a novice when it comes to being rolled in the hay.' The words burst forth from her pent-up anger and resentment, then she directed Tidy out of the water and cantered him to where Sharon and Jack sat their mounts, farther up the beach against a back-drop of brilliant red squill cloaking the cliffside.

'That was just like a scene from *His Slave*,' Sharon laughed, any chagrin she might have felt at being beaten by Debra compensated by seeing her lose control of her mount.

'When did a spring chicken like you ever see an old silent like *His Slave*?' Jack wanted to know, leaning forward in the saddle to give Debra a congratulatory pat on the shoulder.

'A friend of Mummy's video-taped it from a showing on American television.' Her laughter pealed out. 'Oh, Jack, you wouldn't believe what a giggle it is—almost as good as Laurel and Hardy.'

Rodare rode up and he was frowning. 'I'm glad you're amused,' he said to Sharon.

'Oh, don't be such a grouse.' She pouted her lips at him. 'It was really exciting watching you go chasing off along the sands, hell-bent to rescue Debra. I quite thought you were going to sweep her out of the saddle into your arms.'

'My heroics don't extend into the realms of schoolgirl fantasy,' he retorted. 'The chestnut needed to be cooled down, that's all.'

'Which chestnut do you refer to?' Sharon ran her gaze over Debra's windblown hair. 'I do like that colour; is it a L'Oréal tint?'

Before Debra could reply, Rodare spoke and his voice was heavily silken. 'Miss Hartway's hair is naturally her own.'

Sharon raised her eyebrows. 'What would a man know about it??'

His lip curled slightly, and Debra agonised

in silence as she watched him. Was he really going to tell Sharon how he happened to know that her hair wasn't tinted. 'I doubt,' he drawled, 'if a beautician could ever reproduce that shade of hair. There are some things that only nature is in control of.'

'Such as?' Sharon's blue eyes were openly flirting with him. 'I know you Spaniards can be alarmingly frank in your opinions, so what else is nature in control of? Men and women?'

'Unquestionably,' he replied, and shot a look at his wristwatch. 'I don't know about you people but I'm ravenous, so shall we make tracks and go and have breakfast?'

'Egg, bacon and sausage, here we come!' Jack smiled sideways at Debra, but she saw in his eyes a questing look. A look that was still there when they dismounted in the stable yard and handed over the horses to the groom. Rodare ran a hand down the neck of Tidy Boy.

'Larry,' he addressed the groom, 'have you clocked this *castaña*'s speed along those sands?'

'That we have, sir.' Larry broke into a grin. 'He's quite a goer and should be raced.'

'I agree with you. I think it might be a good idea to enter him for the Staunton Stakes; see about it, will you?'

'Happy to, sir.'

'Did you catch that?' Jack murmured to

Debra as they entered the house through the sideway. 'Tidy Boy might turn out to be a winner, so you had better lay a bet on him when the time comes.'

'He moves like silk through a loom,' she smiled. 'I'm just a little bit too light for him and my hands lack the strength he needs to keep him in control. I can see he's got Arab in him from the shape of his head.'

'Have you noticed that similarity in Rodare?'

'Yes.' She stood hesitant as Rodare entered the hall with Sharon. 'I won't join you for breakfast—'

'Oh, but you will!' Jack caught her by the hand and marched her across to the dining-room which was flooded with sunlight through the open windows. An array of covered dishes stood on the sideboard and at Jack's insistence Debra helped herself to scrambled egg and kidneys, reflecting as she did so that life for the Salvadors on their island had stood still in time and the world of convenience foods wrapped in plastic seemed a thousand miles away. She somehow guessed that Rodare was responsible for this maintenance of a timeless, untouched atmosphere at Abbeywitch, as much in keeping with life in Spain as he could make it.

As she followed Jack to the table, she couldn't help glancing round the room with a sense of appreciation. The proportions were

superb, rising to a ceiling of such a felicity of
detail it was almost Moorish, another reminder
of what lay simmering in Salvador veins . . .
there in Jack as well as Rodare, but buried
deeper and not quite so close to the surface of
his personality.

Through the windows as they ate breakfast
there stole the strong scent of flowers and
watered flagstones drying in the sun beneath
broad-leafed trees—camellia begonias, dusky
red roses, and a great bed of mixed carnations
and pinks. Larkspur stood tall and blue in
companion with lupins, and gypsophila
spilled around a pagola. It was the kind of
garden Debra's mother would have loved, for
in their narrow back garden at Newington
Green she had grown as many shrubs and
herbs as possible, with borders of flowers
edged with aubretia, that heavenly mauve
plant which was one of the reasons Debra was
so fond of the colour.

'That was a deep sigh?' Jack glanced up from
his bacon and sausage, which he was greedily
tucking into. At the other end of the long table
Sharon was carrying on her flirtation with
Rodare, who seemed in a mood to be charmed
by her.

'I was thinking how many flowers you have
in the garden here at Abbeywitch, such an
abundance of them, as if they thrive on the sea
air.'

'The island is in the same stream of climate as the Scilly Isles.' He broke a piece of toast and buttered it. 'It wouldn't have suited our infamous ancestor if it had been a cold island, for Spaniards love the sun.'

'The desert in them,' she murmured. 'Shades of the sirocco and the seraglio.'

His lips quirked. 'So you've noticed Rodare with his head inclined to Sharon's lively chatter. She does look the kind of bright flower he might want to lock up with the seven keys of Moorish legend, behind the iron grilles of his *granja* deep in the heart of Andalucia. Those roses you can smell are from cuttings he brought from there, so deep red and velvety they hold their scent for hours, especially in the evening.'

Jack paused to refill Debra's coffee cup. 'You haven't changed your mind about this evening?'

'No.' But she had to brace herself to say it. 'I don't go back on my word if I can help it.'

'You went back on your word where Rodare was concerned.'

'Oh—that.' She buried her nose in her cup of delicious coffee which she knew to be percolated from Brazilian beans especially ordered for the household. 'The entire idea was farcical and I said so.'

'You actually used that word in reference to his—proposal?'

'Yes, I said it was a farce and that couples in this country cared first and foremost about each other.'

'Brave words, my wench.' Jack spooned thick golden marmalade on a wedge of toast. 'No wonder there's such an atmosphere between the two of you—I noticed it this morning. You could have cut it with a knife.'

'I daresay.' She managed to sound cool and casual. 'Anyway, he dredged up some of his Latin courtesy and apologised for calling me a novice where riding is concerned.'

Jack gave a quiet laugh, but his eyes were thoughtful as they dwelt on her face and hair in the stream of sunlight through the windows. She felt her skin warming beneath his gaze and knew what was going through his mind . . . he was curious about Rodare's insistence that her hair was naturally *castaña*, as he had called the chestnut horse.

Indelibly fixed in Debra's mind was an image of herself stretched upon the sand, quite nude beneath dark Spanish eyes which had not missed a detail of her person. How long he had stood regarding her before she stirred awake Debra would never know, but he had stood there long enough to have assessed each particle of her body, including such details as her natural colouring and the tiny mole on her left hip.

'Does he consider you a novice at anything

else?' Jack suddenly asked, almost as if he forced out the words.

'I—don't quite know what you mean, Jack.' She wiped nervous fingers on her napkin.

'I think you do, Debra.'

With an effort she met his eyes. 'Surely by now you know your own brother and his tendency to make most things sound more significant than they are?'

'He's my half-brother,' Jack reminded her, 'and I've never been entirely sure of him. There's a Spanish word called *duende* and in so far as it can be translated it refers to shadow of the soul. It's in Spanish music, drama and the bullfight. A kind of lament. A kind of reaching out for a dream so elusive that in retaliation the crowd sits in the arena and watches a man in a suit of lights put out with a sword the light of life in a bull's eyes, then an additional barbarism is the presentation of an ear to the loveliest lady present at the ritual.'

Jack sat back in his chair and there were brooding Latin shades in his own face. 'The spectacle is so brutally beautiful that I confess to having watched it once or twice on visits to Spain, and I've always been aware that in Rodare there is a ruthlessness allied to great generosity and even compassion. He has something of a matador nature, as many Spaniards have. The game of dare or die appeals to him, but he was born a gentleman and in the main the fighters of bulls are from penurious backgrounds. The *hidalgo* of Spain is very aware of his privileges and his duties and he observes tradition up to the hilt.'

'And when he comes to England?' Debra murmured.

'I'm never sure.' Jack cast a glance at his brother who sat drinking black coffee and looking amused by his blonde companion, who seemed to have a fund of diverting conversation.

'Don't you feel just a little twinge of jealousy?' Debra was a little curious, having been told by Nanny Rose that Sharon had been very friendly with Jack before he met Pauline. 'Miss Chandler seems to be as amusing as she's pretty.'

'She's a light, sweet wine before the headier vintage,' he rejoined, rising to his feet. 'I'm going to take Dean on a visit to Nanny Rose, so come along.'

As Jack held out a hand to her, Rodare glanced in their direction and she just saved herself from accepting that extended hand. 'I'll go and change out of my breeches and boots and join you in her room,' she said, and with a polite nod at Sharon and Rodare she walked out of the dining-room.

Alone in her turret, as she changed into a cool print dress that left her arms bare, Debra let the events of the morning slide through her mind. As she braided her hair and made it into a knot at the nape of her neck, she had an image of herself riding along the sands with her hair blowing free in the balmy wind. She knew what Rodare released in her, it was a response to the primitive, a yearning to let her senses rise above her sensibility as the high tide rose above the sands until only the rocks could be seen.

That image of the ebony rocks with the sea thrashing around them was so vivid that she felt it to be a warning. She held the jade hairpin poised above her nape knot, then stabbed it home like a sharp resolution.

Never again would Rodare treat her as if she was just a body for him to enjoy . . . someone he fancied as if she were a piece of candy to melt in his mouth.

She was fiercely glad that she had retained her chastity, which some girls seemed to discard as if it were an undergarment they no longer enjoyed wearing. But for Debra it was a symbol of her independence and the right to make a choice. It was the seal of approval upon her own thoughts, actions and dreams.

With a tilt to her chin she studied her reflection in the vanity-table mirror . . . the mirror which had once held the reflection of Pauline. Had Pauline stood here and placed her hands against her body and felt the movement of the child she had denied was her husband's. She had flung the denial in Jack's face and defiantly she had told him that Dean belonged to another man.

Debra drew away from the mirror, as if Pauline might appear at her shoulder and whisper the name of the man. She turned and hastened out of the turret and was glad when she reached Nanny Rose's room and heard, as she opened the door, the sound of Dean's happy chuckling.

Nanny Rose was in an armchair by the window, cuddling Dean in her arms . . . and Mrs Salvador was also in the room and it was too late for Debra to make a retreat for Jack spoke her name.

'Come along in, Debra. I was just telling Mama how well the book is going and that we've earnt the holiday we're taking today.'

Crossing that room to the group near the window was for Debra an ordeal, for she didn't believe for one second that Lenora welcomed her back to Abbeywitch. When they looked at each other it was impossible for them to forget their last confrontation.

'So there you are, Miss Hartway.' Lenora's voice was polite and she even managed to fix her lips in a smile. 'Dear Jack is quite insistent in telling me that you are responsible for his return to us. Needless to say, had we suspected for one moment that naughty Mickey Lee knew where he was hiding, then I would have insisted that my stepson shake the information out of him. You, of course, wheedled it out of him.'

Debra caught the underlying suggestiveness in the words, but she decided that the best way to deal with Lenora was to pretend that her claws left no scratches.

'He's just like a big child,' she said quietly. 'You get more out of children with a smile than you get with a scold.'

'Really?' Lenora raised an elegant eyebrow. 'I do happen to have borne two children of my own, Miss Hartway, and I don't think dear Jack would ever say I was a scolding mother. Both my children have been as loved and spoilt as darling Dean.'

'We know we have, Mama, so don't get prickly.' Jack lightly kissed his mother's cheek. 'And as I'm a big spoilt boy I want you to pamper me by being nice to Debra who may agree to take Miss Tucker's place as my right-hand girl.'

Lenora greeted this as Debra expected, with a sharp query in a voice of silk. 'You did say right-hand, Jack?'

'I did, Mama,' he said drily.

'One way or the other, Miss Hartway,' Lenora's silken tones seemed to thread a little, 'you have the knack of making yourself indispensable to the men of this family.'

'Mama,' Jack spoke warningly, 'you've lost

me one proficient secretary and I don't intend
to lose another. If Debra leaves this house a
second time on your account—'

'My account?' His mother looked highly in-
dignant. 'Your half-brother had more to do
with her leaving than I did, or hasn't she told
you of her involvement with him?'

'Debra has told me all about it.' But he spoke
with just a touch of constraint. 'Anyway, let's
drop the subject. I'm glad to be home and I
think we should all forget our differences and
be one big contented family.'

He leant down and kissed the top of Dean's
head. 'You agree with me, don't you, infant?
Miraculous age, isn't it? He thinks life revolves
around the dinner bowl, a nice splash in
the bath and lots of toys—what's that you're
playing with at the moment, son?'

'He's taken a shine to my good luck medal,
Mr Jack.' Nanny Rose wore the medallion on a
long chain around her neck. 'Mr Rodare gave it
to me; he said it wasn't likely lightning would
strike me twice but I had best be on the safe
side and be protected by St James of Spain.'

'Rodare and his superstitious nonsense!
Jack, don't allow the child to put the medallion
in his mouth!'

'It won't harm him, madam.' Nanny Rose
gave Lenora a look between tolerance and
mischief. 'It's pure gold, the chain as well.'

'Really?' A frown almost gathered Lenora's

brows together, and then she disciplined her face into its polite, slightly disdainful mask. 'I'm gratified that you are feeling so much improved, Nanny. I would gladly look after darling Dean all the time but I am such a martyr to my nervous headaches. He's a dear child but he will persist in banging that drum which Zandra foolishly gave him. I tried taking it away from him but he went into such a tantrum.'

'I'm back on my feet now, madam,' Nanny Rose assured her. 'I'm only too happy to take up my duties again.'

'That's brave of you, Nanny.' Lenora glanced at her jewelled wristwatch. 'It's almost time for noon coffee with Millicent. She's a late riser but I do enjoy having her for company, along with dear Sharon. Will you join us, Jack?'

'I can't spare the time, Mama. Rodare and I have decided to burn the Devil tonight and we've got to organise the effigy—'

'Jack,' his mother cut sharply across his words, 'your father dispensed with that custom, he always said it was tantamount to inviting trouble—'

'Now who's being superstitious?' he mocked. 'Come on, Mama, it's only an additional bit of fun.'

'Irresponsible, adolescent fun!'

'Ah well,' he cast a lopsided smile at Debra,

'it does all of us good to be irresponsible once in a while because the business of being an adult isn't always easy. I'm hoping to persuade Zandra to donate her scarlet jogging suit, which stuffed with hay should make an effective body for the effigy. The head is going to be the problem.'

'Make it from a pumpkin, if you can get hold of one,' Nanny Rose suggested. 'Scoop out the fruit and carve eyeholes and a mouth in the pumpkin case, then you can mount the head on a stick and fix it in the body.'

'We'll need horns for the head,' Jack laughed.

'And a cloven hoof and a tail,' Debra reminded him, rather taken with the idea of seeing the Devil burnt.

'This is too much!' Lenora exclaimed. 'I hope you know what you are doing, Jack?'

'Dicing with danger,' he said, a mischievous gleam in his eyes. 'I must get hold of that deliciously awful jogging suit—have you any ideas about the Devil's horns, Nanny?'

'A pumpkin head will look wicked enough, Mr Jack.'

'I'm surprised at you, Nanny, for encouraging him,' Lenora scolded. 'You're a God-fearing Welsh woman who usually exhibits some common sense.'

'It's God-fearing, madam, to want to burn bad Old Nick.' Nanny Rose smiled and rocked

Dean in her arms. 'Burn, Devil, burn, and don't you dare return!'

'Nanny Rose!'

The two women locked eyes and suddenly there crept into the room a silence filled with the awareness of Pauline's untimely death, and the lightning which had struck Abbeywitch and left the smell of sulphur hanging over the house.

'Very well.' Lenora moved towards the door as if she were making a stage exit. 'It's quite obvious, Jack, that you are in a wilful mood encouraged by everyone but your mother. Burn your effigy, if you must—at least we'll be rid of the sight of Zandra looking like a pillar-box on the run!'

As the door closed behind his mother, Jack broke into a laugh. 'Now we know who Zandra takes after, don't we? Though I suspect that Mama would have made the more significant actress.'

'There's no denying it, Mr Jack, your mother knows how to put on an act.' Nanny Rose gave him one of her long looks. 'According to Mrs Lee, who got the information from Mickey, the bonfire is twelve-foot high.'

He nodded. 'We lugged a ladder to it last night and when it was finished it was such a beauty we decided to burn the Devil on it.'

'Is Father Restormel going to approve, Mr Jack?'

'He's a Jesuit monk, isn't he? He's bound to be delighted.'

'It's pagan,' Nanny Rose reminded him.

'Isn't everything?' He suddenly stretched his arms in the sunlight. 'I'd better be off to my art work—want to help me, Debra?'

'Debra's going to stay and have a chat with me, Mr Jack.'

'You can be a martinet when it suits you.' When he reached the door he turned and added with a smile: 'I'll have tea and biscuits brought to you both, not forgetting "joose" for my son and heir.'

The door closed behind him and with a smile denting her lips Debra sank down in the slipper chair; the room in which Nanny Rose had recuperated was much grander than her previous one.

'It's lovely to see you back to your old self, Nanny.'

'And what about you, my girl, are you back to your old self?'

Debra looked mystified. 'I haven't been struck by lightning.'

'Haven't you?'

'If by lightning you mean the *señor*.'

'I could have meant Mr Jack.'

'We both know who you meant—may I hold Dean on my lap?'

'If you haven't got the trembles.'

'Why should I—?'

'Girl, we know each other well enough to talk without beating about the bushes—hold open your arms and I'm warning you Dean's getting to be quite a weight. Going to be tall like your Papa, aren't you, my duck?'

As Dean snuggled against her, Debra studied his upraised face. They wrinkled noses at each other, then all at once she felt a great need to share a burden of another kind with Nanny Rose. 'If I tell you a secret, Nanny, will you promise to keep it?'

'I've kept many a secret in my time, Debra. It goes with the job, being trustworthy.'

'What I've got to tell you has been weighing on me—Dean is a Salvador, isn't he? You've seen their look in him, haven't you?'

'Many a time.' Nanny Rose gave Debra a sharp look. 'It's bound to be there, with Mr Jack for his father.'

'The fact is, Nanny, Pauline told Jack the baby wasn't his, that night on the yacht—the night she fell from the deck and was drowned. That was why he left Abbeywitch in such a terrible state of mind, and the awful thing is—it could be true.'

'Never—'

'It could, Nanny, because of something Mickey Lee told me the day he took me to see Jack. He said he'd seen Pauline making love with a man on the beach though he wouldn't say who the man was. Then I met Jack and talked with him and he finally came round to the idea that Pauline had lied to him about Dean. I managed to convince him that she said it in a fit of temper, because she wanted to leave him and he would have stopped her from taking Dean with her.'

Debra stroked the soft dark hair away from Dean's dreamy eyes, for he was half-asleep in her arms, with his thumb in his mouth. 'I wish I was certain she lied to Jack, but I'm not—'

'You believe he's the son of Pauline's man on the beach?' Nanny Rose shook her head in disbelief. 'That silly, silly girl, what could have got into her?'

A blade seemed to twist inside Debra . . . why, in God's name, hadn't Rodare slapped her face for saying what she had said to him? There could only be one answer, and he had provided it last night when he had walked away from her.

'If Pauline told Jack the truth about her baby,' Debra said, each word like a weight on her heart, 'there's only one other man on the island who could have been her lover.'

'Mr Jack's own brother?' Nanny Rose looked appalled. 'A man such as he, haughty and proud, and thoughtful in his own fashion. How can you think such a thing, Debra?'

'Because I have no choice.'

'What does that mean?' Nanny Rose stared

at Debra, reading her stricken face. 'You've accused him of it?'

'I—I'm afraid so.'

'You might well be afraid, my girl. As if he'd lay hands on his own brother's wife? As if he'd stoop so low? How can you hold such hate of him in your heart?'

'Oh—' Tears cruel as acid filled Debra's eyes. 'I don't hate him in the way you mean, Nanny. It's loving him that I hate!'

The words were out, they were spoken and there was no recalling them. They had spilled from Debra with all the sad impetuosity of her tears, making Dean blink his black lashes in surprise as a teardrop fell on his face.

'Dear, dear.' Nanny Rose sat shaking her head to herself, her fingers twined in the chain of the golden medallion. 'And there's Mr Jack thinking you'll stay on at Abbeywitch.'

'There's no way I can, Nanny Rose.' Debra wiped the teardrop from the soft warm cheek of Pauline's baby. 'The next time I leave it will be for good.'

'Better so, my girl. Nothing good can come of Mr Jack wanting you when you're wanting his brother.'

'I don't—want him.'

'Spare me the lie, Debra. There's been enough lying from the sound of things, and hand me back the boy.'

Debra did so without comment. She didn't

stay to drink tea with Nanny Rose, she went sadly out of the room and wandered along the gallery to the beautiful rose window at the far end, like a great jewel whose colours glowed deep ruby, emerald and gold. A multicoloured web which held Debra in its strands as she stood there and realised the truth of what she had said to Nanny Rose.

There was no way she could remain on Lovelis Island, living in this house and never knowing when the master of it would stride into the hall and announce his return from Spain.

Work on Jack's book was coming to an end, and Debra knew that she must refuse his offer to stay on as his right-hand girl. 'Right-hand?' his mother had queried, and Debra had caught her meaning. She didn't want Jack to get any ideas about the part the left hand played in a relationship between a man and a woman.

It was in Spain where the right hand was ringed by a man, and as if running from her thoughts Debra sped down the staircase and was hurrying out of the sideway when she blundered into the very person she wanted so much to avoid.

'*Dios*, what is all this hurry, a touch of Midsummer madness?'

She shuddered to a halt in his grip, except for her heart which raced madly when she met his eyes. 'Believe me, *señor*, I've never felt so sane.'

'Then where were you going in such haste?'

'Nowhere in particular.'

'Then let me suggest that you come with me to Penarth in order to find this pumpkin which Jack insists upon.'

'Oh, the pumpkin head.'

'*Si*, the pumpkin head,' he said drily.

'No, I'd rather not come with you, thank you.'

His hands gave her a shake. 'It will be cool on the water and I refuse to accept no for an answer.'

'Typical of you to force people into doing what you want,' she said freezingly.

'So always I force you?'

'Yes.'

'In which case, come along!' Her wrist was gripped and like a mutinous child in rebellious silence, she was led down to the beach and ordered on board the motorboat. Mickey Lee stood there on the sands watching them, a big dark figure against the afternoon gold of the sky.

As they sped away from the island Debra wondered what Mickey Lee was thinking as he stood there rock-like, watching them out of sight on the sunlit water.

CHAPTER THIRTEEN

PENARTH was crowded with people enjoying the Midsummer market fair and the scene was a lively one, with the sun shining down on summery dresses and white shirts. There was a roundabout with painted horses and children laughing on the backs of them, and it was all such a contrast for Debra, so different from the last time she stepped from the quay and crossed the cobbled pavement.

Today she noticed the shaggy palm trees and the picturesque little houses facing the quayside, their granite walls softened by trailing plants, their slate roofs gleaming.

'To think that in days gone by Penarth was raided many times by the Spaniards,' Rodare remarked. 'I am with you right now because my notorious ancestor was one of them.'

'I'm sure it delights you to have him for an ancestor,' Debra rejoined. 'You certainly have his look.'

She didn't need to look at Rodare in order to see his buccaneer resemblance to the Spanish captain who had sailed his ship into Cornish waters, intent on pillaging anything he and his crew could lay hands upon. Then one morning they had anchored off Lovelis Island and he had rowed ashore alone and found unexpected plunder in the shape of a girl. Young and innocent, and probably scared out of her wits, she wouldn't have stood a chance of fighting off his advance.

'Did he never have a portrait painted of his stolen bride?' Debra found herself asking Rodare.

'It hangs on the white wall of my *sala* in Andalucia,' he replied. 'Don Rodare had her painted not as the grand lady of the house but wearing the dress of a fisherman's daughter, her hair blowing in the wind and looking exactly as she must have looked the day he abducted her from the beach. Their romance started with tears, but from the look in her eyes the Don soon convinced her that tears were a waste of time.'

Debra had often wondered about the companion portrait and now she heard his explanation it left her unsurprised. It would appeal to him to have in his Andalucian house the likeness of the girl from Bride's Cove. He had only to look in a mirror to see his own likeness to the man who had built Abbeywitch.

'Do you want to take a look around the market?' he asked. 'These stalls with their bric-à-brac are interesting and you might find something you would like to buy.'

'I haven't any money.' She shrugged. 'You

did a bit of abducting yourself, didn't you,
señor?'

His eyes shamelessly scanned her face.
'Don't worry about money, I have sufficient.
Come, let us enjoy ourselves now we are here.'

'You—you take the prize!' she exclaimed.

'It's in the blood.' His dark eyes dazzled her
and she turned her head away from him and
walked in among the stalls where the local folk
and the holiday-makers were clustered in
lively groups around the goods on display.

Each time Debra paused to look at something she would be aware of Rodare close
behind her, dark and tall in a leisure shirt and
pale-mushroom trousers, the golden links of
his watch blending with the gold of his skin.
Sometimes his arm would reach across her
shoulder and he would pick up an item that
took his eye, and she would feel the touch of
him and despise the thrill that went up and
down her spine.

'What have you found?'

'Oh—this.' She had picked up a small vase
and was rubbing at the grime that concealed
the delicate latticework of its design. 'I think
it's quite pretty but you can't see the colour for
the dirt; it's grimed in.'

'Let me see.' He took the vase from her and
studied its curved shape and fluted neck, and
wetting a finger he rubbed at the latticework
until a delicate rose colour began to show

through. He turned it bottom-up, but sprawled over a possible maker's mark was the price in black lettering.

'This you must have,' he said casually to Debra, and beckoned the stall-owner. It was wrapped in a sheet of newspaper, paid for and handed to her. As they walked away from the stall he told her not to drop the vase because it was probably quite valuable.

Debra gave him a startled look. 'Really?'

'I think so.' His lip quirked. 'Now you have proved that you have a good eye for a bargain; it's probably hard-paste porcelain and will clean up like pink silk.'

She flushed with a sense of pleasure she couldn't conceal. 'You should have it, *señor*, as you've paid for it.'

'Come, what would I do with a little vase meant for a vanity-table?'

'But if it's valuable—'

'All the better that you should have it.' He took her elbow in his grip as they crossed the road, his eye having been caught by a fruit shop. 'I wouldn't care to present a young woman with a shoddy gift . . . it isn't my style.'

The sudden ring of arrogance in his voice brought a reluctant smile to her lips . . . darn his eyes, why did he have to be such a mixture of devilment and generosity? So aloof at times, and then a man who deliberately tried to break down her defences.

They entered the fruit shop, redolent of luscious aromas from a rich variety of summertime fruits, piled in colourful mounds with greenery interwound in overhead beams in order to create a sense of coolness.

'May I help you, sir?' The girl behind the counter turned to Rodare with a very willing look in her eyes.

'What I need,' he said, 'is a pumpkin.'

The girl didn't look too surprised by his request. 'You want it for pie-making, then?'

'No.' His eyes smiled. 'My brother wants to make a spooky head out of it, for it's to be part of our Midsummer revels.'

'Oh, I see.' His smile had brought an apple-like flush to the girl's cheeks. 'We get more requests for pumpkins around Hallowe'en but we may have one in the back room, if you don't mind waiting while I take a look?'

'I shall be grateful if you can find one.'

Five minutes later he and Debra were walking along in the sunlight, collecting amused glances from passers-by. The pumpkin was a bit shrivelled and an odd colour, but Rodare carried it with a total lack of embarrassment.

'Hungry?' he abruptly asked Debra.

'Why, are we going to sit on the seawall and eat some of that sad old thing?' she wanted to know.

'Tonight it will grin among the flames. No, I thought we might go and each lunch at The

Garden Café, if you feel inclined to break bread with my hateful self?'

'Last night you were hateful.' She flushed at the memory.

'I would have said I was something else, but it's too warm for argument here on the pavement, and I am myself longing for a glass of wine, lobster and crusty bread. Have I tempted you?'

He was the essence of temptation, six feet of it, from his black hair to his hand-tailored brogues. He was also strangely endearing with that pumpkin in his arms.

'All right,' she said. 'I'd hate to deprive you of your lunch.'

'No matter what else you deprive me of?'

She tightened her lips and refused to answer that question. 'The Garden Café sounds nice,' she said, in cool tones.

'You won't be disappointed,' he assured her.

The place was rustic and charming, the garden tables shaded by trees that filtered the sun. Rodare ordered white wine right away and stowed the pumpkin in a nearby flower bed.

'It seems a shame,' Debra murmured.

'What is a shame?' He was taking a casual look at the menu.

'Using the pumpkin for a devil's head.'

'You said it was ancient.'

'I know, but in the story of Cinderella a

pumpkin was turned into the glass carriage that took her to the ball.'

'Your head is filled with fairy tales.' He gave her an amused look over the top of the menu card. 'What a child you are at times.'

'Just because I happen to have some imagination?'

'A colourful imagination is fine so long as you don't permit it to distort your vision. Now what do you fancy as a starter? Will you have lobster or do you prefer melon and smoked salmon?'

She picked up her own menu card and decided on the avocado pear with shrimps.

'And to follow?'

She glanced up and his eyes were fixed upon her . . . she looked right into them and was lost in their darkness. A kind of panic took hold of her, for try as she might she couldn't seem to cope with the feelings he aroused in her.

'Don't look at me like that!'

'How do I look at you?'

'Like a man who always wants to finish what he starts. I—I didn't come with you today because I wanted to come. You made me!'

'I'm perfectly aware of that.'

'And what do you hope to gain by it?'

He slowly raised an eyebrow. 'My dear girl, this is merely a farewell lunch. Tomorrow I am going home to Spain, for what is there to keep me at Abbeywitch? Jack is there to be in charge of things and is it not significant that tonight we burn our various devils?'

As he spoke those words, the waiter came to the table with the wine and this gave Debra the chance to recover from the shock of his statement. There he sat, in all his dark dominance, but already he was slipping out of her life and by this time tomorrow he would be stepping on to Spanish soil—he would have become a stranger whom she would never see again.

A coil of pain seemed to wind itself around her throat and she could barely say, 'Thank you,' as the waiter poured wine into her glass.

'*Salud.*' Rodare raised his glass to her, then drank from it. 'I hope my news has put an edge on your appetite—have you yet decided on your main dish?'

She stared at the menu card and for the sake of her own pride she had to pretend that she was unaffected by his imminent departure from England. 'Do you recommend the white meat of chicken, *señor*, garnished with mushrooms and onions?'

'I'm sure it's delicious, *señorita.*'

'Then I'll go for that.'

'Excellent.' For himself he ordered *tournedos* and a selection of vegetables, but first they had their fish courses to eat, and Debra felt as if she would choke on every mouthful even though the avocado pear and shrimp had a heavenly taste. In fact, she told herself, it was like chew-

ing on heaven and hell, having him there at the
other side of the table, hearing his voice with its
Spanish intonation, facing at last the full torment of her feelings for him. Her idealistic
dreams of love faded to a pale grey beside the
black misery of what she felt right now.

As her eating pace slowed, she felt him
watching her and quickly she lifted her glass of
wine and half-emptied it with a flourish which
she hoped looked careless.

'I expect it will be very hot in Andalucia,' she
said, gaily.

'Hot as the very deuce but I revel in it.' He
broke a lobster claw and withdrew the white
meat on his fork, dipping it casually in mayon-
naise and carrying it to his mouth. 'One day
you should visit that region of Spain; I feel sure
you would find it most interesting. Perhaps
Jack will bring you there.'

'Jack?' She gave him a startled look.

'Why not?' He shrugged his shoulder. 'He
may wish to research and I understand from
him that you are considering becoming his
full-time editor and secretary.'

'But I haven't quite—made up my mind—'

'Why not?' he said again, beckoning the
waiter to refill their glasses. 'Jack is obviously
pleased with you, in and out of the den.'

He spoke the words so smoothly that they
almost slid away from her before she realised
their import. Then her thoughts fled to her

strawberry picnic with Jack in her turret, and when she met Rodare's eyes she felt her fear confirmed. He knew that Jack had been in her room last night . . . somehow he knew!

'Yes, I am sure you are quite invaluable to my brother,' he added, almost as if goading her into argument with him. But she decided not to be goaded. What purpose would it serve? He was leaving in the morning and what she decided to do about Jack's offer of a permanent job was her business. Right now she was too confused by misery and potent white wine to be able to sort out her problems.

Her chicken dish came to the table and once again she had to force herself to look as if she was enjoying every mouthful . . . God help her on the trip back to the island. Already she felt nauseated and could feel tiny beads of cold sweat breaking out on her brow. Suddenly, in a voice of iron, Rodare spoke:

'Put down that knife and fork, you damned little fool! Do you think I don't know what you are doing to yourself?'

She did as he ordered and sat back in her chair. She took several deep breaths of air and was vaguely aware that the waiter was at the table again and Rodare was ordering coffee.

'It's the heat,' she said at last. 'It's such a warm day.'

'Quite.' He had pushed aside his own plate. 'That and the way you take so much to heart.'

'W-what am I taking to heart?' Her voice scraped her throat. 'The fact that you're leaving? Is that what you mean?'

'Meeting you, Debra, has been an interesting experience, in view of the fact that you are the only girl I ever asked to be my wife.'

'You felt obliged to ask.'

'And you felt obliged to refuse.'

'Of course I did.'

'Will it be the same story when Jack proposes to you?'

She stared at him, her eyes wide with amazement. 'There's nothing like that between your brother and me! I like working for him, he's kind and considerate but—'

'Aren't kindness and consideration what you are looking for in a man?' Rodare probed her face with his dark eyes. 'Jack has all the virtues while I, so you flung at me last night, have all the vices. I'm the devil who comes to Abbeywitch, pretending to be a man of honour when all the time I'm a seducer, first of my brother's lawful wife, then of his secretary. Let me tell you—'

He stopped, breaking off abruptly as the waiter brought their coffee and proceeded to pour it. As usual Rodare took his black—black like his scowling brows—and when they were alone again Debra could feel the threat emanating from him across the table.

'Ah, think what you will!' He picked up his

coffee cup and drank from it. 'It's over, and tomorrow I shall be in Andalucia.'

Debra went to speak but he looked away from her, showing his profile which looked rigid and forbidding. In that moment there wasn't a thing about him that looked English, he was entirely the proud and dignified Spaniard. He had closed a door between them and she had felt it thud against her heart.

'I—I'm sorry,' she managed to say, but he didn't bother to answer her.

As they skimmed back across the water to Lovelis Island she found it impossible to break the silence between them. She sat quiet in the stern of the motorboat holding on her lap the little pink vase wrapped in newspaper. She felt as if she would remember this trip for the rest of her days, until she was a little old lady like Nanny Rose who had given herself to a career instead of a man. And like Nanny Rose she might one day say to a younger woman:

'When I was a girl I met a big, dark-haired man who lit lightning in the heart and struck sparks with a look, and it's only once in a lifetime that a girl meets a man like that.'

Then all at once something struck Debra. 'Oh—' She glanced helplessly at Rodare. 'We forgot the pumpkin!'

'Did we?' he said. 'How unfortunate.'

She lowered her gaze and said no more and when he beached the motorboat she jumped quickly ashore and hurried to the cliffside steps. She ran all the way to the headland, clutching her little vase as if afraid fate would snatch it from her and leave her with nothing at all. When she reached her room she quickly unwrapped it, took it into the bathroom and gave it a careful wash. As Rodare had promised, it cleaned up beautifully and gleamed in her hands like pink silk. She selected a place for it on the vanity-table and stood back to admire her only tangible reminder of Rodare, the rest lay in her heart, and in her mind.

'Oh, God!' She sank down on the cane settle at the foot of the bed and her eyes were grey with remorse. How could she have believed him to be Pauline's man on the beach? As if Mickey Lee, with his big boy's mind, would ever again have accepted Rodare's authority if he had seen him making love to Jack's wife. Jack, who had so much of his trust and loyalty!

Debra wrapped her arms about herself and rocked back and forth in pain . . . her indulgence in pain and self-pity interrupted when fingers tapped upon her door. When she failed to respond the door opened and a maid entered carrying an envelope on a small tray.

'This came with the mail, miss, and I'm sorry it got overlooked. We've been that busy today, what with the big dinner tonight and Madam wanting everything just so.'

'That's all right, Kitty. Thank you.'

Kitty lingered, staring at Debra's wan face. 'Are you all right, Miss Hartway?'

'I've a bit of a headache—the sun's been hot today.'

'And not a breath of breeze about. Cook's been grumbling because of tonight's special dinner. Goose, of all things, to have to roast on a sweltering day!'

'Goose?' Debra groaned inwardly. 'I'll take an aspirin and hope for the best.'

'You'll be eating with the family tonight, miss?'

'Mr Salvador has invited me, and as it's Midsummer Eve I didn't like to refuse.'

'There's magic about on Midsummer Eve.' Kitty broke into a laugh between shyness and boldness. 'You'd best put a sprig of rosemary and a silver coin under your pillow, miss, and you'll dream of the man you're going to marry.'

'So you're superstitious, Kitty?' Debra had to smile.

'Aren't you, Miss Hartway? Anyway, it's worth a try.'

When Debra was alone again she tore open the envelope and withdrew the neatly typed letter. It read:

Dear Debra,
    We hope you can complete work on Jack Salvador's new book without delay. Felicity

Cooper is leaving us to take up a position with Harmony Publications, and Malcolm Monroe is taking over her section.

We would like to offer you the position of chief editor of our Juvenile books so let us hear from you as soon as possible.

Best regards,
Yours sincerely,
Harrison Holt.

Debra stood there with the letter clenched in her fingers, then all at once she decided where her future lay. Tomorrow she would tell Jack that she was going to accept Mr Holt's offer. It was a definite step up the ladder at Columbine and proof that the Holt brothers thought her capable of handling a responsible position with the company.

She straightened out the letter and returned it to the envelope, and she thought of what Kitty had said about the sprig of rosemary and the silver coin . . . she wasn't going to need those because the future she had in mind didn't include a dream husband.

She didn't take an aspirin, but she did kick off her sandals and take off her dress and then open her windows wide in the hope of catching a little breeze. She lay on her bed and tried to empty her mind of its teeming thoughts. They seemed to buzz back and forth like dodgem cars and the music of the funfair at

Penarth was their accompaniment.

Discordant, she thought, like the mood of the lunch she had shared with Rodare. Her head turned restlessly on the pillow. How inadequate to say she was sorry, and almost with contempt he had turned his head away from her.

Who was it who had planted that appalling suspicion in her mind? It certainly hadn't been Nanny Rose who had been horrified that she should entertain it. And though Lenora Salvador had said cutting things when she had discovered Rodare in her room the night of the party, she had not implied that he was in the habit of being found in the wrong bedroom.

Debra remembered quite suddenly . . . it had been Stuart Coltan, saying in his insinuating way: 'They liked to dance together so perhaps they liked doing other things together.'

Stuart was the snake in the grass who had whispered his venom and then watched it have its effect on her. Stuart and Pauline, the realisation struck her like a blow that brought her completely to her senses so that she wanted to run and find Rodare and beg him to forgive her.

But it was too late for regrets. The clock couldn't be turned back to last night when he had kissed her and wanted her because the moon had lit a little madness in his heart.

Debra lay with her face buried in the crook of her arm and in a while, like a misery-worn child, she fell asleep, unaware when the curtains began to flutter as the sun cooled and the sea deepened in colour. Her exhaustion was complete and she slept on, the room slowly darkening around her.

Moonlight was flooding into the room when she awoke, and she sat up with the guilty realisation that she should long ago have started to dress for dinner.

As she reached to the bedside lamp her arm protested, for she had slept on it heavily. She gave a gasp of dismay when she saw the time . . . it was twenty minutes to eight, which gave her very little time in which to shower and dress.

It was a special occasion and every one would be dressed accordingly, and here she was, still drowsy from a heavy sleep, rubbing a numbed leg as she stumbled to the closet and opened it. Even though her brain screamed she couldn't seem to make the scream come out of her mouth. Stuart Coltan was standing there among her dresses; he was wearing his white dinner-jacket and his pink shirt with the string-tie, and in his upraised hand he held Mickey Lee's claw-hammer.

'I'm in your room this time, Miss Prim,' he said, and his eyes danced with a crazy blue light. 'This time you're tucked well away from the brothers, aren't you, milady? I can do to you what I did to Pauline and not a soul will hear you scream when I do it. Bunch of fools, even if they live high on the hog in this high-toned house of theirs.'

He laughed and swung the hammer in his fingers like a pendulum. 'They think she drowned in the sea but I know differently. We swam ashore, the two of us, to make love on the beach. When the fun was over she started her usual monologue about telling Jack if I didn't marry her—marry her when I had rich and devoted Zandra on the hook? I told her to shut her mouth and when she just kept yelling at me I picked up a rock and closed her mouth with it. She fell in the rock pool and that's where she drowned.'

And each awful word fell into place and made sense as Debra drew away from him, badly frightened and yet defiant . . . this wasn't a man who confronted her with his confession of murder, this was a vicious, whining brat who had found a hammer to play with.

'Why pick on me?' she found enough voice to ask.

'Because I happen to feel like it.'

'You're mad,' she said, and knew the Midsummer moon was looking in through her wide-flung windows . . . a mad, livid face just like Stuart's.

'Oh no,' he shook his head and grinned his

brazen grin, 'it's big Mickey Lee who's mad
and he's the one they'll blame when they find
you, your chestnut hair—'

'I'll join you in hell before that ever happens!' The voice was iron like the hammer-
head, savage with intention, and it came from
the direction of the door. 'Lower the hammer
carefully, my friend, and then hand it to me.'

'Sure, I'll hand it to you, *el señor*!' Stuart flung
it viciously and it swiped Rodare's shoulder as
he took a flying tackle at Stuart's legs and
closed on them with powerful hands. The two
men went crashing to the floor and items of
furniture overturned as they wrestled and
jabbed, each one of them driven by a desperate
need to gain supremacy.

Debra didn't stand there like a petrified fool,
she ran as fast as her legs could carry her
downstairs and into the drawing-room where
Lenora presided in her regal velvet. Zandra in
rose-red georgette half-rose from a chair, and
Jack in a dark dinner-suit was about to hand a
drink to a creamy blonde all in blue.

'Jack!'

'Good lord—'

'Stuart's gone crazy and Rodare's up there
with him—do come!'

Debra ran back the way she had come, in her
bare white feet and ivory-coloured slip, her
hair like a dark flame about her shoulders.
When she ran into her room Rodare had Stuart

in a secure arm-lock and the actor was blubbering like the spoilt, spiteful brat that he was.

'Put on a wrap,' Rodare ordered her.

She obeyed him, breathing quickly as she tied the sash. Jack loped into the room, pulling up short at the sight of his brother, his black hair all over his brow as he held on grimly to Stuart.

'Don't go telling him!' Stuart yelped when he saw Jack. 'He'll kill me—'

'That is what I'd like him to do.' Rodare looked murderous himself. 'I would like to see my brother break your evil neck!'

'Stuart,' Zandra came running into the room, 'what are they doing to you, darling?'

'He killed Pauline.' It was the word 'darling' that Debra couldn't bear to hear on Zandra's lips. 'He was hiding in my closet a-and he was going to kill me—with that!' She indicated the claw-hammer which lay where it had fallen after striking Rodare on the shoulder. 'He was g-going to use that so Mickey Lee would take the blame—'

'What's she talking about, Stuart?' Zandra stood there in her brilliant dress, her eyes fixed upon him in her brother's unrelenting grip. 'I want to know what you were doing in her room—answer me!'

And as if he heard again the same hysterical tone which had driven him to violence the night he and Pauline had swum from the yacht to make love on the beach, he turned on Zandra a look of crazed hatred. 'You and your demands, who do you think you are, a princess with the right to order people about? You and your mother, a pair of real Queen Bees, one minute full of honey, the next full of stings!'

He stopped abruptly, then slowly turned his gaze on Debra and he was grinning. 'You had your chance, baby doll. I could have gone for you but you went all hoity-toity on me. Only *el magnifico* was good enough for you, and then when you'd got him you ran out on him! Just like every dame I ever knew, you're all mixed up. You don't know whether you want the moon or the sun—the stars or the dirt!'

Again he stopped, then all at once he was blubbering again, and Zandra watched him in a kind of horrified fascination. He squirmed and twisted and was almost pathetic in his white dinner-jacket and his pink shirt.

'He killed Pauline?' Jack said heavily.

'Yes, *amigo*.' Rodare glanced at Debra, and his iron look seemed to soften for a fraction of a second. 'You are all right, *niña*?'

She nodded, unaware that she was clasping her wrap around her as if she were cold. 'You arrived like the cavalry, thank heaven!'

He didn't explain why he had come to her room, not in front of everyone, but Debra felt sure he would tell her why later on . . . she knew it had something to do with the way they had been with each other during the trip back from Penarth.

'It would give me intense satisfaction to burn this *cerdo* on tonight's bonfire,' he said crisply. Then he marched Stuart out of the room and Jack followed in a numb sort of way. Poor Jack, Debra thought, he now had to come to terms with the true facts of Pauline's death and they were as tragic as they were deplorable.

Jack, immersed in his writing, his initial passion for Pauline cooling down as he came to realise that they had very little in common. He may have believed her content with her baby, but her sensuality had not been satisfied by maternity.

Debra remembered what Nanny Rose had said about Stuart, that he liked hanging around women, even one like herself who was old enough to be his mother. He had lost no time in noticing Pauline's discontent, and Debra glanced around the disordered turret and wondered how often the pair of them had been alone here, two people from show business who had crossed the barrier into the society of the wealthy Salvadors.

Poor, lost Pauline, torn between two worlds . . . two men. Wanting everything and losing all she had when Stuart grew tired of her. A shiver of compassion shook Debra and she wondered if things would have been different for Pauline had Jack's family drawn closer to her and made an attempt to understand her. Debra sighed. It was too late for regrets, and though she had suspected Stuart's amorality, her own troubled emotions had blinded her to the truth.

As she tightened her arms about her own body, she seemed to feel Rodare's strong arms when they had danced together, their every movement matched, their steps in perfect time. It was then he had taken possession of her, and she ached to be forgiven for ever thinking that he had possessed Pauline. With his Latin shrewdness he had suspected the truth, and he had been the only member of the family to give Pauline his friendship.

Right now Zandra had a self-absorbed look; a pride-affronted air, and not knowing what to say to her Debra started putting the furniture to rights, and it was then she noticed that her precious little vase had been knocked from the vanity-table and trodden to pieces in the furious struggle between Rodare and Stuart Coltan.

Sadly she began to gather up the pieces.

'You knew he was no good, didn't you?' Zandra spoke abruptly, her hands shaking as she lit a cigarette.

'Yes, I knew, but I never dreamt he was quite so—bad.'

'God, it's like a nightmare!' Zandra dragged

deeply on her cigarette and the rose-red tips of her fingers danced in the air with nerves. 'To think I wanted to marry him and he—he killed Pauline.'

Suddenly a terrible thought struck Debra as she knelt there gathering up the broken pieces of her silky pink vase. What if Dean . . . oh no, Dean *was* a Salvador; she had seen in his infant face the look that as he grew up would make him proud and noticeable. He had those blue eyes from Pauline . . .

Eyes blue as Sharon's as she came into the room in her rustling satin dress, carrying a tray with a coffee pot and cups on it. She was surprisingly cool and kind as she poured coffee for Debra and Zandra and insisted that they sit down and drink it.

'You poor dears, what a shock for you both.'

Debra held her cup in both hands and drank from it gratefully. The sight of Stuart lurking in her closet among her dresses was fading like a detail in a dream, losing delineation even as she sat and started to feel warmed by the hot, sweet coffee.

'We—we can't let this spoil things,' Zandra said suddenly. 'Father Restormel is coming from the Chapel to bless the fire and his being here will be like an exorcism. Sharon, what are my brothers doing about—Stuart?'

'Rodare has taken him to the mainland. Mickey Lee's gone with them because poor

Jack is in a bit of a state, which is only to be expected.'

'Jack's with Mama?'

Sharon nodded. 'Only an hour ago everything was so pleasant and she was showing me photographs of her wedding day, and when Jack was baptised. Isn't life a surprising thing!'

'There's more drama in it than in the theatre, I sometimes think.' Zandra was beginning to recover her poise and her second cigarette was steady in her fingers. 'Mama has always loved Jack the best of the two of us, but that's the way of mothers, unless they're little sensation-seekers like Pauline. She had everything in Jack and Dean and yet she couldn't keep her hands off Stuart—she drove him to it, that's the truth of it!'

'Perhaps.' Sharon cast a significant look at Debra, then she said brightly: 'Isn't little Dean the image of his grandfather? I was amazed when your mother showed me that photograph of his grandfather taken in Spain, where they tint them so well. That chubby child has the same deep-blue eyes.'

Debra had been listening in a kind of dream, but suddenly the significance of Sharon's remark struck her wide awake. Dean *was* Jack's child. Dean had his grandfather's eyes. Dean owed nothing at all to his mother's association with Stuart Coltan. He was Pauline's baby by Jack Salvador and that night on the yacht she

had flung a lie into his face, hurting him deliberately because she had wanted dross in the
place of gold.

'Thank God,' she said, and didn't know that
she spoke aloud.

'Yes.' Zandra rose to her feet. 'You are right
there, Debra, and as I said before, we mustn't
let Midsummer Eve be spoilt. We'll leave you
to get ready—come along, Sharon.'

'You will be all right, Debra?' Sharon
hovered, her hand on Debra's shoulder.
'You've had such a fright so perhaps we
shouldn't leave you on your own?'

'I'm fine now.' Debra smiled and decided
that she liked Sharon Chandler, that her first
impression of her had not been wrong. She
was a warm-hearted girl who would make the
perfect daughter-in-law for Lenora Salvador.

'Don't be too long,' Sharon said. 'We'll see
you downstairs.'

The door closed behind the two figures in
their glamorous dresses and once again Debra
had to approach her closet in order to find
something suitable to wear. She couldn't quite
suppress a shudder as she put her hand inside
the closet and withdrew the white dress she
had worn the night she had danced with
Rodare.

Yes, she would wear this dress in which to
say *muy bien* to him, and in a quietly resigned
mood she bathed in the scent from her

favourite sachet, slipped into her nicest under-
wear and sat down at the vanity-table in order
to comb her hair and arrange it so her neck was
left slim and vulnerable for the style of her
dress. She still looked rather pale so she applied light touches of blusher, lightly made up
her lips and hung around her neck the pearl
pendant and chain which were now as good as
new, thanks to Rodare.

Yes, in retrospect, she should have guessed
there was something more amiss with Stuart
Coltan than a tendency to react like a destruc-
tive child when he was denied his own way.
She fondled the pear-shaped pearl and her
eyes were reflective. She had assumed he was
merely vain and flirtatious, but remembering
the crazy smile in his blue eyes she shivered
and hastened with her dressing.

Later they would all go out on the headland
to watch the blessing of the fire, so Debra
decided to take a coat downstairs with her. It
was a white angora jacket and Debra carried it
over her arm as she descended the dark mag-
nificence of the staircase lit by the blazing
glitter of the chandeliers. She smiled a little and
thought to herself that she should be trailing
mink or sable in the leisurely wake of her silver
shoes. Inevitably she thought of herself walking down these stairs with Stuart when he had
said they were both ambitious.

He had been unbalanced and greedy, but

Debra knew that her own ambitions were linked to her mother's hard-working struggle to provide her with a good start in life. She had a good position awaiting her at Columbine, and one day, perhaps, she would be able to look back upon events at Abbeywitch with a composure she didn't feel right now.

'There you are.' Jack came forward from a shadowed alcove and held out a hand to her. 'We've turned dinner into a buffet so come along in and eat something.'

She let him take her by the hand and directly they entered the dining-room she saw Lenora in conversation with a lean man in the dark robe of a monk. 'Come and be introduced to Father Restormel,' Jack said, and as she walked with him across the room she thought of what Zandra had said about exorcism. When her hand was taken by the monk's and she looked into his eyes she felt a sense of peace, the kind that comes when the spirit has been in turmoil.

'I hear that you are a very brave young woman,' he said, and as if it were the most natural thing in the world to do, he made the sign of the cross on her forehead and with a look he seemed to say: 'Forget the evil that men do and think only of those who do good.'

Encouraged by Jack and Sharon, she managed to eat a slice of roast goose and some salad accompanied by a glass of Krug. She chatted with them but wondered all the time if Rodare would suddenly walk into the room and see her in her white dress and forgive her for being young and unworldly and confused between her dreams and the reality of desire.

But it wasn't until they all stood out on the headland, with the flames of the Midsummer fire leaping skywards, and no burning of the devil after all, that Rodare came at a leisurely pace towards them, as if he had all eternity instead of only a few more hours in which to tell her why he had come to her room.

'Mickey is putting the boat away,' he said. 'He will be here soon to admire the bonfire he helped to build.'

'Rodare?' His stepmother's voice held the question they all wanted to ask.

'Taken into custody,' he said, 'and tomorrow the official enquiry will begin, which means I must cancel my return to Spain in order to be here. I fear it will all be stirred up again, Jack. There is no avoiding it.'

'At least we now know everything,' Jack said quietly. He turned his gaze to Abbeywitch, a wonderful sight in the moonlight, as if thinking of his son fast asleep in the care of Nanny Rose. There would come a day when Dean would learn how his mother died, but time would dim the brutality of her death. The flames leapt high in their golden dance, and a quiver went straight to Debra's heart as an arm stole around her waist and a deep voice murmured in her ear:

'Come quietly with me, I have something to say to you.'

Like a figure walking in a dream she went where he led, until the fire was only a glow in the distance and they were alone above the waves beating on the beach. Then Rodare turned her to face him and in the moonlight his face was strong but his eyes were tender. 'How young you look in your white dress, and how much I want you.' He said it quite simply. 'That is what I came to say to you, *querida mia*, but if you don't want me then I shall do my best to accept defeat with good grace.'

'You saved me,' she said softly.

'*Dios mio*, I don't want your gratitude!' He snapped his fingers at the very idea. 'Between us it is fire and passion and need—or it is nothing, so take your choice!'

'But is it love?' she murmured, entranced by the fire in his eyes.

'Love?' He threw wide his arms. 'It is all this—the moon and the stars and the sea. We knew the day we met and we shall know it the day we die so we might as well surrender to it. And if you need to hear me say it, then listen while I say it—I love your hair when it blows in the wind, and I love how spirited you can be. I love it when I touch you, and I am lonely when you aren't there to touch.'

'Lonely?' she breathed.

'Ah, that touches you to the quick!' And with sudden ruthless impatience he caught her close to him and held her white-clad body with an urgency that stirred into life the last remnants of her doubts and fears. Like sparks they danced through her blood and then were quenched by what she saw in his eyes.

She saw there the fear that she would elude him again.

'Rodare,' her hand pressed against the nape of his neck, 'I—I need you to forgive me—you know what for.'

'Ah, that.' His gaze moved slowly, almost tormentingly over her moonlit face. 'Perhaps I should punish you first.'

'Punish me?'

'Like this.' And gathering her even closer to him, he brought his lips down upon hers and kissed her without mercy.

Merciless he was, but by some miracle, some decree of fate, Debra knew they belonged together . . . but could they be together here on Lovelis Island?

Side by side they stood on the headland, their arms twined about each other, and he had released her hair so the moon made it shine.

'What of Abbeywitch?' she quietly asked.

'It's a wonderful house,' he said, 'but you were right when you called it my burden. I want no burdens but that of making you happy, *querida mia*, so what I think I shall do is to let it belong to Jack. He is more a part of it than I am, for I am a Spaniard and there is only one place in the world where I want to live with my wife and raise my family, and that is in Andalucia.'

With strong and loving hands he turned Debra to face him. 'Will you live with me and be my love in Andalucia?'

Her eyes were a little tearful in that moment, then she raised a loving hand to stroke his Spanish face. 'How generous you can be, Rodare, to give away your birthright.'

'I wasn't born,' he smiled, 'until one fine day I met a shameless hussy on a beach . . .'

'Oh, you're going to hold that against me!'

'I don't intend to ever forget it.'

'Then I shall—'

'What will you do?'

'Go to Columbine and be chief editor of their children's books. I've been offered the chance, you know, *el señor*.'

'I'm sure you would make an excellent chief editor of children's books, but what of me?' he asked. 'Don't I count?'

'Oh yes,' she sighed, 'more than anyone in the world.'

'Dare I believe you?' He framed her face in his hands and searched her eyes by the light of the moon. 'How much does Jack mean to you?'

'I admire him as a writer and I like him as a man.'

'I saw him coming from your turret last night.'

'He had picked some strawberries and we shared them.' She spoke with the simplicity of truth. 'That was all we shared, Rodare, and I think you know me well enough to believe me.'

'True,' he smiled. 'The girl who thought I kissed and caressed her because I thought she was just a toy for me to play with. Will you believe that the look of you, the ways of you, drive me wild with wanting you? Will you at last believe me?'

'Yes,' she said, and not a shred of doubt was left in her heart . . . this was love and it was both a dream and a consuming need to share his desire. And below where they stood so closely embraced the sea had an unearthly beauty, sharing with them the mysterious aura of two people who had found each other's love.